VAMPISH: BLOOD BONDS

G.K. DEROSA

Paperback ISBN: 9798833706503

Cover Designer: Sanja Gombar www.fantasybookcoverdesign.com

Published in 2022 by Mystic Rose Press
Palm Beach, Florida
www.gkderosa.com

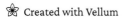 Created with Vellum

To all my amazing readers!
~ GK

VAMPish

CONTENTS

Emblems

Royal Vampires

Children of the Night

Royal Sicari

CHAPTER
ONE

P *hoenix*

"No, it's not possible." My knees wobbled, darkness seeping into my vision and distorting the sprawling chamber of Sky Lair. I waited for the smack as my legs betrayed me, but instead strong arms pulled me into a firm chest.

"It's okay, Red, you're going to be okay," Ransom whispered.

How could I ever be okay again? I tightened my hold around his neck, like he was my anchor, the only thing keeping me from capsizing in this tumultuous sea of uncertainty. Not only had my parents lied to me my whole life, but the man who'd banished my family from Moon Valley, was my father? How could he have been so cruel?

"I'm sorry," said Hunter. *My brother*. The fanging supreme alpha of all shifters was my half-brother. I wasn't sure I'd ever be able to process that. Then again, a few days ago, I never thought I could shoot fire or that scorching flames could float across my furry body without leaving a mark.

Mother fanger, what happened to my life?

"I'm sure this is a lot to take in," he continued as he sank into a chair in front of the hearth. A very pregnant Sierra perched on the armrest beside him. "I know it has been for me. If I'd ever suspected it all these years for even a moment, I would've come looking for you."

Ransom steered me to the sofa and guided me down next to him. I was numb, my body performing the actions on autopilot.

"How?" I blurted. "I want to know how this happened."

"I'm afraid I don't have many details. I had to threaten my father's personal guard, Walt, to get the little I managed." He blew out a breath and resettled in the massive chair. "My mother died rather suddenly when I was only seven. The healer said she died of a literal broken heart. There were certain things happening in my personal life at the time that could've accounted for that, but now that I consider the timeline, you would've been about one year old. Maybe the truth came out--"

"My mom loved my dad," I blurted. "She wouldn't have done that to him. She couldn't have. They were fated mates..." My life was crumbling, everything I'd known, everything I'd held onto about my parents was a lie.

"Phoenix, I wish I had answers for you. I don't know how my father became involved with your mother, but as alpha, there were few things he desired and didn't eventually attain. I knew he'd sought solace in other women after my mom's passing, but before?" He shook his head, a grimace twisting his lips. "I had no idea." He cleared his throat and

Sierra's hand tightened around his, her knuckles whitening. "Walt admitted your father discovered the truth about your bloodline. He was furious and attacked Tyrien."

"That's why we were banished."

He nodded slowly. "An attack on the alpha's life is grounds for immediate death. The fact that he spared your father makes me believe he must have cared something for your mother, for you."

I swallowed down the thick knot in my throat. Everything I'd ever heard about Tyrien Silverstalker had been awful. He was the monster who had banished us, who'd condemned us to a nomadic life on the borders. He was cruel and selfish. If we'd been living safely behind the borders of Moon Valley, my parents never would've been killed by Ronin and his men.

None of it would've happened.

"The past doesn't matter anymore, Nix." Hunter slid forward in his seat and offered me his hand. Unraveling my fingers from Ransom's, I took it tentatively. His rough palm glided against mine, and a current of energy traveled between our flesh. That odd pull I'd felt earlier returned, a strange tightening between my belly button and sternum. "We're family now, and there's nothing I won't do to protect you. Whatever you need, it's yours."

The depth of emotion in his emerald-green eyes sealed his words. How had I not noticed before how similar they were to mine? How had I not sensed our connection? I only hoped what Ransom had said was true and that this man, my brother, was nothing like his—*our* father.

"Thank you," I finally managed. My eyes lifted to Sierra's; her lips were spread into a broad smile. Then my gaze dipped to her belly. "I appreciate the offer to help, but this is my fight. I won't let you or your family get caught in it."

"You *are* our family," said Sierra.

My chest tightened and despite the life-altering news, I didn't think my heart could feel any fuller. "I promise to come to you if we can't figure this out on our own."

Ransom nodded. He'd been so silent if it weren't for his unrelenting hold on me, I would've forgotten he was there. Very uncharacteristic for the typically chatty vampire.

"I mean it, Phoenix, when this is over, I'd like you to return to Moon Valley. I want to get to know my sister."

My chin dropped, emotion tightening my throat too much to speak. Kenna could finally return home and live a normal life, safe among the wolves. I'd have to speak to Deacon as soon as possible to get her transferred.

"My sister, Kenna, if you could keep an eye on her, that would be all I could ask for."

"Of course," Sierra answered.

"I'll have Deacon contact you to set it up."

"Done," said Hunter. "Whatever we can do."

"There's one more thing." Ransom lifted a finger, finally releasing his hold on me. "Could you put us in contact with Azara, the dark lord of the Underworld? I'd like to pay her a visit."

"Sure, I'll have Vander arrange it." Hunter turned to me, brows knitted. "Are you sure it's safe for you to be gallivanting around the Underworld when the god of death is after you?"

I opened my mouth to reply, but Ransom interrupted. "She's not going. She'll stay safe and sound within the walls of Sky Lair."

"The hell I will."

Sierra laughed and whispered something to Hunter, but I was too busy glaring at the infuriating vampire beside me to listen in.

"I'm going if you're going," I cried.

"We'll have to discuss this later," he growled.

"I could go for you, if you want." Hunter directed his question at me, which I appreciated.

"No, I want to meet this female warlock," Ransom interrupted. "If Red's well-being depends on hers, we all need to be on the same page."

"If you think you'll convince Azara to hide out, you'll find you're gravely mistaken. You'd have a better time convincing Nix." Hunter smirked. "She didn't become the only female dark lord for nothing."

"Which is exactly why I'm going." I shot Ransom a sidelong glance. "Who knows what he'd do if he was left to his own devices."

"Ouch, Red, that hurt."

"She's not wrong." Sierra shrugged, a mischievous smile playing on her lips. "Ransom's known for doing reckless things when it comes to protecting the ones he loves."

Heat rushed up my neck, and I'd suddenly had about enough of this new family bonding. I jumped up and made a beeline to the door. The truth was I needed a minute alone to process all of this. "Sorry, just remembered I needed to do something. See you later." I sprinted through the doorway, praying my vampire shadow wouldn't follow me. I sent a splash of threatening vibes through our connection and hoped he'd get the hint.

I needed to be alone.

This thing between Ransom and me was all-consuming. I couldn't think straight when I was around him. And I needed to right now. As monumental as the discovery of my real lineage was, right now, I had a bigger problem to contend with. Both Ronin and the queen wanted me, and I had to stop the rebel king from summoning Thanatos and breaking the shadow curse.

That was what I needed to focus on. Not on whether or not my parents really loved each other and everything I'd known had been a lie.

I released a breath and slowed my pace when the sound of trailing footsteps never came. Now I had to figure out how to make it through this labyrinth and back to my room. I couldn't accomplish anything hiding out here in Draeko. But my vampire guard wouldn't let me out of his sight. He wouldn't even let me go to the Underworld.

Let me, ha, that was a joke. This bond was messing with everything. A tiny part of me was relieved we hadn't been able to complete the mate bond. If I felt this tied to Ransom already, I couldn't imagine what it would be like once the mating link was solidified.

Maybe it was my parents' fault I was so screwed up and falling for a fangin' vampire.

I was rambling now, my brain spinning with all the events of the past week that I hadn't had time to process. I turned the corner and finally the hallway looked semi-familiar. This was definitely Spark's wing. My ears perked up searching for sounds from my team, but the halls were quiet. I hoped they hadn't left yet. We needed to firm up the plan before they returned to Nocturnis.

Ronin had to be stopped.

Maybe if I could prove to the queen I could take him, she'd repeal the bounty on my head. If I could work with my team and the other sicari, I knew I'd be able to take out Ronin.

I turned down another corridor and a familiar figure leaned against the door, her long, violet hair tumbling over her shoulders. *Violet.* I snorted. I still couldn't get over the fact that Ransom's nickname for me was a cheap knock-off.

"Sorry, I hope you don't mind the company," said Sierra as she straightened.

I did. I did mind it, but how could I tell that to my high alpha and new sister-in-law? I'd fully expected Ransom to track me down, but not her.

She must have sensed my mood through the pack link or maybe it was the scowl on my face because she backed away from the door. "I don't have to come in if you don't want... I just wanted to check on you. I know what it's like when family secrets come out, and I only wanted to offer a sympathetic ear if you needed it."

I shrugged and closed my hand around the knob.

"It was either me or Ransom, and I figured you guys could fight about the Underworld later."

"Thanks," I finally managed. I knew I was being rude, but there was only so much I could take in one day. I motioned for her to come in, then scanned the quiet room. No Vera or Seline. Where were they?

"Hunter is going to be the best brother to you, Nix. He's had a tough few years, and finding out he had family out there, you should've seen how happy it made him."

A stab of guilt jabbed at my insides. I was being selfish, only thinking about how all of this affected me, and I'd never even stopped to consider what it was doing to him. "It's not about that Sierra. I'm glad Hunter's my brother. He seems great, and Ransom's only had good things to say about him, about both of you. I hope we'll have a chance to get to know each other soon. It's just all of it together is too much."

Sierra nodded and laced her arm through mine. Guiding me to the bed, she plopped down beside me. "I know it's hard to believe, but I understand what you're going through.

I never knew my father. He died when I was young, and everything I'd thought was true growing up turned out to be a lie. It's a long and boring story I'll tell you about one day, but the point is that everything happened the way it was supposed to. Everything I suffered, all the loss, it made me the person I am today. It led me to Hunter." She hugged her belly, and a smile tilted her lips. "And our new family."

"I'm really happy things worked out so well for you guys, but our situations aren't quite the same."

She nodded. "I know they're not, and I won't pretend to understand what's going on with you and Ransom. But I do know that mated pairs are stronger together. To me, it seems that you could use all the strength you can get for what's to come."

"We tried—" the words exploded from my mouth before I could stop them. With everything going on, I hadn't had time to consider the ramifications. Sure, I was slightly relieved but a larger part of me, of my wolf, was devastated. She wanted to be bound to him.

"It didn't work?"

I shook my head. "Well, we didn't—" Good goddess this was embarrassing. "I couldn't bite him because of my wolf."

"Ohhh." Sierra's eyes widened.

"Yeah, not something we'd thought about. I could kill him during the blood exchange."

"Because you'd have to *bite* him?" Her brows furrowed. "That's what Ransom told you?"

"Yes. Isn't that how it works?"

She nodded slowly, but something unreadable flashed across her eyes. "Yes, traditionally."

"Anyway, even if I were able to bite him, there's no guarantee it would work. Ransom died, Sierra."

"I know, believe me, I don't think I'll ever get the image out of my head."

"I'm sorry." I snagged my lower lip between my teeth and bit down. Not the most sensitive thing I'd ever said.

She suddenly stood and patted me on the shoulder. "Don't give up, Nix. Miracles do happen."

I chewed on my lip as I considered telling her about the appearance of the goddess Luna when I was a kid. Ransom had told me she'd had a visitation as well, and I willed my mouth to form the words, but before I got the nerve, she'd turned heel toward the door.

Weird.

"I'll let you have that alone time you wanted now, Nix. I just remembered I needed to yell at Ransom about something important. But if you need anything, we'll be here until this evening. I know Hunter would love some time to get to know his little sister."

I opened my mouth to ask about Ransom, but she waved a nonchalant hand as if she'd read my thoughts and again, maybe she had. I smiled, the words little sister sounding odd to my ears. I'd always been the big sister, the strong one who had to look out for Kenna. A swell of warmth bubbled up at the idea of being looked after, of being protected. It was a feeling I'd never felt before.

CHAPTER
TWO

R *ansom*

"YOU LIED TO HER!" Sierra's finger stabbed me in the chest. She'd stomped into the sitting room like a whirlwind.

"Lied to whom? About what?"

"Don't you dare play this game with me, Ransom De La Sangue."

Hunter stared up at his mate, the look of surprise mirroring my own. "What's going on?"

"You lied to Nix about the mate bond."

I could practically feel my face pale, all the blood rushing out. *Curses.* "I didn't lie exactly."

"But you didn't tell her that it was possible to complete without her biting you back. She feels terrible. She thinks it's her fault." She paused, glaring at me. "I felt her pain through the pack link. That girl really cares about you, you idiot."

I shifted in my seat and reached for the tumbler on the table. Taking a long pull, I finally faced my old friend. "I panicked, okay? I never thought she'd agree to forever with me, a vampire! So when the biting thing came up, I gave her the out."

"What if she didn't want the out? I doubt it was a decision she made lightly."

I tsked. "Sierra, don't you remember what the first few weeks of the burgeoning mate bond are like? The pull toward each other, it's irrational, relentless and completely overpowering. Logical thinking hardly comes into play. I know Red, and after the initial lust dissipates, she'll be stuck with me. Mated to her greatest enemy."

"You're just being stupid," Sierra hissed. She nudged Hunter, staring expectantly. "Tell him not to be so stubborn. Remind him about all the crap you put me through because you were so *noble*."

Hunter chuckled and raised his hands in surrender. "She's right, Ransom. I told you not to make unilateral decisions. You need to tell her the truth. If you're worried she'll get caught in the heat of the moment, have the discussion with clothes on."

Sierra giggled, and I shot her a narrowed glare. "You two are having way too much fun with this. I'm glad my incessant torture amuses you."

"You kind of deserve it," said Sierra. "Now, vampire up and tell Nix the truth."

"You're ruthless, Violet. And to think, you used to be my favorite."

She threw me a smile that had my heart staggering on a beat. "I just want you to be happy, Ransom. Because despite what you think, you deserve it."

I dragged my hand through my hair and let out a huff.

"You're assuming this will work, when in reality we have no idea if it will. My wolf is still dead, remember?"

"It won't hurt anything to try."

But it would. The truth was that giving into that tiny bit of hope could wreck me. I was already walking on a tightrope most days, so close to falling. Red was the only thing that kept me steady. If the mate bond didn't work and I lost her, I'd plunge into the darkness forever.

I grumbled an inarticulate response. There was no point in rehashing my instability with my old friends. "Enough about my love life, matchmakers. Can you get me that meeting with the dark lord?"

Hunter nodded. "I'll get on it as soon as we return to Moon Valley."

"Thank you, brother. I need to know exactly what we're up against before I take down the mad king."

"I was serious earlier, Ransom. Whatever we can do to help, you've got it. Not only is Phoenix family now, but I understand the ramifications of serviles running free into my borders. I'll make sure the Etrian Assembly understands it as well at our next meeting."

"I'd appreciate that. I worry that the other realms aren't taking Ronin's threat seriously."

"I'll make sure they do."

HUNGRY. Hungry. I prowled the corridors of Sky Lair, my throat parched and my stomach howling. I'd just fed from that dragon girl a few hours ago and already I was craving more. It was a damned good thing my desire to protect Red kept me from leaving the confines of the fortress to search for another blood source.

My pride kept me from asking Red for another donation. We hadn't exactly left things on a good note after she'd found me with that girl, and I wasn't sure where we stood on her offer to provide blood.

The smack of approaching footsteps turned my attention down the hall. My nostrils flared as I inhaled the familiar scent, the same scent that perfumed these hallways. Spark appeared around the corner with Seline at his side. The she-wolf clung onto him like sweat and desperation. Not a good look.

"Where's Nix?" he barked as he approached.

"I don't know. I'm not her keeper."

The dragon snorted on a laugh. "Since when? Lately, I can't get a minute alone with her without you showing up."

I shrugged. "It's not my fault if she enjoys my company."

"Right... She's just addicted to your blood. I knew that undercover mission was a bad idea."

"Oh Sparky, you don't know the half of it. If only it were my blood she was addicted to." I licked my lips and shot him a wink. Gods, he was so easy to rile up.

"Whatever you think you have with her isn't real," he growled, lunging closer. "It's a side-effect of your damned blood."

"Spark, come on, let it go." Seline's arm slapped across his chest, trying to force him back.

I actually felt bad for the girl. It was clear to everyone but her that the dragon was still in love with Red.

"Think what you want, Sparky." I smirked. "Now, what do you need with Red? I can find her for you if you'd like? With my damned blood, as you put it."

His lips twisted into a scowl, but his head finally dipped. "Yeah, I just heard back from Cal and Archer. They have news."

I nodded and closed my eyes, searching the connection between us. The string tightened, and I let my instinct takeover. My feet began to move of their own accord, and I gave them free rein.

Five minutes later, we emerged just outside the walls of Sky Lair to a snow-covered lawn. Hunter and Red were in wolf form, and I couldn't help the twinge of envy as the pair frolicked in the snow. Red's fur was its usual auburn tinge, and no flames coated her body today. Instead, the siblings were taking turns blowing fireballs from their mouths and knocking cans off an old railing.

How delightfully mundane.

"I still can't believe it," Sparky muttered beside me.

I'd forgotten that her precious team had never seen Red's wolf in action. I stopped, enthralled by her movements. Her sleek fur glistened beneath the moonlight, muscles quivering below the brilliant red hair. She moved like a wraith, unencumbered by her physical form as she darted around Hunter's wolf.

Thanatos, she was perfect.

My wolf stirred, that ghostly presence brought to life at the beguiling sight of his mate. What if the mate bond did bring him back? What if I could run free on lupine legs once again? I shook the thought out, the hope too risky to even consider.

Red finally caught sight of us and with a quick nod to Hunter, galloped in our direction. As she moved, a crimson mist rose around her legs. By the time she reached us, she was back in human form. Naked. My eyes bulged out along with a lower part of my anatomy.

"What's going on?" she panted.

Spark's eyes lit up as they razed over her milky white skin, and hot, fiery jealousy ballooned in my chest.

I tugged my shirt over my head and tossed it to her. "I'm sure Sparky will be happy to share once he can drag his eyes back up to your face."

With a scowl, she pulled my tee over her head and crossed her arms over her chest. Not like she needed to now. "So what's up?"

"Cal and Archer were called in to see the queen."

Red's fear lanced through our bond, the feeling so acute I barely suppressed the urge to clap my hand over the pang in my chest.

"Where's Vera?" Her worried gaze lifted over the three of us.

"She went back as soon as we got word from Lucíano."

"What's the queen doing to them?" she squealed.

"Nothing yet. Just questioning them about your whereabouts."

I muttered a curse. Despite their training, they wouldn't be able to block the queen's compulsion forever. They'd break, and they'd spill the truth.

"That's why Vera left," Spark added. "She'd given them both potions to block compulsion, but if the queen holds them for long, it'll wear off. She's going to try to sneak them some more."

"While they're in the queen's custody?" she shrieked.

"She had to try," said Seline.

Red's jaw clenched, determination written across her face. "You have to leave now, Spark, both of you. Tell the queen the truth that I was here, but I left."

"No." The big dragon shook his head. "Where will you go?"

"I can't tell you. It's safer that way. The less you guys know the better. The queen can't take it out on you if you don't know anything, right?" Red eyed me.

15

The truth was that I wasn't so sure. Carmen Rosa was a good woman, but her people and her throne meant everything to her. Would she kill some sicari if it meant getting to Red? I wouldn't put it past her.

"You can't live on the run," the annoying dragon continued.

"I'll protect her, don't you worry, Sparky." I patted his shoulder, and he recoiled from my touch.

"Nix doesn't need you. She was doing just fine before you showed up in her life."

"Spark!" Red barked. "Enough. We don't have time to argue. We'll stick with the plan just like we talked about, only it looks like I'll be on the move instead of enjoying the comforts of Sky Lair."

Hunter appeared behind Red, his wide shoulders looming over her. "Phoenix is right, Rhydian. You need to return to Nocturnis. Your father must remain in good standing with the Etrian Assembly and harboring a fugitive of the queen will only worsen the cause. We're going to need each of the houses of Azar on our side if war erupts."

"When it erupts," I interjected.

"Fine then, it's settled." Red moved toward her friends and wrapped her arms around Spark's neck.

I fisted my hands at my sides as his arms curled around her. It was a fanged good thing she had my shirt on, or I would've lost it.

"Be careful when you go back there," she whispered to Sparky. "You're in charge now, and I'll kill you if anything happens to you or our team."

A rueful smile rounded the dragon's lips. "I'll do my best."

She hugged Seline next and despite the drama within this love pentagon, the embrace seemed legit.

"I want daily reports, Sparky. And you let me know the moment Cal and Archer are released from the queen's custody."

"Yes, sir." He saluted her before turning on his heel. But before he got far, he turned back and shot me a narrowed glare. "You better protect her, or I'll hunt you down and kill you myself."

I waved him off with a smirk. "Like you could ever catch me." Red jabbed me with her elbow, and I buckled over for her benefit. "I'll guard her with my life, dragon boy," I called out.

The pair disappeared back into the fortress, and an icy breeze blew over the mountaintop. Red shivered, and I drew her into my side without thinking. Surprisingly, she stayed put. It was likely because she was freezing, but I enjoyed the moment just the same.

Hunter cleared his throat, and the moment of bliss passed. "Sierra and I have to head back to Moon Valley shortly." He dragged his palm over the back of his neck, and I relished in the supreme alpha's unease. It was so rare to see the great wolf flustered. "I'm sorry for the upheaval my news brought, but I'm glad we had some time together."

"Me too." Red gave her new brother a tight smile.

Hunter's hand landed on my shoulder. "I just heard back from Vander, and Azara's awaiting your arrival. When will you go?"

"Tomorrow," Red answered before I could get a word in. "*We* will head out tomorrow."

I let out a frustrated sigh and shrugged. "You heard the boss, tomorrow it is."

CHAPTER
THREE

P *hoenix*

A SMATTERING of ash coated the dull earth all around us. Still in a crouch, I scanned the barren landscape of the sixth realm where the portal had dumped us. A few crags jutted out in the distance, that same ashy hue covering the peaks. No lush green like in Marlwoods or the fluffy snow of Draeko. The land itself seemed dead, cursed.

A chill skittered up my spine despite the oppressive heat. Why would anyone choose to live in the Underworld?

A handful of demons eyed us as they lumbered by. A particularly nasty looking guy with a leathery face and antler-like projectiles sticking out of his head snarled at me as he passed. And my question was answered: these creatures wouldn't exactly blend in if they lived in the other realms.

"This way," said Ransom, tearing me away from ogling the locals.

Behind a wall of jagged rocks and boulders stood a white marble fortress. The structure was so at odds with the stark surroundings I wasn't sure how I'd missed it when we'd first landed. It was light and bright, reflecting the tiny shards of sunlight that eked their way through the ominous clouds.

My heart froze, eyes darting to Ransom. Sunlight? I released a breath when my vampire buddy still stood, untouched by the sun's rays. I'd almost forgotten about the potion Vera had gifted him before our departure. She was also working on getting him a solari ring, but I hadn't shared that bit of information with him just yet. He needed to earn that bad boy and after his recent behavior at Sky Lair, he was nowhere near the day-walking prize.

Every time my relationship with Ransom took a step forward, he'd do something to mess things up and we'd end up right back where we started. I hated it. Hated the uncertainty, the back and forth, push and pull. But I couldn't stop...

As we approached the immense alabaster structure, the ground began to rumble. My arms shot out to keep me balanced, and bardy teetered in my palm. The wall of rocks split, creating a path to the towering fortress.

"Guess this is the entrance," said Ransom.

We walked up the pathway and a few yards before we reached the entrance, the thick metal double doors opened. A young woman with hair as black as midnight stood in the archway alongside a massive dragon shifter. His silvery gaze raked over us, and he moved closer to his mate.

She cracked a smile. "Welcome to the Underworld."

"Thanks," I managed. "I'm Phoenix and this is Ransom."

"We've been expecting you both. Please, come in." She

backed away from the door and motioned inside. "I'm Azara as I'm sure you've guessed and this is my mate and husband, Talon."

The dragon eyed us as we entered, irises like molten steel. Damn, he was scary AF. Light giggles drifted across the hallway and a little girl raced by, dark curls flying behind her. "Momma! Dadda!" The tiny toddler wrapped her arms around Talon's tree-trunk sized legs.

He bent down, the scowl carved into his face disappearing as he hauled the child into his arms. "Serafina, where is Lumi? I told you to stay upstairs while we have company."

From the corner of my eye, I couldn't help but notice the look of longing on Ransom's face as he watched the big dragon with his child. A pang streaked across my heart at the sight. I shoved the useless thought aside. Ransom was a vampire, and anyway, he'd made it clear he had no interest in children from the beginning. Then why was he looking at the little girl like that?

A woman appeared a moment later, graying hair flowing loose from her bun and a long tail chasing after her. "There you are, you naughty little thing." She dipped her head at Azara then Talon. "I'm sorry, she got away from me."

"It's okay, Lumi." Azara squeezed the demon's shoulder. "I know what a rascal Sera can be." She pried the girl loose from Talon's arms and after a quick hug placed her in the nanny's arms. "Be a good girl, and Mommy will give you a treat later."

She giggled and clasped her arms around the demon's neck. "Yum, yum."

"Sorry about that." Azara's cheeks rosied as she regarded Ransom and me.

"Impressive; dark lord and mommy," Ransom quipped.

The tension in the air dispelled a notch, and Talon

pointed us toward a sitting room off the main foyer. The modern vibe continued inside with sleek furniture and bright colors. It was as if the interior designer had tried everything in their power to offset the dreariness of the realm with an explosion of color inside.

Once we were all seated, the dragon shifter steepled his hands and sat forward in the chair. "Please tell us more about why you're here. The supreme alpha was rather vague in his explanations."

"I apologize for that." I straightened, mirroring Talon's position. "I wanted to be the one to share the news in person." Clearing my throat, I began. "Let me try to make it short and sweet. Azara is in danger. There's a battle going on in Nocturnis between two factions of vampires. Ronin and the Children of the Night want to remove the queen from power. He's gotten it in his head that the way to do that is by summoning the god of death, Thanatos, to break the shadow curse, and he needs Azara's blood to do that."

The pair eyed me incredulously.

"Maybe we need to hear the long version," said Azara.

"Okay..." I drew in a breath and started from the beginning. Once I finished the whole story, the two of them still looked at me like I had grown a third eye.

"I know it's a lot to take in," Ransom interjected, "but it's all true. You can speak to the queen herself if you'd like."

"But you just said the queen wants you dead." Azara's curious gaze ran over me.

"Or imprisoned. Basically, she just wants to keep Ronin and Thanatos from getting to me."

"Which means she could want to do the same to Azara." Talon's jaw clenched.

"It's possible," said Ransom, cutting in, "but I doubt she'd be stupid enough to go after a dark lord, let alone one who sits on the Etrian Assembly and is a favorite grand-daughter of Lucifer."

My jaw nearly dropped. *Shift.* How did I not know that? I needed to brush up on my Underworld history.

"What about my mom?" Azara's eyes chased to her husband's. "If it's the blood of any female warlock, she would be in danger too."

"Luna is safe in the human world. You know your father would never let anything happen to her."

She nodded slowly.

"And your daughter?" Ransom's question drew my thoughts to the cute little raven-haired girl.

"She's half dragon," Talon answered. "She's not a warlock."

"Either way, I'll let Mom and Dad know what's going on. Either one of us could be this Ronin's target."

"I'm more concerned about Thanatos." Talon's dark brows drew together. "Do you think this warlock you spoke of could really return him to corporeal form?"

It was a good question and one we hadn't paid much attention to. The gods hadn't walked the earth for centuries, not before the first vampires were made. "I don't know," I finally muttered.

"We were all hoping it was just the ravings of a mad man," said Ransom, "but I'm not so sure anymore."

Talon turned to his wife. "Talk to GG and see what he thinks."

"Good thinking."

"GG?" I asked.

"Azara's maternal grandfather, Garrix, is the High Warlock of the Coven Council and arguably one of the most powerful men alive."

Ransom nodded as if he recognized the name. Damn, I

was way behind on Azarian history *and* politics. I needed to up my game ASAP.

"We need to make sure Ronin is unable to assemble the last few ingredients to complete the spell. We have no idea how many he's acquired, but we know for sure he's missing the final three—you, Azara, Red here, and the vampire with a soul."

Talon's eyes raked over Ransom. "That's not you?"

"Nope. One hundred percent soulless here."

His brows knitted together again. "So how do you fit in exactly?"

"I'm with her." Ransom jerked his thumb at me.

"Interesting," Talon mumbled, and heat swam up my neck. "I thought she was a sicari. Isn't her job to kill vampires?"

"It is," Ransom answered, a cocky grin lighting up his face. "She just couldn't resist me."

Azara chuckled, and I was a second away from punching him.

"That's not exactly true," I hissed.

"Anyway," Talon interrupted, "Azara's safety is always my utmost concern, so you don't have to worry about this Ronin guy on our end. I appreciate the warning nonetheless."

Azara's hand closed over Talon's leg, and it was such a sweet, intimate gesture, my chest tightened. "We both appreciate it."

I began to rise, sensing the end to our visit, when I realized we had nowhere to go after this. We couldn't return to Sky Lair or to Marlwoods. I wouldn't put my new brother and his family at risk. So where would we go now?

"Wait," said Azara. "I was thinking that Lucifer might be able to help."

The prince of hell?

Ransom's eyes sparkled. "It's true. If anyone would know anything about the god of death it would be him. Hasn't he been around for millennia?"

Talon rolled his eyes.

"Don't let him hear you say that. Luci still thinks he's in his prime," Azara said with a laugh. She snapped her fingers, and a pen and paper appeared on the coffee table.

Whoa, pretty cool.

It was easy to forget the demon war lord was also a crazy powerful warlock. No wonder she'd survived the notorious Darkblood Prison.

As she scrawled out a message on the scrap of paper, she began to mutter the words of a vaguely familiar spell. I'd seen Vera use her fire messages more than a couple times. It was her preferred method of communication trumping simple, human text messages of course.

"There." The note floated up into the air before catching fire and disappearing in a puff of smoke. "I'm sure Luci will get back to us shortly."

"Luci." Ransom chuckled under his breath.

"He only allows his precious Azara to call him that, so don't get any ideas," Talon warned.

Ransom grinned and pressed his lips into a tight line. "Wouldn't think of it."

Talon narrowed his eyes at my vamp buddy, then he wagged a finger at him. "Don't I know you? From Moon Valley, right?"

Ransom tensed. "Yes," he finally mumbled. "I was from the Royal pack."

"I thought you looked familiar."

"Yes, you too. I remember you and Hunter were friendly as children."

24

Talon's eyes glazed over, his expression going wistful. "That was a long time ago."

What was a dragon doing playing with wolf pups? Something about the look on his face told me not to ask. Maybe I wasn't the only one who'd been displaced as a child.

A spark lit up the air between us, and a note drifted onto the table. Azara picked it up and quickly scanned the paper. "Luci's very interested, but he's tied up right now in Rio." She rolled her eyes. "He said he can be back here by morning, if that works?"

I shifted nervously beside Ransom. There had to be a motel or something in the Underworld, right? I did not like the image that conjured up, but what other choice did we have?

"If you could kindly point us to the nearest five-star establishment—" Ransom began.

"You're welcome to stay here of course," said Azara, cutting him off.

"Oh no, we couldn't—"

"It would be our pleasure," Ransom interrupted.

"Ransom!" I whisper-hissed.

"What? It's not like we have anywhere else to be this evening." His eyes grew wider. It wasn't that I didn't understand the obvious, I just didn't like staying in the home of a stranger.

"Azara's right," said Talon. "Stay. I'd like to hear more about your story, Phoenix. I'm former SIA and that island you trained on sounds incredible. We need something like that for the SIA's recruits."

I scanned the beefy dragon up and down. *Supernatural Intelligence Agency*. Now, that totally made sense. "Sure," I finally muttered.

"Perfect." Ransom clapped his hands. "Now, what is there to do for fun around the sixth realm?"

Azara laughed. "I think I'm going to like you, Ransom."

"That's what all the girls say." He shot her a wink, and she laughed again.

A scowl etched into her mate's wide jaw as he glared at the annoyingly flirty vampire.

"No, but seriously, do you think you could conjure up some blood, Az? I'm starving."

"I'll have Lumi go fetch some." She rose and wound her arm through Ransom's. "Let's let these two have their talk, and I'll tell you all about the best clubs in the Underworld."

Talon's jaw twitched, and the faint grinding of his teeth reached my sensitive ears.

"Sorry, he's harmless really," I found myself blurting.

He lifted his gaze to mine, and the anger seemed to dissipate. "I know. I'm not worried really. Her demon's got a wild side, and it's been tough for Azara down here in the Underworld. She misses her family, her old life. It's not exactly the most exciting realm."

"I can imagine."

"Anyway, tell me everything about the Isle of Mordis."

CHAPTER

FOUR

R *ansom*

THAT AZARA WAS a barrel of laughs. Who knew dark lords knew how to party? And ones with babies too... My mind whizzed back to the little girl who'd come running to greet her mommy upon our return. The void in my chest gaped, the emptiness threatening to swallow me whole.

Red. Where was my little sicari? She always seemed to fill the vast chasm. I followed my nose to her tantalizing scent, then paused at the door. Azara had given us adjacent bedrooms at Red's request, but I had zero intentions of letting her sleep alone tonight. Leaving her in the dragon's care was one thing, but not overnight while everyone was most vulnerable. Though the alabaster fortress was crawling with demon guards, I could never be too sure as to the extent of Ronin's reach, or Thanatos' for that matter.

Bringing Lucifer into this fight was a true piece of luck. Who better to battle the god of death than the devil himself?

Closing my fingers over the handle, I gingerly twisted. The room was dark, and I could barely make out Red's form beneath the covers. Was it that late? How long had we gone out for? Even the baby was still up. Which meant only one thing... Red was avoiding me.

I crept inside and tiptoed all the way to the edge of the bed. Red was on the opposite side, her face turned to the wall. I watched the steady rise and fall of her chest, trying to determine if she was asleep or just pretending. My guess was the latter.

We still hadn't discussed my little mishap at Sky Lair with the girl or what it meant for our relationship. I knew she was angry, but she had to have forgiven me by now, right?

I searched the bond for a hint of her state of mind, but all was quiet. Perhaps she truly had fallen asleep. Yesterday had been an emotional day for her. She legitimately could've been exhausted.

But somehow, I could feel her presence...

I tugged my shirt over my head and undid the zipper of my jeans, eyes intent on her the whole time. She didn't move. I wasn't even sure she was breathing. Totally faking. I pulled the covers back and crawled into bed beside her. Still nothing.

I was certain she would've shooed me off by now.

That's it, it's time to call in the big guns.

I rolled over to her side, threw my arm around her waist and pressed my body into her back. Still nothing. *Hmm...* It was time to play dirty. My fangs lengthened, and I dragged the pointy tips over the back of her neck. Goose bumps exploded across her flesh, and a faint gasp escaped.

28

"Mother fanger!" she shouted and whirled around.

I couldn't help the dark chuckle that burst from my mouth as she glared at me.

"What are you doing?" she hissed.

"Midnight snack?"

She narrowed her eyes, twin slitted emerald pools of anger. "Didn't you have enough on your little night out with Azara?"

A swell of jealousy crashed through our connection, smacking me in the chest. "Seriously? You can't honestly think something would ever happen between me and the dark lord of the Underworld? Who's married to a huge dragon ex-SIA agent and has a child with him? How bad do you think I am?"

"I don't know, Ransom," she spat.

"Now I'm hurt, Red. After everything, you trust me so little?" I jerked up, sitting straight.

"Well, apparently my mom cheated on my dad with Tyrien, and they were fated mates. I guess it happens."

"Hey, what's wrong?"

"Everything. Nothing. I don't know." She crossed her arms over her chest. "It's the blood lust. That's what I don't trust." Her lips screwed into a pout, and the blazing anger dissipated into disappointment.

Which was worse. Much worse.

"I'm trying," I muttered lamely. It sounded weak to my own ears. It hadn't even been forty-eight hours since I fed on that girl. My arm snaked out, reaching for Red's face. I cupped her cheek, and I was shocked when she didn't smack me away. Her eyes met mine, sadness lingering in the deep green depths. "I'm sorry. I want to be better for you. I just keep screwing up."

"Then don't. Be better."

"If it were only that easy." My thumb stroked her soft skin, and that lupine presence in my core awoke. *Mate. Mate. Mate.* The incessant chant began its unearthly torture. I'd promised Sierra I'd tell Red the truth, and I would eventually. But first, she was right, I needed to get a handle on the blood lust, the insane cravings. If I couldn't prove I was trustworthy, nothing else mattered anyway. Red wouldn't be mated to a bloodthirsty animal.

"Help me," I murmured. "I can't do it without you, Red. Without you, nothing matters."

A rueful smile curled her lips, and I ran my thumb across her pouty bottom lip.

"You're going to be my undoing, you know that?" she whispered against my finger.

"I sure as hell hope so." I shot her a smirk and captured her lips. It had only been a few days since we'd been together, but it was already too much. My body craved hers, even more than it craved blood. I needed the connection, the spark of life I felt only when I was with her.

My tongue entangled with hers, my fingers digging into the hair at the back of her neck. I held her close, flush against my body. But it was never close enough. My flesh burned for hers, to become one with hers. My arousal pressed against my boxers, hellbent on breaking through the barrier between us.

Mate. Mate. Mate. That damned chant picked up in rhythm and intensity.

Red's eyes snapped open, meeting mine.

"Did you hear that?" I murmured against her mouth.

"Yes," she rasped out, and a hint of disappointment dribbled through our connection.

I pressed my lips into a tight line to keep from blurting the truth—that maybe just maybe we had a chance to complete the bond. I vowed to become the man Red deserved first, then I'd tell her. And I'd start by finally taming this bloodlust. It would be the only way she'd truly trust me. Then I'd kill Ronin and Thanatos. Hell, I'd burn down all of Nocturnis if it meant keeping her safe.

"I love you," I whispered, the words tumbling out as a sort of consolation prize.

A faint sigh slid between her lips as her eyes drilled into my own. "I know you think you do."

My brows slammed together, and a streak of pain lanced across my heart. "Excuse me?" My arms loosened around her waist.

"How can you tell? With the blood bond, the impending mate bond *and* the blood lust? How do you know how you really feel?"

As I scrutinized her expression and the tangle of emotions whirling between us, realization hit me. She wasn't questioning my feelings for her but rather trying to figure out her own. Gods, she was as messed up as I was. I supposed finding out you were Tyrien's daughter could do that to someone.

"I just know, Phoenix." I forced a smile, despite my insides crumbling. I hadn't realized how much I wanted her to love me, how much I needed it. If she believed in me, I could do anything, but without her love, none of it was possible.

Her lips brushed mine, tentatively. I felt stiff against her. I'd bared myself to her, but still she wasn't ready to give into this thing between us. Would she ever be?

"Sometimes I wonder what it would be like without the bond," she whispered, leaning her head back to meet my eyes.

I snorted on a laugh. "You never would've given me the

time of day, little sicari." I swept a tumble of auburn hair behind her ear. "I guess it's a good thing that fate had other plans for us."

"Fate or the gods?" Her brow arched.

"I suppose we can ask Thanatos when he decides to show up." She shuddered against me, and I immediately regretted the words. "I'll never let him have you, Red. Whether you like it or not, you're mine, and I won't let anyone take you away from me. Not even the god of death himself."

She smirked. "Even though I'm more than capable of taking care of myself, thank you."

I pulled her tight against my chest. The fire from earlier had fizzled, but I still needed her close. It was funny because the truth was, Red would be *my* undoing.

CHAPTER
FIVE

P *hoenix*

I GAPED at the figure coalescing from the shadows. Power emanated from his impressive form, dark and ancient and all-consuming. The heavy fog cleared, and the prince of hell stood before us in all his glory. I sucked in a breath. I never in a million years thought I'd come face to face with Lucifer. Or that he'd be so devastatingly gorgeous.

In a three-piece midnight-black suit complete with a matching pocket square, the original fallen angel peered at me from across the room. His face was perfection, the chiseled cheekbones, strong jaw, cleft chin and skin like porcelain.

I swallowed hard and dropped my gaze. His beauty was overwhelming.

"Azara, my dear." He closed the distance between himself

and his granddaughter. "I see the Underworld is thriving under your rule. Well done, as always."

"Nice of you to show up, Lucifer," Talon grumbled. "I hope St. Barth's won't be too dull without you."

"Ugh, the surly dragon, and I was in Rio this time." He wiggled his fingers in his direction. "I still think you could've done much better, Azara."

"Luci!" she hissed.

The devil rolled his eyes. "Now, where is my little great granddaughter?"

"Sleeping," Talon barked. "And no, you can't wake her."

"Besides, I asked you here about the god of death, remember?" Azara eyed her grandfather with a look similar to the one she'd given her naughty toddler.

"Ah, yes." Lucifer turned his dark gaze on me, and Ransom inched closer. "You must be the wolf with the mortal bite?"

All the words stuck at the back of my throat. *Good gods, say something, Nix!* My mouth opened and closed but no sound came out.

"She is," Ransom answered coolly.

"And you are?" He eyed my vampire bloodbuddy.

"Ransom De La Sangue." He dipped into a dramatic bow.

Lucifer's eyes narrowed as he regarded him, and a chill skirted up my spine. "Hmm, very interesting."

"What's interesting?" I blurted, suddenly finding my tongue.

"You'll find out eventually." He smirked.

"Lucifer loves to speak in vague platitudes and riddles," Talon muttered.

"Sit, Luci." Azara pulled a chair out and motioned for us all to sit. "We were hoping you could give us some information on Thanatos. Could a warlock really give the god corporeal form? And does he have the power to break the shadow curse?"

Lucifer's dark brow arched. "It's been centuries since gods have walked the earth. No one has been stupid enough to attempt to bring one back." He crossed his legs and shrugged. "I suppose it's possible."

"Do you know Thanatos?" I asked.

"I've encountered the Reaper in the past. It's been more than a few centuries at least. He used to roam the hallowed ground of the Underworld, but that was long ago."

"Well, we need to know how to kill him," Ransom interjected.

Lucifer grinned, wagging a finger at my vampire shadow. "I like you. You don't mince words. You cannot kill the god of death; he is a god. However, if he manages to return to earth, he can be banished back to oblivion where he belongs."

"Okay, so how do we do that?" I asked.

"I can't just give you all the answers..."

"Luci!" Azara stood and loomed over her grandfather. "It's not just Phoenix he wants. He needs *my* blood to break the spell too."

"My dear Azara, sometimes things need to play out as fate dictates."

Talon hissed out a curse and slammed his fist into the table. I nearly jumped out of my skin. "Are you seriously telling us you won't help?" he growled.

Lucifer didn't even flinch. He steepled his hands, fingers drumming against each other. He leveled a glare at Talon, and my skin crawled. "Control your mate, Azara, or I will."

"You're being unreasonable, Luci." Azara crossed her arms over her chest and narrowed her eyes at her grandfather, as if he weren't the most intimidating male to walk this earth.

"As I said before, certain things must play out as intended. Trust me, I wouldn't allow my great grandchild to grow up motherless. If Thanatos does return, we can reconvene at that time."

"What if it's too late by then?" Talon barked.

"It won't be. Thanatos knows better than to cross the devil himself."

"Well, this has been an absolute waste of time," Ransom muttered.

Lucifer shot him a wicked grin. "You, my vampire friend, have only just begun your journey. To be mated to the wolf with the mortal bite will prove to be your downfall."

How the hell did he know? A violent chill raced up my spine, and a tremor zipped through my body. "What does that mean?" I cried out.

"You'll see."

Talon growled. "See what I mean? Vague answers and gloom and doom. Don't listen to him."

"That's not news to me, Lucifer." Ransom threw the prince of hell his own smirk. "I always knew she'd be my undoing."

"I'm sure it'll all be worth it." The devil eyed me then returned his dark gaze to Ransom. "I will say this: hold her close if you wish to keep her from Thanatos's clutches. The god of death is vengeful and consumed with wrath. He's on his own mission—has been since the dawn of time. I've felt his presence closer lately. If he succeeds in breaking the shadow curse, all of Azar will suffer."

"Then why can't you do something?" I shouted.

He folded his hands on the table. "It's not my place. As I've said, things must play out as they are meant to. For now."

I glanced over at Talon. He was right. This guy was full of it. The dragon rose, the chair legs screeching across the stone floor. "Thanks for nothing, Lucifer. If you don't have anything else to share with us, you're welcome to see yourself out."

He stood and with an elaborate bow, dipped his head to Azara. "Always a pleasure, my dear. Say hello to the warlords for me. I don't miss them one bit." He chuckled. "You're doing a wonderful job keeping them in line."

"Yeah, yeah," she muttered.

"Don't hesitate to call if you need me!" His words drifted into the fog as a wave of black consumed him.

"Well, that was a complete waste of time," Ransom repeated.

"Sorry." Azara's lips puckered. "Luci is...facetious."

"More like crazy." Ransom's arm curled around me.

"As difficult as Lucifer can be," Talon began, "I'm certain that if Azara were truly in danger, he'd step in, which leads me to believe the situation isn't critical."

"Yet," I added.

Ransom tightened his hold around me. "It's simple, we'll just have to stop Ronin's warlock from bringing Thanatos back in the first place."

"Sure, easy-peasy."

He dipped his head to the dark lord and her mate. "Azara, Talon, we appreciate the hospitality, but it's time for us to be on our way."

"I'm sorry we couldn't be of more help," she said. "Lucifer can be a little fickle at times, but Talon's right, he'll step in when necessary." She moved closer and lowered her voice. "It's true then? You're mates, even though he's a vampire?"

I opened my mouth to respond—to say what I wasn't

quite sure, but Ransom cut in before I could get the words out.

"It's complicated," he interjected.

Talon stepped to Azara and wrapped his big arm around her. "It always is." He smirked.

The dark lord snapped her fingers, and a whirling portal churned to life in the middle of their sitting room. "What's your next stop?"

Ransom's eyes met mine, and I nodded. It was time to go back to Nocturnis and face Ronin head on. "The Darklands, please."

"Good luck," said Azara. "And keep us in the loop with any developments on Thanatos, and we'll do the same."

"Thanks again," I shouted over the blustery winds.

Ransom's fingers entwined with mine, and we jumped into the spiraling abyss.

THE PORTAL SPAT us out along the river, the dark waves splashing over the walkway. I glanced across the bridge into Royal lands, and my chest tightened. The queen's betrayal still stung. I knew she was only trying to protect her people, but we could've worked together somehow. I still hoped we could. Which was probably stupid. Gods, I barely recognized myself anymore. When had I become this weak, sniveling girl? I was a badass vampire-killing sicari, and it was time I remembered that. No more hiding, no more tiptoeing around Ronin.

It was time to fight.

I unstrapped bardy from my back and thumbed the worn wooden shaft.

"Red, are you trying to make me jealous?" Ransom shot me his trademark smirk, revealing that dimple.

"No, but I was thinking that it's time to kick some rebel king ass."

"Agreed." His fangs dropped, and he flashed me a wicked grin. "But first, we need a new hideout."

"Fine by me. I was never really a fan of the safehouse."

"Don't worry, Red, I have something much grander in mind for our first love nest."

A laugh burst from my lips. "You're relentless."

"I know. And you love it."

I rolled my eyes at him, but I couldn't help the smile from pulling at my lips. The truth was that I *was* falling in love with him. Despite everything, in spite of all the terrible things he'd done and would likely continue to do. But I couldn't voice the words just yet because it would make them real. Letting myself love Ransom felt like admitting defeat somehow. Which was so messed up.

"Right this way, darling." He sketched a bow before wrapping his hand around mine once again. We took a few steps along the pathway on the river's edge when approaching footsteps stopped us mid-stride.

Ransom's nostrils flared, and his mouth twisted into a scowl. "Serviles."

"Great. Welcome back to the Darklands." I tightened my hold on bardy as adrenaline began to surge through my veins.

The pack of starving fangers turned the corner, and their watery gazes settled on us. In the center of the group, a familiar blonde head poked out. *Ugh, Dinah.*

Her eyes focused on Ransom like twin lasers of crimson, and her fangs extended. "Handsome Ransom, fancy meeting you here. I'd heard rumors you were back in town. But since

Rocco saw you at the blood brothel, I hoped you'd finally abandoned your little wolf." She shrugged. "Guess not."

"I just can't shake her, Dinah. You know how it is. Once you go Ransom, you never go back."

Oh, barf. I jabbed my elbow into his side to shut him up.

"As lovely as it is to see you again, Dinah, it was bad luck for you. You see, I'd rather not have Ronin know Red here is back in town. So as much as it pains me, I'm going to have to kill you now."

Her dark eyes grew wide. "You wouldn't dare."

"I'm afraid love makes you do foolish things, my dear."

I was pretty sure her eyes were going to pop out of her head, and I couldn't deny the tiny swirl of satisfaction. Although I didn't think blurting his feelings to Ronin's right-hand vamp was the smartest move on his part.

"You don't love her, you idiot. It's her blood. You're obsessed with her."

"You're probably right," I interjected. Better for her to think that than figure out the truth. Love was a weakness, after all. "But either way, Ransom's right. We can't have you running back to Ronin now." I dropped down and grabbed the stake strapped to my thigh. The serviles began to growl and hiss, slowly stepping toward us. With bardy in one hand and the stake in the other, I lunged.

My body went into autopilot, the calmness of battle icing my veins. I moved through the herd, slicing a path toward Dinah. After everything that female fanger put me through while I was in Ronin's prison, I was going to enjoy ending her.

The serviles began to disperse as bardy got to work, their shrieks and howls ricocheting across the night air. Ransom moved beside me, beautifully lethal. As the pack thinned, Dinah staggered back, the fire in her eyes dimming.

I saw it. The moment she decided to run. Her eyes widened, and she spun on her heel.

Ransom was busy with two serviles, so I took off after her. She leapt atop the river wall and dashed across the slate stone. Pumping my arms, I willed my legs to move faster, but damned that vampire speed. A growl vibrated in my chest, and that furry presence made itself known. The change came instantly. One second I was running on two legs, and the next I was down on all fours, a fiery fiend streaking through the night.

I leapt onto the wall, my four paws more sure-footed than my human feet and raced after the fleeing vamp. I vaguely registered Ransom's shouts from behind, but I didn't slow down. I needed this. It felt good to be free, to fight, to kill. This was what I'd spent my whole life training for. With any luck, Dinah would lead us right to Ronin.

I could feel the flames hovering over my fur as I ran, feel the heat but somehow the fire didn't burn me. It was the craziest thing. Dinah's blonde head bobbed just ahead now. I was gaining on her. My wolf was insanely fast, almost vampire speed. But not quite.

Dinah jumped off the wall and zipped down a dark alley-way. I chased after her, my wolf completely taking over. I was the predator, and she was my prey. Ahead, I could just make out a cinderblock wall. She was trapped. I slowed my pace and drew in a deep breath, steadying my frantic heartbeats.

Dinah backed against the wall, fear streaking across her obsidian irises.

I flashed her my fangs and tipped my head back. A deep howl echoed across the narrow alley. *Time to die, mother fanger.* I sat back on my haunches and lunged.

A glimmering portal opened right beside Dinah, and the vampire darted into the whirling winds. I slammed my front paws down, claws digging into the crumbling asphalt. Indecision stopped me in my tracks. Drakin had to be on the other side of that portal and Ronin too. This was my chance.

The portal began to close. Pushing myself off my back legs, I leapt toward the churning winds. My paws reached for the whirling vortex, but a hand closed around my tail, jerking me back. What the...? I let out a yip. The brilliant azure faded, and the mystical doorway slammed closed as I hit the floor.

"What the hell were you thinking, Red?" A pissed off vampire loomed over me, his fingers clenched tight around my flaming tail.

I growled at him and bared my fangs.

He released me and glanced at his burnt hands. Wincing, his scowl grew deeper. "Oh no you don't, wolfy. How could you even think of doing something so reckless? That portal could've delivered you straight into Ronin's hands."

I huffed out a wolfish sigh, then focused on the magic that lay beneath my fur. I couldn't fight with the overly protective vampire if I couldn't yell at him. The crimson haze surrounded me, and a second later I was back in skin.

"We're trying to find Ronin, remember?" I shouted, crossing my arms over my bare chest. It was damned hard to look intimidating when you were butt naked.

"Find him, yes. Not deliver yourself to him with a big red bow."

"Ransom, if this partnership is going to work you have to trust that I know what I'm doing. I was slaying vamps way before you showed up in my life."

"So you expect me to just sit there and watch you get killed?" The depth of emotion swirling through the onyx abyss of his irises pierced my soul. I relented, loosening my fighting stance.

"No," I mumbled. "But you have to let me fight my own battles."

He shook his head, clucking his teeth. "Fine, Red, next time you jump half-cocked into a portal to who knows where, I'll let you. But I'll be right behind you."

A faint smile parted my lips. "Deal." I swept my hair behind my ears and glanced back in the direction we'd come. "You took care of all the serviles?"

"Of course, I did."

"Guess it doesn't matter now that Dinah got away. She'll go straight to Ronin and tell him we're back in town."

Ransom shrugged. "You wanted a fight, Red. I have a feeling you're about to get one." Chewing on his lower lip, he regarded me, a renewed fire in his eyes. "Now put some clothes on or I'll be forced to have my way with you right here in the middle of the street." He tugged his shirt over his head and drew it over mine in a move so quick, all I saw was a black blur. Then he threw his arm around my shoulders and steered me back toward the main avenue. "Now, let's get home."

CHAPTER
SIX

R*ansom*

IT WASN'T THE RITZ, but at least it was a penthouse. I paced the length of windows that stretched the span of the master bedroom. Unlike my old place, this one had a generator, which meant electricity and running water, along with decent furniture which had been a fantastic bonus when we'd stumbled across it late last night.

Red was exhausted despite her protestations otherwise. She'd slept soundly all night as I stood guard. Now that Ronin knew we were back, it was only a matter of time before he made an appearance. Then there was the queen. She'd be on the lookout for Red too.

How had we gotten into this mess? And more importantly, how would I get her out?

Maybe it was time to take matters into my own hands. I could go to the queen and attempt to negotiate for Red's life. I knew exactly how to get her to comply with my demands. My gaze drifted to Red, her peaceful form splayed across the bed, brilliant auburn hair like a crimson halo. I had to protect her at all costs. My mate. I may not have completed the bond between us, for multiple reasons, but I loved her all the same. I couldn't imagine loving her any more. My cold, dead heart constricted at the thought.

We couldn't fight our enemies from both sides. I had to speak to Carmen Rosa and force her to see things my way. I eyed Red again, and my chest tightened. I hated leaving her alone, unprotected. But she was right. She was strong, and I had no doubt she could handle herself. Besides, if all went well, I'd be back before she awoke.

I slipped on my shirt and jeans before tugging on my leather jacket. As I walked by the bed, I paused, stealing one more glance at her. Bending down, I brushed my lips over her forehead. "Sleep, my love. I'll be back soon." As I straightened, I caught sight of Red's favorite weapon leaning against the opposite wall. I marched over to it, seized it in my hands and couldn't believe the surge of jealousy I felt over an inanimate object. She loved this weapon more than anything. With a rueful smile, I set it beside her on the bed. If anyone dared disturb her, they'd have bardy to contend with.

SNEAKING into the queen's private chamber was too easy. I'd have to mention that if she didn't kill me first. I stood at the balcony and peered into her room. As predicted, she was still asleep. I'd learned a few things about the queen's habits during my tenure at Royal Castle. I also knew she made her guards remain outside her bedroom. Which made this little impromptu visit all the easier for me.

Silently, I unlatched the window and climbed inside. The second my boots hit the floor, Carmen Rosa jolted up. She appeared small across the vast bed, thick crimson curtains concealing her from view. Her wild eyes snapped to mine, and the tension in her jaw dissipated. "Ah, Ransom. What an unexpected pleasure." She drew her hand through her dark locks, tying them back, then rose, pushing the elaborate drapery back. The long lacey train of her nightgown trailed her slender form as she moved toward me.

I'd been invited into that bed more than once during my days at the castle. For whatever reason, I'd never taken her up on the offer. Something about it seemed wrong. Though she'd never replace my real mother, as my sire, I held onto the familial tie.

She stopped mere inches from me, dark eyes boring into mine. "Why have you come, my son?"

"I don't want you as an enemy, Carmen Rosa. I've come to bargain for Phoenix's life."

Her eyes sparkled as a knowing smile crossed her crimson lips. "You're in love with the girl. How very trite, Ransom."

"The heart wants what it wants." I steeled my nerves, grinding my teeth. Better for her to think I was stupid than learn the truth about our mate bond.

"The heart," she chuckled, the shrill sound sending a wave of goose bumps rippling across my flesh. "It's the blood, you fool. Whatever you think you feel for her and she for you is only a result of the blood you've shared."

"Potato, potatoe."

She shook her head. "What is it that you think you can offer to change my mind? You understand that I'm only doing what I must to protect my people."

"I understand. And I'm offering you another solution."

"Go ahead."

"I believe you've overestimated your former friend, Ronin. We've done some of our own research and not only is he missing Red's blood but also that of the female warlock and vampire with a soul, if not more. If he can't have the other two, his need for Red becomes obsolete."

"I'm following..."

"Withdraw the bounty on Phoenix's head, and let's work together as we'd planned. We'll take Ronin down before he can summon Thanatos, and this will all be history by week's end."

She leaned against the door to the balcony, staring out into the dark night. "While that sounds lovely, it's not quite that easy, my child. Ronin's army grows more powerful by the day. While you and your little wolf were in hiding, the rebel king has amassed hundreds more serviles, as well as generals. You see, what he's offering is too tempting to even my most loyal subjects."

"More reason for us to move quickly."

She cocked a dark, perfectly sculpted brow. "What exactly are you suggesting?"

"A guarantee. If we do not put an end to Ronin's plotting in let's say two weeks, I'll make sure he's never able to complete the spell to break the curse."

"How?"

"Simple, I'll kill the only two female warlocks in existence." A stab of guilt pummeled my insides, but I swallowed it down burying it in the dark depths. I had to do everything in my power to save Red. Even if it cost me my non-existent soul.

"Easier said than done."

"Not really. The dark lord trusts me. Her mate too. I have no doubt if I asked her to convene with her mother to discuss the situation, she would do it. I'd have the element of surprise at my side."

Carmen Rosa clucked her teeth. "Well played, Ransom. I never thought you had it in you. Although, I should've guessed given your parentage."

I swallowed down the bitter guilt. While I had no desire to end Azara or her mother, the truth was that I would do it to save Red. I'd do anything.

"Just one thing." She lifted a finger to her lips. "Why do I need you? I could have the dark lord and her mother killed just as easily as you."

"Doubtful. Plus, why would you want that? Such a blatantly aggressive move would surely have you ejected from the Etrian Assembly. Azara sits on the council in the place of her grandfather, Lucifer. Targeting her would be an affront to the governing body of Azar, and everything you've fought so hard for would crumble."

Carmen Rosa's lips twisted. "It seems like you've thought of it all, haven't you?"

I nodded and threw her a satisfied smile. "It would benefit us all to work together. You have to agree."

"Hmm. Perhaps."

"I'll give you until tomorrow to consider. If not, we'll go after Ronin ourselves and risk getting captured again. You wouldn't want that now, would you?"

Something like pride gleamed across the queen's pitch irises. "No, I wouldn't."

I pivoted on my heel and marched toward the window. "I

look forward to receiving your answer," I called out over my shoulder before I jumped.

I hit the stone floor below and raced back toward the Darklands, thoughts of my little sicari guiding my feet and my troubled heart.

CHAPTER
SEVEN

P*hoenix*

"DID YOU FEED LAST NIGHT?" I suspiciously eyed the vampire dancing around the kitchen. Ransom seemed much too chipper for this early in the morning.

"I did not. I told you I'd try to be better, and I'm sticking to it." He poured the steaming hot coffee into a mug, sauntered across the living room, and handed it to me.

"So aren't you hungry?"

His fangs dropped, and a mischievous smirk flashed across his face. "I'm always hungry for you."

I couldn't help but laugh at his ridiculously cheesy line. The laughter quickly fell away when I remembered I had promised to let him feed from me. But that had been before he'd attacked the girl at Sky Lair. I gripped the mug between both hands, relishing in the soothing heat. I wanted to help

Ransom, I did, but would I just end up hurting myself? The things I was starting to feel for him... They scared the crap out of me.

Fang it. I needed his help to destroy Ronin and to accomplish that I needed Ransom operating on normal capacity. For now, my blood was the best I could offer. I pushed my hair back, exposing my bare neck. "Here, just do it."

"Damn, Red, you really know how to suck the fun right out of it."

I shot him my best eye roll. "No one's forcing you to take it."

He slid onto the couch beside me, batting sooty lashes. "I could never say no, Red."

My entire body prickled at his proximity. He swept aside a few strands of hair and dipped his head. Anticipation pooled low in my core as he inched closer. His breath skated over my skin, drawing a wave of goose bumps. I shuddered and Ransom stopped, eyes lifting to meet mine.

"Are you okay?"

"Yes," I rasped out. "Just do it."

A smirk curled the corners of his lips, and he hauled me into his lap. Cradling me against his chest, his fangs descended. I let out a faint gasp as the pointy tips pierced my skin, then another one as a wave of pleasure surged through my veins.

Mmm. Vampire venom. They should bottle the stuff and sell it on Amazon. My head spun, and I was lost to the mesmerizing sensations. It could've been a minute or an hour later, but when Ransom finally released me, I was clinging onto him like a baby koala. My fingers were tangled in his shirt, and my legs were wrapped around his torso. Mother fanger, how had that happened?

Ransom's arm tightened around me, pressing me closer

to his chest. He licked his lips and those twinkling eyes met mine. He always looked different right after he'd fed, more alive, more human. And still his unearthly beauty shone through.

"Thank you," he mumbled thickly. His thumb grazed my bottom lip, and he tipped up my chin. Damn, I'd been caught staring slack jawed.

"Anytime," I forced out.

"You know, you don't have to do this. We can find another way to wean me off the human stuff slowly."

"I know, but it's the one thing I can do for you. I know there are a lot of things unsettled between us right now, but this... I want to give you this."

He nodded slowly as if he truly understood. And maybe he did. Maybe this bond between us helped him understand the tangle of emotions I felt for him. I wished I could give myself to him fully, but after the betrayal and the constant back and forth, I was terrified.

Finding out my mom had been unfaithful to my dad had only made it worse. How could I trust my own feelings when I'd been so blind to the truth for so long?

My phone buzzed, pulling me from my spiraling thoughts. Only Spark and my team had this number, a gift from the dragon alpha when we were back in Draeko. I flipped it open and scanned the message. A curse slid through my clenched lips.

"What?" Ransom's dark brows jumped up.

"Ronin's on the move with a huge horde of serviles. Spark thinks they're making their move to take the castle."

"That's not good." He bit into his wrist and offered me his arm. "Guess it's time to get ready for battle."

I nodded slowly, already salivating. I longed for the high from his blood, the rush of power. If we were really going to take Ronin on, I'd need it. I swept my tongue over his flesh, drinking him in and my mind flashed back to when we'd slept together. How was it so easy for us to exchange blood, and yet we couldn't when it counted most? I resolved to bring up the logistics of completing the mate bond later.

I released him, the intoxicating effects of his blood coursing through my system. Immediately, I felt stronger, like tiny bolts of electricity crackled through each and every nerve-ending.

"Where is Ronin exactly?" he asked, drawing me back to the present.

I grabbed the flip phone off my lap and typed out a quick message. Spark's response came back in seconds. "Less than a mile outside the compound gates."

"Then we don't have much time." He took my hand and tugged me off the couch. Before I could object, he scooped me into his arms. "We can't wait around for your slow wolf today."

"Oh, bite me," I teased.

"Any time, any day, Red."

RANSOM STOPPED as we reached the crest of the hill, sending my hair whipping across my face. "Oh goddess," he hissed out. I sucked in a breath as I took in the scene below. Growls and snarls rent the air, the scent of blood assaulting my nostrils. *Mother fanger.* There were hundreds and hundreds of them. Vampires dotted the landscape. Where had all these serviles come from? There were at least ten times more than last time.

The fangers flooded the compound, the wrought iron gate that surrounded the outer perimeter had been trampled. I jumped out of Ransom's arms as I scanned the destruction below. I could just make out the sicari teams and queen's guards battling it out in the front lines. "We have to get down there."

Ransom's hand closed around my forearm and held me back. "Wait. Not until I have eyes on Ronin." He scanned the mass of clashing forms below, the cries and howls of battle echoing around us, and I followed his line of sight. I doubted the king would be in the middle of the fray. Last time he'd stayed back, right about where we were now standing.

The hair on the back of my neck rose, and I spun around.

"So nice to finally see you again, Phoenix." Ronin's deep voice had the remaining hair on my body standing at attention.

Ransom darted in front of me. His arm slapped across my chest and forced me behind the flesh and blood armor of his body.

Drakin coalesced beside the rebel king a second later, his form smoke and air. I eyed the warlock, trying to assess who stood before me, but I couldn't tell.

Ransom was so stiff beside me, his muscles vibrated with tension. "Stay away from her," he growled.

"So protective..." He tsked. "I've told you time and again that I don't wish to kill the young sicari. I only wish for her to join the winning team. It's the same thing I've wished for you all along, Ransom."

"And I've told you repeatedly that I'm not interested."

"So you say." He cocked a dark brow, his bald head glistening beneath the moonlight. "I think Phoenix would be interested if she knew what I had to offer in return."

"There's nothing I want from you," I spat.

"I believe you'll reconsider once you know what it is." Ronin ticked his head at the warlock. "Show her."

Drakin's lips curled into a snarl. His navy eyes blazed a brilliant azure, and he opened his hand, revealing a shimmery orb in his palm. It drifted up, until it hovered at eyelevel. I let out an internal breath of relief; still the warlock, not Thanatos.

"Cool shiny ball," said Ransom. "What other parlor tricks can your pet warlock do?"

Ronin waved him off and directed his dark gaze at me. "Look closely, Phoenix, and tell me what you see."

I couldn't see anything with my vampire bodyguard planted in front of me. I scooted around him, but his arm closed around me like a vice grip. "He's trying to bait you."

"I just want to see what it is," I countered.

The orb grew larger until it completely blocked out the top half of Drakin's form. I squinted trying to make out the images more clearly. Twinkling lights and faint music swirled within the magical bubble, and something familiar about the scene rose to the surface. I inched closer, and my heart staggered on a beat.

It was my family. My parents, Kenna and I stood in front of the Christmas tree at Rockefeller Center. It was the one photograph that I'd rescued from the fire. All the air evacuated my lungs, and my knees began to wobble. Oh gods, he knew about Kenna.

Had he gotten into my head somehow when I was held captive? How could I have not realized? I tightened my grip on bardy and forced steel through my veins. "What do you want? Why are you showing me this?" I growled.

A smug smile curled Ronin's lips. "Do you remember what I used to ask you when I'd come visit you in your cell?"

"The month in chains was kind of a blur, vamp-hole. You're going to have to be more specific."

"I asked you to think about what you wanted most in this world. And what you'd do if I could give it to you."

Ah, yes. Now it was all coming back to me. The guy was delusional because the only thing I wanted was my parents back, and they were dead... My stomach somersaulted midthought. I must have paled because Ransom's arm came around my waist to steady me.

"What are you saying?" I managed.

"Once Thanatos walks freely on this earth, the veil between the living and the dead will be no more. He has the power to bring back any who have died."

My head spun, the darkness swimming around me. It couldn't be. It wasn't possible—was it?

"I'm pretty sure it's not that easy, Ronin," Ransom spat, his voice grounding me.

"Well, not for vampires anyway, that's a trickier situation."

I struggled beneath the tidal wave of panic constricting my lungs. Digging bardy's pointed end into the ground, I used the staff to keep me up. Between my trusty weapon and Ransom I had to at least pretend I could stand.

Ransom snorted.

"You dare question a god?" Ronin replied. "Thanatos has dominion over all the dead. It would only take a snap of his fingers to bring Phoenix's beloved parents back."

My father wasn't even my real father. The absurd thought streaked across my mind. Could he bring back my biological father, Tyrien, too? Did I even want to know the man whose blood ran through my veins? I shook away the notion. No, after everything I'd heard about the supreme alpha, he deserved to remain dead and buried. But my parents? I could finally get all the answers I needed. Find out exactly what happened and how I'd ended up as Tyrien's illegitimate daughter.

"It's not possible," I muttered, more to myself than the mad king. People couldn't just come back from the dead, not after ten years. My eyes flitted to the orb, to our smiling faces.

"Oh, ye of little faith." He ticked his head at Ransom. "Didn't your vampire lover come back from the dead? That was all through the power of Thanatos."

"That's different," I spat.

"It is, and it isn't." An arrogant smile parted his thin lips. "I'm so close now, Phoenix. Soon Thanatos will once again walk this earth and if you choose the right side, you and your parents will walk beside him. Beside us." He raised his hands, motioning to all the serviles below. "Where do you think I got my army?"

My stomach roiled as I glanced at the horde of zombie-like serviles.

"With Thanatos's help I was able to reanimate my Children of the Night. And that was only with the god functioning at half power, if that. Imagine what he could do once he's in corporeal form."

I swallowed hard. I so did not want to see that. If he really could resurrect the dead, it would be chaos.

Ronin ticked his head at Drakin, and he closed his palm. The orb blinked out of existence, my family vanishing into oblivion. "I didn't realize you had a sister, Phoenix. Imagine my surprise. Now I'm wondering if she too inherited your mortal bite."

"She didn't," I spat as terror seized my chest. "She's just a kid. She hasn't even shifted yet." I slammed my jaw shut the moment the words were out. Dammit.

"There's still hope then."

But there wasn't. She wasn't Tyrien's daughter, she wasn't blessed by the damned goddess Luna, only I was. "Stay away from her!"

"I'd be happy to, as long as you cooperate."

"She won't," Ransom snapped. "The only way you get what you want is with Phoenix bleeding out on some witchy altar. And I'll never let that happen."

Ronin clucked his teeth. "So dramatic, son. Who says Phoenix has to die? I only need some of her blood to complete the spell."

"Some?" I blurted.

"The ancient texts are rather muddled. It's difficult to ascertain the exact quantity."

Ransom opened his mouth to argue, but I cut in. "Let's say you only needed a little bit. You're telling me that if I give you my blood, you'll leave my sister alone, stop hunting me and bring back my parents? And the only downside for me is the end of the shadow curse?"

"Red..." Ransom's weary eyes searched mine.

"I just want an answer."

"Precisely. Once Thanatos is earthbound, I won't need your wolf. Together, he and I will rule Azar and you can go back to doing whatever it is that you enjoy with your vampire lover."

Ugh, that phrase grated on my nerves. But I had more important things to worry about than Ronin's opinions of my relationship status.

"He's obviously lying," said Ransom. "Once Thanatos has been summoned, who knows what the crazy bastard will do? There are reasons why the gods no longer roam the earth."

Ronin's dark eyes twinkled as he regarded the vampire beside me. "If I were you, I wouldn't be so quick to banish the idea of the reappearance of the god of death. Perhaps he could help with your own little dilemma."

A growl vibrated Ransom's chest, the sound so loud I was fairly certain even the rebel king and his warlock heard it from across the way over the cries of battle.

Ronin raised his hands, a placating grin on his face. "Don't say anything right now. I'll give you a few days to consider my offer. By then, the queen will be dethroned, and I have a feeling you'll be looking at things a little differently."

My brows shot up, and my head spun over my shoulder to the masses below. Had they really infiltrated the castle? "We have to go." I grabbed Ransom's hand and jerked him down the hill.

"Don't forget to consider my offer, Phoenix." Ronin's singsong echoed behind me as I descended, leaping over mounds of ash and random body parts.

My heart slammed against my chest, faster and harder the closer I got to the herd. Were we too late? Had they breached the castle? And where was my team?

I cursed Carmen Rosa for forcing me into hiding. If I'd only been here...

"Red, to your right!" Ransom's cry reached me just in time, jerking me from my whirling thoughts.

I swung bardy and decapitated the attacking fanger. Carving a path through the center with the help of my vampire bodyguard, we moved through the hundreds of bloodthirsty serviles. As we raced deeper into the thick of things, it wasn't just vampire body parts I was forced to jump over. I compelled my eyes up, refusing to look down at the fallen sicari. It wouldn't be my team. Spark knew the herd was coming. They would've been prepared. I'd taught them better than that.

We passed the trampled gate, and the mass of serviles

finally thinned out. Just ahead I could make out the line of sicari holding them off. The fangers had nearly reached the drawbridge. Some had hazarded a jump and their bodies dangled, impaled on the stakes hidden beneath the murky depths.

A brilliant flash of purple sent my head swiveling to the right. I immediately recognized Vera's dark hair as she unleashed a wave of magic across the attacking serviles. She stood atop the stone pedestal that led onto the bridge. "Vera!" I shouted. Her eyes met mine for an instant before a fanger leapt at her. "No!" I screeched and pumped my arms faster, racing across the battlefield.

"Red, wait!" Ransom called out behind me, but I didn't stop. I had to get to my friend. The vamps closed around me, and I lost sight of her.

"Move! Out of the way!" I shouted.

A second later, Cal's alabaster wings appeared over the crowd, their heavenly glow lighting up the dark night. Vera lay across his arms, unmoving.

"No, no, no!" I barreled through the remaining vamps between us, slicing my way across decaying bodies. Ransom raced beside me, snapping necks and ripping hearts out like it was his day job. When we reached the bridge, I let out the breath I'd been holding.

Spark, Seline, and Archer all stood around Callan and Vera. My friend's eyes were closed, but her chest rose and fell in a steady rhythm. Tears filled my eyes, emotion clogging my throat. "Is she okay?"

Callan nodded. "She hit her head on the stone floor when the fanger lunged. She could probably use the rest. She's been overusing her magic trying to fend off the attack."

I quickly wrapped my arms around my team. "Thank the gods you guys are okay."

"We are, but we can't say the same for the queen's castle." Archer motioned at the looming fortress behind us and the serviles scaling the walls. "There's just too many of them."

"And we're the last line of defense," said Spark.

"Sounds like we're all screwed then." Ransom smirked.

I ignored his comment and scanned the field. To my right, I recognized a few more of the sicari teams still holding the bridge, but Archer was right, we were greatly outnumbered.

"Hold the line!" River shouted from a few yards back. The sicari teams' leader bellowed instructions to the remaining slayers.

But it was no use. The entire compound was overrun. From over Spark's head, I could make out the building that used to house the remaining sicari. Serviles spilled from doorways, shattering glass and trampling the fine furnishings.

"Has anyone seen the queen?" I cried out over the chaos.

"I saw some of her personal guards hightail it back inside a few minutes ago," Spark answered. "I'm pretty sure they were her ticket out of there."

"Do you really think she'd abandon her throne?"

"If it meant her life, yes," Ransom answered. "There's no such thing as a good dead queen."

The serviles continued their advance, their snarls and cries ricocheting across the stone. We wouldn't be able to stay here much longer.

"What now, boss?" Archer tossed me a smug smile. "Or is Spark still in charge?"

I exchanged a look with my old friend. "Spark is still our temporary team leader. We'll do what he recommends."

His eyes grew wide as he regarded me. "Right," he

mumbled. Turning to the team, he scanned the same weary gazes I'd been watching. "Every good leader knows when it's time to retreat. And I think this is it."

"Excellent choice, dragon boy." Ransom grinned.

"Where to?" Callan asked, his wings flapping leisurely, so he and Vera hovered just a foot above the ground.

"Nix, any ideas?" Spark turned to me.

"Well..." I glanced over at Ransom and shot him my very best smile.

"No, no, not the penthouse, Red," Ransom whined.

"I like the sound of that," Archer chimed in.

"Don't even think about getting comfy there, Fae boy."

I elbowed Ransom in the gut. "It's our best option for now. We'll regroup and come up with a plan tomorrow."

"Fine," he muttered. "But all you girls better not hog the bathroom."

CHAPTER
EIGHT

R*ansom*

I COULDN'T BELIEVE the Scooby gang had raided our love nest. I huffed out a frustrated breath as I watched the witch and the angel making out on *my* couch. Okay, well, technically nothing was really mine, but it should've been. Mine and Red's.

What a hell of a day this had turned out to be, and to think it had started out with such promise. Which reminded me, Carmen Rosa's time was nearly up. Surely, she'd take me up on my offer of a truce now that she'd been ousted from her precious castle.

Sparky trudged across the living room and settled down beside me on the kitchen island. I shot the dragon a narrowed glare, but he didn't even flinch. Dammit. I needed to work on my game. He didn't find me the slightest bit intimidating anymore. That was what love did to a man. "I just heard back from River. The entire compound has been taken over by the Children of the Night. Ronin's probably settling his fanger ass into the queen's throne as we speak." The dragon directed his statement at Red who stood by the window, staring out into the Darklands.

When she didn't reply, I took advantage. "This should be interesting. I wonder how the Etrian Assembly will react to that. Why don't you tell your alpha daddy, dragon boy?"

"Fang off," he gritted out.

"Both of you shut up." Red marched over, hands planted on her hips. "As much as I hate to admit it, Ransom's right. We need to see how this plays out with the Etrian Assembly."

I snorted on a laugh. "They won't do anything. They're too busy sitting on their gilded thrones to stop a mad man's revolution."

"You don't know that," Spark snarled back. "My father understands what Ronin's planning. He'll tell the others, and they'll never allow it."

I shrugged. "Maybe, maybe not."

"Azara knows too," Red added.

A twinge of guilt rocketed through my insides at the mention of the dark lord. The dark lord-slash-female-warlock that I'd promised to kill if things went sideways. Did I hope it wouldn't come to that? Of course. Would I do it if it meant saving Red? Also, of course. Love ruined rational men, and I was slightly unhinged to begin with. I was totally fanged.

Seline appeared from one of the bedrooms and her gaze caught on Spark. She darted over and positioned herself between her current lover and his ex. "So what do we do for now?"

"Let's just wait until the dust settles," said Red. "At least now we'll know where to find Ronin when we need to."

"You don't think that warlock of his will have the castle warded up till kingdom come?"

"Probably, but since when has that stopped us?" She shrugged. "And anyway, Ronin's waiting for my answer, remember? I'm pretty sure that'll give us a ticket inside."

"At the low, low price of your life."

Red rolled her eyes at me. "I don't think Ronin really knows how much of my blood he needs. Vera couldn't figure it out so why would Drakin? He's not that all-powerful. It would explain why he always wanted to keep me around. He doesn't know exactly what he'll need from me."

"Whoa, whoa, whoa," said Spark. "I think we missed something here. How are you even considering going to see him?"

Red quickly summarized our encounter with the rebel king during the battle as Spark and the rest of the team stared expectantly.

"Do you think he can really resurrect your parents?" Vera asked.

Red chewed on her bottom lip, a nervous habit I found irresistible, and I wondered if her friends knew the truth about her biological father. "I don't know," she finally mumbled. "But even if he could, I wouldn't sacrifice all of Azar to bring them back."

A glossy sheen curtained her expressive irises, and I understood the truth in her words. She was a real-life hero-ine. She'd always put the good of all over her own selfish desires. Unlike me. It was a good thing she had me in her life to make the selfish decisions for her.

Ransom, it's time to talk, my child. Carmen Rosa's voice

echoed through my mind, and I nearly crawled out of my skin.

What are you doing in my head? I drew up my walls, trying to force out the invasive presence.

No, don't block me out yet. We need to talk.

The rumors about the queen's telepathic abilities were true then. Why had she never made them known to me before? I slowly slunk away from the group and drifted toward the windows. Had the queen found us? I scanned the streets below, but not a shadow stirred. *What do you want?* I kept my eyes on the surrounding darkness, searching for the queen or her guards.

You said I had until tonight to get back to you regarding Phoenix. I'm doing just that.

A smile curved my lips. *Now you want our help? Now that you've been ousted from your throne.*

Does the deal still stand or not, Ransom? As you can imagine, I'm not in the most patient mood this evening.

Well, I'm just thinking that the deal isn't quite as attractive anymore. Without a castle, without your guards, you don't exactly have a safe place to offer Red any longer. How would this arrangement benefit us?

I'm still the queen, despite the temporary loss of the castle.

Are you though? I singsonged.

Don't push me, Ransom.

Why not? It's not like you'd waste your precious resources coming after Red now.

No, I wouldn't, but we can still work together to bring Ronin down. Isn't that what your precious sicari wants anyway?

She had a point. Red still desired Ronin's demise above all else. And having one less enemy to contend with, despite the queen's current status, would be beneficial, but I had to sweeten the deal somehow. *Fine, but I have an addendum to the initial agreement.*

What is it? Her frustrated sigh resounded across my mind.

I need your word that if Phoenix ever gets captured by Ronin again, you'd do everything in your power to get her out. And not like last time, Carmen Rosa. I mean legitimately moving heaven and hell to find her.

Yes, fine. I agree. Is that all?

For now. I smirked.

Good. Now, I assume Phoenix and what remains of her team are within your reach.

Sure. I eyed the streets below one more time. *Still quiet.*

I need all the remaining sicari assembled. River and his team are with me, and we are working on finding the others. Tell the witch to await my message. Ronin will not sit upon my throne for long.

We anxiously await your instructions, my liege.

The connection between us closed, and I quickly threw up my mental barriers. If the queen had been able to speak to me telepathically all along, why hadn't she come after Red a long time ago? My brows drew together. Perhaps, she never really wanted to harm Red after all, and she was content with having her wolf in hiding.

A hand landed on my shoulder, and I spun around, bristling. "Geez, Red, put a bell on or something."

"What's going on? Why are you being so quiet?"

I took her hand and towed her into the bedroom we'd shared just the other night. "I talked to the queen."

"What? How?" Her brows shot up.

I pointed at my temple. "Apparently, the queen's telepathic abilities aren't just rumor."

"She contacted you out of nowhere?"

I nodded. Sort of true. "In any case, given the situation, she's no longer a threat to you. She needs our help."

Her eyes narrowed as she regarded me, as if she could ferret out the truth. "Just like that? She's given up on keeping me locked up or flat out killing me?"

I sat on the bed and crossed my legs, trying hard for that casually sexy look. "Red, she did just lose her throne. She's not exactly in a place to make demands." I patted the empty spot beside me. "Anyway, she needs you and River to round up all the remaining sicari. She's trying to summon up her forces to take back the castle."

Red ignored my invitation and stood in front of me, arms pressed against her chest. "Ransom..."

"What?" I gave her my most innocent smile.

"This all seems a little too convenient."

Curses. My little sicari was too smart. Either that or she knew me too well. That was highly disconcerting. "I may have promised her something in return."

"I knew it!" She pointed her finger at me triumphantly, and I couldn't help the smile from curling my lip. "What was the deal?"

"I may have told her that I'd eliminate one of the other critical components of the spell if things got out of control."

"What does that mean?" she growled, stepping closer.

Lie. Lie. "I told her I'd kill Azara and her mother if I had to." *Dammit!*

Her eyes widened to astronomical proportions as her mouth curved into a capital O. "How could you?" she shrieked. "Azara welcomed us into their home! How could you even consider killing her? She's a dark lord of the Underworld and Lucifer's granddaughter! Are you out of your mind?"

I leapt up and captured her hands between our bodies.

"Yes," I snarled back. "I'm out of my mind with fear that someone would take you away from me."

She struggled in my grasp, jerking her wrists free. "Well, if you keep this up, the only person that's going to take me away from you is *you*." She jabbed her finger into my chest. "You have to stop doing these terrible things in my name. I'd rather die a hundred times over than let you kill someone to save me. Don't you understand that?"

"I do! I know perfectly well how stupidly selfless you are. Which is why you need me to make the hard choices to protect you."

"Ransom!" She grabbed me by the collar, those emerald irises ablaze. "You can't keep doing this. Don't you see that the harder you fight to keep me, the more you're pushing me away? I can't be with someone, I can't love someone who I can't trust, mate bond or not." She shoved me back and I fell onto the bed, my heart sputtering out a dismal beat. She marched out of the room and slammed the door behind her. It had a depressing ring of finality to it.

69

CHAPTER
NINE

P *hoenix*

"NESTOR'S BEEN IN TOUCH." Vera marched into the kitchen with a sleepy Cal at her heels. The past few days in the penthouse with the whole team had gone surprisingly smoothly. With the exception of the occasional heated argument between Ransom and Spark, no one had killed each other which I viewed as a win, considering the circumstances. Luckily, the space was large enough for everyone to keep some distance.

Even Ransom had kept away after our last fight, choosing to sleep on the couch instead of "our room". I hated that I missed him, missed the comfort and safety of falling asleep in his arms. But fated mate or not, I couldn't be with someone with so little regard for human life. Ransom's love for me made him even more reckless, more volatile. I huffed out a breath as I watched him from the corner of my eye. He stood at the floor-to-ceiling windows, staring out into the darkness. He didn't even turn around when Vera entered.

Given the temporary truce with the queen, I'd let go of the idea of approaching Ronin with a deal. I had nothing to offer him besides my blood and as much as I wanted my parents back, I couldn't have that and risk an apocalypse of the dead rising.

I placed my mug down on the oversized island and glanced up at my friend. If the queen's warlock had reached out, there must have been a plan in place. I'd been itching to get back out there. "What's going on?"

"They've rounded up all the remaining sicari, or at least those that hadn't deserted or were too wounded to fight."

"How many are left?" Archer appeared in the doorway of his room, platinum hair sticking up in wild spikes.

"Including us, River and his team, thirty-two."

I hissed out a breath through clenched teeth. We'd been a hundred and thirty-nine strong when we arrived at Nocturnis. After the attack on the sicari residences and the infiltration of the castle, two-thirds of us were gone.

"Damn..." muttered Cal.

"What's going on?" Spark poked his head around the corner, and Seline appeared beside him. The pair had been sharing one of the bedrooms, and I was surprised by how okay I was about it. Spark would always hold a special place in my heart, but I'd moved on. My gaze unwittingly flickered to the unusually quiet vampire in the corner.

"We have to get ready to move," I finally answered, turning to my team.

"I thought the queen wanted you dead?" Spark cocked a curious brow at me.

"Ransom already took care of that little problem." From the corner of my eye, I caught him stiffen.

"We're all on the same side again?" Seline asked.

"Looks that way." I turned to Vera. "What else did Nestor say?"

"The queen wants to meet with all of us this afternoon to go over the plan. Nestor will open a portal to summon us through so the queen's location remains secret."

"Great." Spark clapped his hands. "I don't know about you all, but I'm ready for some action."

"I need coffee," Seline grumbled, trudging around him.

I grabbed the pot, filled a mug, and handed it to her. "Anyone else? We need to bring our A-game today, guys. With our numbers down, each of us has to make it count."

"Coffee all around then," said Ransom, finally turning to face us. "Why don't I open up a vein to spike your drinks with? Because you're going to need a hell of a lot more than caffeine to survive this."

"Ransom..." I growled.

"No, Red. I won't be shushed. They deserve to know what they're getting into." He shot me a glare. "You all do. With Ronin holding the castle, he has the upper hand. Your numbers are down by a third, and the queen is sending you into a bloodbath. You're expendable. Don't you all get that?"

"You're not helping," I shouted.

"Yeah, this is kind of what we do, fanger." Spark rolled his eyes. "We fight for the good guys."

"Good, bad, it's all so black and white to you all." Ransom shook his head, his lips curling into a sneer. "You'll never get it until you realize there's a whole world of gray out there." He pointed across the dark streets below. "Ronin may be crazy in wanting to summon Thanatos and take the queen's throne, but he's not all wrong. Why are vampires forced to dwell in the darkness? Why can't we consume human blood like we were made to? No one asked to become what we are. I sure as hell didn't. But I still have to deal with it, every damn day."

I watched him, my eyes growing wider with each word. Where was this coming from? Was this just about our fight?

"I was a wolf just like you, Seline, less than a year ago. Hell, I was the alpha heir to a prominent pack. And now, because of some twist of fate, I'm relegated to the darkness, to live out the rest of my immortal life enduring relentless hunger. It's not fair. Those serviles, they didn't ask for any of this. The Royals get to do what they want, eat from whomever they please and no one bats an eye. The whole system is fanged up if you ask me."

The entire room was quiet. He paused and sucked in his lower lip.

"Vampires aren't born this way, remember that. We were all something else before this was forced upon us. We all had lives, had families. I'm not saying Ronin is right, but he's not all that wrong either."

"So what are you saying?" I finally blurted.

"Are you not going to fight with us?" Vera asked.

That dark gleam lit up his eyes, and his typical smirk returned. "No, I'll fight. I go where Red goes. Call me stupid, call me whipped, but it is what it is. I just wanted you all to realize what you were fighting for."

Heat blossomed across my cheeks as my team's gazes zipped from Ransom's to mine.

"Aw cute, the fanger's got a crush," Archer singsonged.

I shot my teammate a scathing glare, and the Fae's gaze dropped to the floor. After another beat of silence, I faced my team. "Ransom's not some fanger with a crush. He's my fated mate."

The silence took on a whole other level as all eyes bored down on me. Including Ransom's, which was the heaviest of them all. He darted across the room so fast I blinked, and he stood before me. Those eyes seared into me, the deepest, most profound obsidian. When he was this close, I just wanted to drown in them, to lose myself forever in him. Despite my logical mind telling me what a bad idea that was.

His mouth descended on mine, and my lips curved to his despite the audience. I knew I shouldn't love this man, knew giving into my feelings for him was the worst decision ever, but that was the problem: logical thoughts had no say in it. What I felt for him was bone deep and there was no denying it.

When he finally released me, a ridiculous smile played on his lips. "Thank you," he mouthed.

"Um, is anyone going to explain this?" Archer asked. "Or are you two just going to make out some more?"

"I thought his wolf died when he did," said Seline.

"We're not really sure how any of it is possible," I answered once I'd caught my breath from the searing kiss.

I could feel Spark's heavy gaze on me from across the room, but I wasn't ready to meet it. At least now I hoped he'd understand why I'd ended things with him. Dragons had mates too.

"Wait a second," said Cal, rubbing his chin. "Could Ransom be the vampire with a soul?"

"No!" Ransom spun at the Nephilim, nostrils flaring, and fangs extended.

Cal held his hands up. "Whoa, chill, I'm just saying it makes sense. I've never met a vampire who can still shift."

"I can't shift," Ransom snarled.

"Then how are you two mates?" Spark asked.

Ransom's arms came over his chest as if they could

somehow deflect the barrage of questions. Maybe blurting out the truth hadn't been the wisest move.

"We're not sure exactly," I finally answered when Ransom's lips remained sealed shut. "But my wolf can sense his somehow."

"That's what brought your wolf out." Seline's eyes widened in understanding.

"I guess so."

Spark's eyes lifted to mine, and the storm of emotions sailing through the brilliant amber shook me. "Have you completed the bond?" His tone was flat, lifeless.

"I don't think that's any of your business," Ransom snapped.

I slowly shook my head at my friend.

My mercurial vampire mate grunted and stomped into the back bedroom. My gaze trailed his movements for a long moment before returning to my team's curious faces. I owed them an explanation after lying to them for weeks.

After I hashed out the story, a heavy silence blanketed the room. "It doesn't change anything," I said after another endless minute of quiet. "I don't know what this thing between us means, not with his wolf being gone." I pivoted to Cal and raised a brow. "Is there someone within the Sons of Heaven that could determine if Ransom still has a soul?" I figured his heavenly counterparts had to have some sort of intuition on the subject.

He shrugged, lips screwing into a pout. "I'm not sure, but I can find out for you." He ticked his head at the door Ransom had disappeared into. "Your mate seems pretty adamant he doesn't have one though."

"Ignore him. The whole dead wolf thing is a touchy subject."

"I'll see what I can uncover."

"Thanks, Cal."

Vera squeezed her boyfriend's hand and rewarded him with a smile.

"Enough sitting around, guys." I stood and faced my team, my fingers itching to reach for bardy who leaned against the wall by the door. "In a few hours, we go to meet the queen. If we can't take Ronin down, we're all out of a job, so let's make sure we don't fang this up."

A whoop broke out, echoing across the high ceilings of the penthouse. "Everyone grab what weapons you have left and meet me in the apartment downstairs in thirty minutes. It's vacant and big, so we can get in a quick training session before we go."

"Wait a second, if there are other livable apartments in this place, why have we all been stuck on top of each other?" Archer asked.

"Because, you Fae brat, this is the only one with a generator and running water." I pointed at the door with a smirk. "You're more than welcome to stay down there if you'd like."

Archer snorted on a laugh. "I don't think so, Nix."

I turned toward the hallway and called out over my shoulder, "See you down there in thirty." Then I pivoted to the room at the end of the hall. There was something I had to do first.

I peered through the crack in the door before I entered. Ransom lay across the bed, eyes closed. I watched the steady rise and fall of his bare chest for a few more seconds before I steeled my nerves and marched in. I didn't know what exactly I was going to say to him, but something had to be said. It wasn't that I magically forgave him for promising to kill Azara to save me, but hearing his speech back there changed something.

All this time, I looked at vampires—at him as the enemy.

I never considered the truth, that they were as much victims of circumstance as I was, as my parents were. With those words, my view of the world pivoted, and suddenly everything was different.

I crept onto the bed beside him, my flesh lighting up at his proximity. We'd been at odds for too long, and the burgeoning bond between us was angry. It longed for completion, burned to be made whole. Placing my head on his chest, I snuggled into his side. My blood sang.

After days fighting, it was like the pinnacle of pleasure without any of the sex. My thoughts bounced back to that night when we'd failed to complete the bond. My wolf nudged at my ribcage, butting her big head against my insides. She still longed for that connection. Her loneliness, her grief seeped into my conscious thought.

Despite all the terrible things Ransom had done, I would've tried to complete the bond just for her sake.

A muffled groan slid from Ransom's parted lips, drawing my attention to his mouth. His eyes were still closed, but the steady rise and fall of his chest had accelerated. Maybe even in sleep he could feel me too.

A low growl filled my belly, confirming my suspicions. My wolf mostly made her presence known when his was around. My thoughts flew to Callan. Would one of the angels be able to give us an answer? Would Ransom even agree to go to Celestia to find out?

Ransom sighed and rolled toward me, trapping me beneath his strong arm and muscled leg. I smiled into his chest as his arm tightened around me. I peeked up at him, but his eyes were still closed. So I settled into him, his warmth and steady breathing making my own lids heavy.

I must have nodded off because I awoke in a panic to check the time. My arm was wrapped around Ransom's bare torso and pinned in place by his heavy bicep. I tried to wriggle free, but he groaned at the movement.

Ugh. I was stuck. I was crushed against Ransom's body, my mouth pressed to his chest. Thirty minutes had to have passed by now, and my team would be waiting for me. I hated waking him especially when I didn't have time to say all the things I wanted to now.

I tried to slide my arm out from under his, or loosen his hold around my waist, but it was no use. *Come on now...* I pushed against his chest, but his arms were like steel vices.

A dark chuckle filled the air between us, and my eyes shot up to his. "Ransom," I squeaked.

"You've got another thing coming if you think I'm going to let you go now." He arched a mischievous brow. "You sneak into my bed and press your body against mine like you mean it... what did you think was going to happen?" He shot me his trademark grin, revealing that devastating dimple.

"Ransom, I wanted to talk, I still do, but I'm supposed to meet with my team to train."

"Not right now you're not." He rolled his hips against mine, and his arousal pressed against my upper thigh.

"Ransom..." I groaned, but even I could hear my conviction faltering.

He didn't waste any time to take advantage of my floundering. His lips descended on mine before he rolled me on top of him. I grumbled against his mouth as I straddled him, my traitorous body melding to his.

"You're already late, Red. A few more minutes won't make a difference. Especially not for what I have planned for you." A wicked grin curled his lips before he claimed my mouth again.

I was helpless when I was trapped against him. All

logical thought flew out the window as my body simply reacted to his. "Make it quick," I mumbled against his lips.

"Oh, Red, I love it when you talk dirty." His hands skated down my back, cupping my butt and pressing me harder against his lower half.

A burst of pleasure lit up my core as he rubbed against the bundle of nerves at my center. "Oh, gods," I groaned.

Ransom took that as an invitation, his deft fingers making quick work of my bra, then top. As my shirt hit the floor, I glanced down at the man splayed out beneath me. The man. My mate. In that moment, he wasn't a vampire, he wasn't a fanger, he was just perfect.

And *mine*. My wolf growled.

Ransom's eyes drifted to my chest and for once I didn't think it was my boobs that had caught his attention. His ghostly wolf whined in return, the sound whistling in his chest. I lowered myself against him and palmed his sculpted pecs.

"That was a new sound," I whispered.

His head dipped, but he didn't say a word.

The closer we got the more his wolf seemed to surge to the surface. His thundering heartbeats battered my palm, as if his heart were desperate to break free. I smiled at the persistent beat. To think he had died... I squeezed my eyes shut to banish the panic-inducing thought.

His hand came over mine, pressing it to his firm chest. "Thank you for what you said out there."

I nodded slowly. "I should've told them the truth a long time ago."

He brushed his lips over mine again before pulling back and pinning me in his devastating gaze. "I've completely fallen in love with you, Red. It's undoubtedly the stupidest thing I've ever done, but I can't bring myself to regret it."

My eyes locked on his, and I could feel the truth from those dark depths. "Good."

A rueful chuckle parted his lips. "Not exactly the answer I was hoping for."

I smothered his objections with my mouth, and it only took him a second to yield to my tongue's demands. For now, it was easier to give into the desire, into the pleasure. Those things were easy, uncomplicated. What I felt for him was too raw, too uncontrollable, too all-consuming. I'd figure it out eventually, but right now, I hoped this was enough.

TEN

R *ansom*

I followed Red down the dark stairwell still grumbling. Her team had to have finished training by now. There was no reason to drag me out of bed where we could've been having so much more fun. Where we *had* been having so much more fun. After having that tiny taste of her, I couldn't get enough. I wanted to claim her in every way possible.

We'd been close today, but Red's team was on her mind, distracting her. Plus, if we'd had sex again, I would've felt compelled to tell her the truth about the mate bond. Or at least Sierra and Hunter's truth. Even if we attempted what they'd done, it didn't guarantee success.

I huffed out a breath as we reached the floor below the penthouse.

"Oh, stop complaining, it's not that bad." Red shook her head as she opened the door into the hallway. "We could all use a little workout."

"I wanted a little workout. Just with less clothes on." I threw her a wink.

"You're relentless."

"You don't even know." I brushed by her, nudging her with my shoulder. "But I'd love to show you one day." One day when all of this was over, and she was safe.

She nodded, the ghost of a smile flickering across her face before she marched to the apartment at the end of the hall. The door was ajar, and her team's voices drifted into the corridor.

"At least they're still there." She hurried to the door and swung it open.

The dragon and the she-wolf sat on the floor in the corner, fingers entwined. I searched Red's expression for a reaction as her gaze landed upon them, but her face remained unchanged. Was she really over him?

"About time you showed up." The little witch popped up and strutted over with a mischievous smile on her face. "Did you two have your own work out?"

"Oh, please spare us," Archer groaned.

"Sorry, guys." Red's typical take-no-prisoners attitude had dimmed a notch. "I totally passed out." A hint of crimson tinged her cheeks, reminding me of the heated blush that blossomed on her face when I'd made love to her what seemed like a lifetime ago now.

Vera turned to me, still grinning. "What have you done with our real team leader? Who is this lazy imposter?"

I couldn't help my lips from parting. The ways in which Red changed me were innumerable, but to think I had an effect on her was oddly disarming. I just hoped I didn't fang her up.

"Lazy?" Red eyed her friend, then the rest of the team. "I'll show you guys lazy." She pointed bardy at each one of them before tossing the weapon. It flew end over end across the room and landed with a thwack in the opposite wall. The plaster crumbled but the blade remained fully entrenched in the mortar. "Come on, another twenty minutes of weapons work."

A wave of grumbles exploded across the space.

"We already trained for the past hour while you were napping," Archer groused.

Red wagged a finger at him. "But did you have practice with a live, moving target?" Her eyes darted to mine, and a wicked grin lit up her face.

"Are you serious?" I cried out.

She jabbed her elbow into my side and leaned in, her warm breath tickling my ear. "It is kind of your fault I'm late. Consider this punishment."

"Punishment for amazing foreplay?" I hissed out loud. Vera and Seline laughed, and Red threw me a pointed glare. Totally worth it. "Fine, fine. I suppose the least I can do is make sure you all don't get yourselves killed when we take on Ronin."

"And Thanatos, the actual god of death." Sparky stood, jaw clenched tight. "Do we know anything about his status?"

Red shook her head before turning to Vera, who gave us a reluctant shrug. "Ronin hasn't mentioned what exactly he needs to bring Thanatos back, only the items necessary to break the spell."

"They could be linked," I added.

"I don't think so." Vera chewed on her lower lip. "From

my research, Thanatos wasn't exactly banished from Azar. He, like the other gods, who once walked the earth simply left when we were created. I guess they didn't like rubbing shoulders with the likes of us. In theory, any of the gods could come and go as they pleased, but not in corporeal form."

Red's gaze focused on her friend, and a flicker of unease swirled through the bond. "So how exactly do they become corporeal?"

"That's the thing, no one knows. There's no guidebook out there on how to bring a god to earth, which is why I'm guessing Ronin's warlock is just having Thanatos take over his body."

"For now," I muttered.

"Right. Having Thanatos amongst us, with the power that he wields, it would be pretty disastrous."

"Great, and we have no idea when he's coming." Red crossed her arms over her chest, and eyed bardy across the room.

"Or if he's already here," I added.

Red grunted. "For now, we do what we can, which means making sure we're all at the top of our game." She moved to the center of the room and held her hand out. The whole team joined in the circle a moment later. "Whatever happens we're in this together, and we fight till the end."

A chorus of whoops broke out as everyone's hands joined the huddle. I even threw mine in at the last minute.

"And no matter what," Sparky added, "we won't let Ronin or Thanatos anywhere near Nix or her freaky blood." He shot her a smile, and my ghostly wolf snarled. Whether Red had truly moved on from her dragon boyfriend was unclear, but it was glaringly obvious the dragon heir was still in love with my mate.

Mine. My wolf's voice echoed through my head, and

goose bumps puckered my skin. I hadn't heard him so clearly since before...

"Of course not," I snarled, my body moving closer to Red's. I'd do anything to protect her, even going so far as allowing the Scooby gang target practice.

Once the huddle disbanded, I stood in the center of the room. "Now, first a few ground rules." I lifted a hand and began enumerating the restrictions. "No weapons near my heart, obviously. I draw the line at vervain bombs—too messy. No hits below the belt because well, that just wouldn't be fair to R—"

Red's hand clapped over my mouth, cutting me off. "I think they get the idea. Just don't kill him, okay, guys?"

Sparky muttered something I'd make sure he regretted later, then he lunged. I sidestepped his attack with ease, and the stake he'd had hidden in his fist clattered to the floor.

"Nice try." I shot him a grin, but the smile quickly faltered as the Nephilim moved in next. His angel sword arced over my head, but it went wide, even for a practice shot. From the corner of my eye, I could make out Red watching each move intently.

Each member of the team got a turn, sometimes they attacked two at a time and though they were very skilled, no one got close to a kill shot. The truth was that no matter how many sicari the queen trained, they'd never surpass the speed, strength or agility of a Royal vampire. Lucky for them, most of the time they only had to deal with serviles, but with Ronin sitting on the throne, would alliances change?

The disturbing thought nearly cost me my arm. I darted out of reach of the Nephilim's blade at the very last second.

"Okay, enough," Red called out.

Cal and Sparky backed off, but the dragon's reptilian eyes

remained locked on mine. I had to be careful with that one. A part of me was certain he'd kill me if given the chance.

Red moved beside me as she faced the rest of her team. "So how'd they do?"

"Eh."

"Oh, shut up, fanger," Sparky growled.

"He's not wrong." Red leveled the dragon with a fiery look that had the front of my pants tightening. Gods, she was so hot when she was angry. "I've seen Ransom fight, and he was taking it easy on you guys."

"No way," said Archer.

"Yes way."

I couldn't help the satisfaction from splitting my lips into a ridiculously wide smile.

"But he's sired by Carmen Rosa." Seline huffed out a breath, fixing her ponytail.

"And a lot of Ronin's generals are from her bloodline. Don't forget the king is a direct descendant, only one line down, and so are most of his men." Her steely gaze razed over every member of her team. "We won't just be dealing with serviles anymore. Now that Ronin's secured the castle, he won't give it up easily. After we meet with the queen today, we need to start training every day again. We're getting weak and sloppy, and that's my fault. I'm your team leader, and I haven't exactly been leading."

"In your defense, you were held captive for a month," I interjected.

Red's hand shot up, silencing me. "It doesn't matter. I've been slacking in my duties and that stops now. And if Ransom's willing, I'd like for him to help with exercises like today's."

I grumbled but nodded, nonetheless. Damn girl had me by the vampy balls.

"Is everyone good with that?"

Muttered yeses filled the echoing space.

"Good." She ticked her head at the door. "Now, everyone get ready. We leave for the queen's new hideout as soon as Vera gets word."

CHAPTER
ELEVEN

P *hoenix*

My boots slapped the alabaster marble with an echoing crash as the portal spat me out in a bright white room. Ransom appeared beside me a second later, then the rest of my team tumbled out behind him.

I scanned the obscenely white space flooded in light from the huge picture windows. Sunlight? My brows knitted. I glanced over at the vampire beside me who thankfully hadn't burst into flames. It must have been some sort of illusion. My gaze swept across the room, enjoying the warm sunlight before landing on a round table in the far corner. The queen rose and Lucíano moved with her, as fluidly as if the pair were physically attached. I recognized the queen's warlock, Nestor, who'd portaled us in, skulking in the shadows. Then from the table, another figure rose, and my heart constricted. Demetra.

My old instructor from the Isle of Mordis's eyes locked on mine. I had to restrain myself to keep from running to her. I hadn't realized how much I'd missed her until this very moment. At some point during my three years training on the island, she'd become a sort of motherly figure.

But a woman like Demetra didn't hug and given the recent issues I'd had with the queen, I wasn't sure where we stood. Had she known Carmen Rosa wanted to keep me locked up or worse?

The tense moment stretched to an uncomfortable level until the queen finally spoke. "Team One, I am relieved beyond measure to find you all alive and well." Her eyes drifted to mine for only a moment before they settled on the rest of my team.

Demetra's demeanor was calm and collected, but her eyes—something dark stirred beneath the deep crimson.

"Again, what am I, my queen?" Ransom dipped into an exaggerated bow.

"Oh, Ransom, so needy..."

He balked, his lips curling into a grimace. "Expulsion doesn't suit you, my queen."

"I have not been expulsed or dethroned or any of the multitude of synonyms I've heard in the past few days. We have merely moved to a more suitable location for the time being."

Ransom pressed his lips together, and I knew he was choking down a snarky comment. I was surprised and relieved that he kept his thoughts to himself for once. Despite my anger with the queen for trying to imprison me, we had to work together for now.

"Of course." Ransom pursed his lips and stood by my side. "And where are we exactly?"

"A secret location for now," Lucíano interrupted.

Demetra still stood by the table, but her eyes never deviated from mine. I wished I could talk to her in private. My gaze drifted from her to the other vampires seated at the round table. It only took me a second to recognize the Royal symbol engraved into the chair backs and the queen's motto *Carpe Cruentum Noctem*, seize the bloody night. It was particularly appropriate now. As I scanned the chairs, I noticed two sat empty, not including the ones Lucíano and Demetra loomed in front of.

Had the other two members of the queen's inner circle not arrived or had they defected to the other side? The thought made my stomach roil. The last thing we needed were more Royal vampires joining the ranks of Ronin's Children.

"So why have you brought us here today, my queen?" Ransom's question drew my thoughts back to the matter at hand.

The queen's dark gaze pivoted to me. "The rest of the sicari should be joining us shortly, but I wanted to take this opportunity to speak to Phoenix and her team alone."

I nodded, firming up my mental barriers to ensure the queen couldn't sneak in. Vera had whipped up a compulsion blocking potion for each of us for extra protection. Ransom had insisted on it. He still didn't trust her and neither did I.

"So talk," said Spark, flanking my opposite side.

Carmen Rosa exhaled a dainty breath. "I deeply regret my behavior last time we met. I was hasty and worried for my people which caused me to behave in a rash manner." She sauntered closer, and a growl vibrated Ransom's chest. The queen's eyes darted to his, and her perfectly plucked brow shot up. Anxiety rippled through my insides as I waited for her to say something. But she never did. Instead, she continued walking forward until she stood about a yard in front of us.

Ransom inched closer. His anxiety surged through the bond, overpowering my own.

"I want to apologize," she finally said. "And assure you that I will never do anything so irrational again. As queen, the pressure I have to protect my people has occasionally driven me to make hasty decisions. I realize now that I went too far in my efforts to keep you away from my enemy. Instead, we should've been working together."

I released the breath I'd been holding and slowly dipped my head.

"Besides, Demetra threatened to abandon me if I ever tried anything so foolish again."

My chest tightened as I caught my old mentor's gaze over the queen's shoulder. Her lips parted into a tight smile.

"So I ask your forgiveness and hope to continue our relationship in a more equitable manner."

"I'd like that," I finally answered, hoping it came off more convincing than it felt.

"Wonderful, so glad we're all friends again." Ransom tossed Carmen Rosa a smile that didn't quite reach his eyes. "Now, what's the plan?" He eyed the round table adjacent to the queen. "And where are Helga and Dmitri by the way?"

The queen's saccharine smile faltered for an instant. "Helga, Dmitri and I have decided to part ways."

"You mean they decided to join Ronin?"

Her crimson lips pressed into a tight line as those piercing eyes leveled Ransom with a glare. "Yes," she hissed through clenched teeth.

"You see, Red, this is the problem." He bent down so his

eyes were level to mine. "Vampires are tired of being forced to live in the darkness, forced to drink Blud. I assure you Helga and Dmitri are only the first to desert the queen's cause."

A rumble broke out among the remaining vampires of the inner circle. "I will always stand with my queen," said Luciano. A few of the others murmured their assent.

"Well, I know you will," Ransom muttered. "Your lips are permanently tattooed to her—"

I elbowed my vampire blood buddy in the gut. There was no reason to insult the guy who was on our side.

Ransom shrugged. "Either way, my queen, your precious inner circle is down from twelve to a mere nine. It's only a matter of time..."

"What would you have me do, Ransom?" she gritted out.

"Talk to the Etrian Assembly! Use your power to make some changes for the better. Do something for your people. If we no longer are relegated to the darkness, if we're allowed to consume real blood, Ronin's offer wouldn't seem quite so attractive, now would it?"

What Ransom was saying wasn't something that could happen overnight, but even I had to agree, he wasn't totally wrong in his thinking.

"It's madness, my son. They'd never agree to any of that."

"Why not?" I asked. "What if we could get some of the other members of the assembly on board?" Hunter would back us up for sure. Then my gaze flitted to Spark. Could we convince his father to vote with the queen? Or Azara. The dark lord of the Underworld sat on the assembly as well.

"It'll never happen, Phoenix. Ronin's right. For centuries the vampires were feared by the other houses of Azar. They'd never allow us to gain power now."

"Then they need to help us fight Ronin and his Children."
I planted my hands on my hips.

"The assembly does not step into civil matters within the houses. They will only take a stand if a major threat arises."

I huffed out an exasperated breath. We were just talking in circles now.

"Okay, then," said Ransom. "I'll ask again: what is the plan?"

Luciano stepped forward, and all eyes trained on the queen's right-hand man. "River is on his way, along with all the remaining sicari he could find. We'll spend the next day or two scouring Royal lands until we find every last one. Demetra will graduate her class of sicari recruits a few months early and we will all train as a team, immortals and mortals alike. The queen has already put out the call for her citizens to join the battle. Then, when the time is right, we will take back the castle."

Okay, this could work. A twinge of optimism lit up the dark depths. With vamps on our side, we could take Ronin down. "What about Thanatos?" The question burst from my lips before I could stop it.

The queen's warlock, Nestor, stepped forward, his brilliant orange hair alight in the bright room. "I'm currently researching the exact manner in which one would return a god to corporeal form. I've been working on it since Thanatos's appearance, but as of yet, I've found nothing. I am awaiting news from the head of the Coven Council, the warlock Garrix. If anyone is capable of summoning a god, it would be him."

"Great, so for now we just wait," Ransom mumbled.

"No," said the queen. "We prepare for battle."

CHAPTER

TWELVE

P *hoenix*

I HATED RETURNING to the penthouse without Ransom, and more than that, I hated that I hated it. I was becoming way too dependent on my vampire wolfy mate. The closer we got, the more blood we shared, the more my body ached at his absence. The queen had asked for him to stay, and I was itching to find out why.

"Pacing isn't going to make him get here any faster." Vera shot me a knowing smile as she grabbed a nasty looking green juice from the fridge.

"I don't know what you're talking about."

She giggled and took my hand, dragging me to the kitchen island to sit beside her. "You can deny it all you want, but you're acting like a bloodwhore jonesing for a fix."

My jaw dropped, eyes popping out. "Geez, thanks a lot."

She laughed again then squeezed my shoulder with a reassuring smile. "I don't know much about the wolf mate bond, but you know who does?"

I shot her an eyeroll because I knew exactly where my friend was going with this. Things weren't bad between Seline and me, but our relationship had been a little tense since my return from captivity. I kept telling myself it had nothing to do with Spark, but obviously I was a liar.

"Go talk to Seline," said Vera when I didn't answer. "She's a wolf, just like you, and though she hasn't found her mate she probably knows a lot more about it than you do."

"Ugh," I grumbled. "We're on the brink of a vampire war, Vera. This is the last thing I should be focusing on."

She shrugged and took a sip of the dark green concoction. My stomach roiled at the sight. "What you should be doing doesn't always line up with what you have to do. Ransom's arrival in your life has been a big change for you. I think if things were more settled in that department, the rest would fall into place."

I cocked a skeptical brow. "So you're saying the fate of all Azar is tied to my relationship with my wolfy-vampire fated mate?"

"Maaaybe."

I laughed, shaking my head. "You just want me to make up with Seline, don't you?"

"It would be nice. Plus, it's messing with the team's mojo."

"Fine, I'll talk to her." Later. From across the great room, I caught sight of a grumpy Nephilim stalking closer. "Ooh, Cal." I waved him over. With Ransom out of the way, it was the perfect time to question him about the vampire with a soul issue.

"What's up, Nix?"

"Did you get a chance to talk to the higher ups of the Sons of Heaven about the soul thing?"

He leaned on the island, wrapping an arm around Vera. "I did confirm it is possible for an archangel to see a soul, but I haven't heard back from Cillian on the specifics. A message has been sent, and I'm sure he'll get back to me soon. He's kind of a busy guy."

"Right." I chewed on my lower lip. I was torn between wanting Ransom to be the one and not. It would put him at risk, painting a target on his back just like my own, but on the other hand, if he still had a soul... My chest tightened, and a faint whine echoed through my ribcage.

"Maybe you and Seline could go for a run," said Vera. She was relentless. "It would probably do your wolf some good to get out."

I shook my head at my friend. "I got it, Mom. Seline and Nix time coming right up." As annoying as Vera could be, she wasn't wrong. My wolf was clawing at my insides. Maybe a run *was* exactly what I needed.

"I'm glad we're doing this," I forced out when the silence became unbearable. Seline had been quick to agree to the run, but now that we were walking toward the edge of the forest, I was starting to regret the whole thing. In wolf form we wouldn't have to talk, which was likely what she'd been counting on.

As much as I hated the awkwardness, Vera was right. We needed to clear the air between us before it affected the team. Plus, if I was being honest, I'd take just about any info on the burgeoning mate bond between Ransom and me.

Especially how to control it from becoming so all-consuming.

"Yup, me too," she finally answered as the crumbling asphalt gave way to a dirt road that led out of the decaying remains of the city.

More silence.

Just spit it out, Nix! Steeling my nerves, I forced all the words out in one big jumble. "So I've been meaning to ask you about the wolf mate bond."

Seline turned to me, her dark eyes wide. "That's what you brought me out here for?"

"Um, yah, kind of. That and I really wanted to run."

She snorted on a laugh and released a breath. "I thought you wanted to talk about Spark. I—I thought you wanted him back or something."

I suppressed my own laugh and shook my head. "Did you really think I would ask you to give him up?"

She shrugged. "I'm not stupid, Nix. I know he's still in love with you. It would just take one word, and he'd go running back."

A spiral of pain and regret swirled through my insides. I'd been pretty crappy to Spark, and still he never stopped caring. "I'm sure that's not true," I finally said.

"Oh, it is. He pretty much told me as much when you first came back."

I sucked in a breath. *Ouch.*

"But then Ransom showed up and now that you told us about the mate thing, it all makes sense."

"Maybe for you it does. I still can't quite wrap my head around the whole thing. I didn't grow up with wolves, so it's just a lot to take in."

"I've never had a mate obviously," she said, "but I've seen

it happen to friends. It's like trying to keep the sun from setting or forcing the world to stop turning. Unless you break the bond, there's really no way out of it."

"You can break a mate bond?"

Her head bounced up and down. "It's not pretty or easy, but it can be done."

Hmm... How had I never even considered the possibility? Probably because the idea of it made my head spin, my lungs constrict, and my stomach roil. Ransom had gotten under my skin and even if we could never complete the bond, I didn't think I could ever truly be rid of him. I needed him like I needed to breathe.

"It's some pretty crazy stuff," she continued when I didn't answer. "I've always dreamt about meeting my fated, but maybe it's just not in the cards for me. And Spark..."

"You're in love with him, aren't you?" I said when her words fell away.

She nodded quickly and my mind soared to the past, to when we'd first arrived at the Isle of Mordis. She and Spark had been hooking up even back then. According to Vera, I'd been the one that had gotten between them.

"I'm happy for you guys." And I actually meant it. "Spark deserves someone who really loves him, and he'd be stupid not to see that's you. Besides, who says your fated has to be a wolf anyway?"

She laughed. "True. As long as it's not a vampire, right?" She shot me a wink. "Too soon?"

"It'll always be too soon." The edge of the forest loomed ahead, and my wolf surged to the surface. "Should we run?"

Seline's gaze lifted to the thick copse of trees ahead. "I'll race you to the tree line."

I reached into my core where my wolf's magic resided and dropped to all fours a moment later. There'd been no shifting, no bones breaking, tendons snapping. I'd just changed. When Seline's gray wolf appeared a few seconds later, her eyes were wide. She must have seen my insta-shift too. Was that a Dragos thing? Or was it a blessed by the goddess Luna thing?

I shook off the thought as my wolfish senses took over, and the sights and sounds of the forest called to me. I took off toward the intriguing scents with Seline's wolf right on my tail. As we moved through the trees, along with my wolf's brilliant auburn hue, I also noticed I was much larger than my wolfy teammate. I didn't have a clear picture of Tyrien Silverstalker in my mind, but as supreme alpha I imagined he must've been huge. My half-brother Hunter was the largest wolf I'd ever seen, dwarfing most of the tigers I'd grown up with. It must have been an alpha thing.

Ooh, alpha Phoenix, I liked the sound of that.

My claws dug into the forest floor as I raced through the trees. My wolf tossed her head back and let out a happy howl. Damn, it had been too long. Lately, the only time I let her loose was for a fight. I'd needed this. The rush of the wind through my fur, the moist earth between my toes. The only thing that would make it better would be Ransom running beside me. The errant thought stopped me in my tracks.

My wolfy chest constricted, and I let out a whine. Would we ever see our mate in lupine form? Was he even still in there? Shaking my big head, I chased away the pointless thoughts. I'd never be able to bite Ransom without killing him, so we'd never be able to complete the bond anyway.

Ugh. This was no good. I was supposed to be letting loose, letting my animal half run free, not being bogged down by my spiraling thoughts.

Wolf-Seline finally caught up to me, and a low growl

vibrated the air between us. She ticked her muzzle to the right, in the opposite direction we'd just come. My ears flickered toward the sound, then my nostrils flared at the familiar scent. Fangers.

CHAPTER
THIRTEEN

P *hoenix*

SERVILES, from the gods-awful smell.

Wolf-Seline sat back on her haunches and cocked her head to the side. I nodded slowly. *We should go check it out.* I tried to broadcast my thoughts to her like I'd done with Sierra and Hunter, but since Seline wasn't from my pack, no mind link existed between us.

Instead, I nudged her in the direction of the sound, then took the lead. As we crept closer, the woods began to thin out, heading back to the Darklands but from the opposite side we'd entered. An old warehouse stood at the edge of the forest, and dozens of serviles milled around the outside.

Oh, shift. This was where Ronin was keeping his horde.

Wolf-Seline padded forward but I snapped at her tail, yanking her back. We needed to get reinforcements. And fast.

If Drakin was still portaling Ronin's headquarters every few hours, it was likely he was doing the same with his servile farm.

I let out a yip and motioned for her to follow. Her big dark eyes widened as they glanced over my shoulder, and an icy chill raced down my spine. I craned my neck, hazarded a glance, and let out a wolfy curse. A dozen serviles surrounded us, creeping out from behind the cover of the trees.

I let out a growl, baring my teeth at the approaching fangers and fire shot through my veins, vanquishing the icy chill from a moment ago. The heat raced over my body and from the corner of my eye, I could already see the flames dancing across my glowing auburn fur.

Wolf-Seline's eyes widened to cosmic proportions, the fiery golden flames reflecting across her dark irises. I let out a howl and lunged at the nearest servile. My teammate moved in beside me, following my lead.

I leapt on one fanger, and a feral grin split my lips as the mystical flames jumped from my body and raced up his torn clothes. I moved through the pack, biting, clawing, and setting the fangers ablaze.

All the while I felt Seline's wolf beside me. I cut through the masses as fast as I could, hoping not to catch the attention of the rest of the herd down by the warehouse. If they caught sight of us, they'd move, and we'd lose this perfect opportunity. Another servile jumped in front of me, and I snapped at him, digging my teeth into her forearm. The vamp collapsed to the floor, black veins spiderwebbing up her arm. She was dead before the flames consumed her emaciated form.

A spine-tingling yelp from behind sent my heart battering against my big wolfy ribcage. I searched the chaos for Seline. Nothing. She'd been beside me just a second ago. I lifted my nose high and sniffed the air. Another howl ricocheted across the battlefield.

I spun on my heel and followed the sound deeper into the woods. Three serviles were bent down around a gray wolf. *No!* Fear lanced across my heart as I raced toward them. I leapt on one, digging my fangs into its neck and tore his head clean off. I spat out the disgusting taste and moved onto the next. Flames leapt from my fur, enveloping the servile in a sea of crimson fire. The last one ran off, but I raced after him, dragging him down with my claws. I leapt on top of him and chomped down on his shoulder. With a shriek, he crumbled to the ground, dark veins spiraling across his wrinkled skin.

With the mad pounding of my heart thundering across my eardrums, I spun on my heel and galloped back to Seline. The moment I reached her, I slid to the floor, back in human form. I sucked in a breath as I scanned her broken body. Even beneath the bloody, matted fur her ribcage didn't look right. It was sunken in, and her breath came in ragged spurts. Panic's claws dragged across my heart.

"Seline, I'm here. Everything's going to be okay." Dammit, where was Cal with his angel healing when I needed him? I cursed myself for not bringing my phone or a com. I never took it when I went out for a run. I'd take her back to the penthouse, and Cal would fix this. Everything would be fine. I gently slid my arm under her neck, and she let out a whimper. "Hold on, Seline. I'm going to get you home." I tried to lift her, and a cry tore from her lupine lips. Her eyes closed, and the rise and fall of her chest slowed.

No. No. No. "Please, Seline. Hold on." Hot tears burned my eyes as I stroked her furry cheek. Every inch of her was covered in bloodied bites and the pool of crimson beneath her fur was growing. Gods, I'd failed her. How had I let this happen? I tried to pick her up again, and this time she didn't utter a cry. Holding her bruised and battered body against mine, I started to run back through the forest.

Gods dammit, why didn't I have wings like Spark or Cal? Or was fast like Ransom? Where was that damned fanger? He was always at my side, except now when I needed him most. I couldn't do anything to save my friend. Seline's body grew heavier with each step, and I could feel the life draining right out of her.

"Ransom, please help me!" I threw my head back and screamed. Which was probably a stupid move since Ronin's serviles might have still been within earshot, and my vampire blood buddy was an entire portal ride away at the queen's new hideout.

"Hold on, Seline, please just hold on." I wouldn't let those fangers take one more person I cared for away from me. I trudged on, trying to backtrack the way we'd come. Moving on two legs made it painfully slow. Seline's body sagged against me, faint breaths parting her lips. "Don't worry, girl, I've got you. I'm going to get you back to the penthouse, and Cal will have you fixed up in no time. You can't give up, okay? Do it for Spark. He'd go crazy if he lost you. I know it."

Her breath caught, and my heart froze in fear. An excruciatingly long moment later, she inhaled faintly. Oh, thank the gods. I picked up my pace, following the paw prints we'd left on the soft earth. How had this gone so badly?

"We're almost there, Seline," I whispered. My arms were sticky with blood—too much blood. Those fangers had ravaged her beautiful wolf. My chest tightened as I glanced down at her. *She's not going to make it.* I ignored my wolf's voice and barely repressed the urge to curse her out. What did she know?

I marched on, my eyes straight ahead. Already, it felt like I'd been walking for hours. When we'd been on four legs, the woods had flown by and now time trudged on inexorable and never-ending.

A crackle of leaves crunching underfoot sent the hair on the back of my neck standing on end. My head whipped back and forth to the origin of the sound. Then that invisible cord around my heart tightened. *Ransom.*

Tears flooded my eyes when he zipped around the corner a second later. His anxious gaze met mine for an instant before dropping to the wolf in my arms. Without a word, he reached for Seline.

My fingers tightened around her fur, and I pressed her against my chest.

"Let me take her, Red," he whispered. His nostrils flared as his dark gaze raked over her.

I lifted my eyes to his, to the churning storm of obsidian. "Can you help her?"

"I'll do what I can." He took her from my arms and gently lowered her to the forest floor. Her eyes were closed, and her breaths were too faint. That beautiful gray wolf looked so small, so frail huddled within the dry leaves and dark earth. Ransom hovered over her for a long minute before finally turning back to me. "I'm sorry, there's nothing I can do…"

A choked sob wrenched free, and Ransom's arms snaked around me.

"No!" I shoved him back. "It can't be too late. Just bring her back to the penthouse. Cal can save her."

"She'll never make it back, Red. It's too late." The anguish in his eyes must have mirrored mine.

I forced down the knot of emotions clogging my throat

and shook my head. "It can't be." I felt it. The moment my tether with reality snapped. I wouldn't let one more person I cared about die. I couldn't. Tears began to fall and I couldn't stop them.

Ransom reached for me again, and this time, I buried my face in his chest, allowing myself comfort in his familiar, musky scent. His hand rubbed small circles along my back as I clung onto him sobbing.

"What happened?" he murmured.

"Serviles. I think I found where Ronin's been hiding them." Damned immortal— My eyes shot up to Ransom's as a swirl of hope kindled, silencing the sobs. I pushed out of his embrace, and the words spilled out. "You can save her."

"What?"

"Turn Seline. It's not too late for that, right?" The words came out in a rush, like they weren't my own.

Fire lit up those onyx orbs. "I won't turn her, Red. Not without her approval."

I glanced down at my friend and muttered a curse. "Please, Ransom. She doesn't have much time." My world began to spin. I couldn't lose her. I couldn't...

"Which is exactly why I won't do it. I won't take away her choice. I know what that's like, and it's unforgiveable."

I slid down to the floor beside her, my thoughts scrambled. I could barely make out her breaths anymore. "Seline, please, can you hear me? Seline, hold on." I glared up at Ransom. "You can save her!"

He let out a rueful chuckle. "Save her? Or condemn her to a life like mine?" His eyes shot daggers as they razed over me. "Did you not hear anything I said yesterday? I would never subject her to this life unless she chose it. You of all people should understand why. Despite everything we've been through, despite the mate bond between us, despite the feelings you claim to have for me, I'll always be just a fanger to you. I won't do that to her."

Grinding my teeth, I hissed, "This isn't about us."

"You're right, it's not. It's about Seline."

"If you don't turn her, she'll die." Darkness crept into my vision. Darkness then smoke. I was choking again. "Her death will be on your head," I forced out.

"Fine."

"I hate you," I gritted out. "I'll never forgive you for this."

"I understand, and I accept that."

A piece of my heart crumbled, as I fought to hold onto my sanity. I was losing it and a part of me knew it. I ran my hand over Seline's head as tears burned my eyes. Holding my breath, I strained to hear the faint inhale and exhale. I moved my hand down to her chest, ignoring the warm blood covering my skin. I felt it. The moment her heart stopped, and her lungs gave up the struggle.

My shoulders heaved as another sob filled my chest. I bent my head to hers and let the tears fall on her unmoving form. This was *my* fault. It wasn't Ransom's, and I knew it. She was my teammate, my responsibility and she was dead because of me.

Ransom's arm came around my shoulders as the tears streamed down. I wanted to shove him off, but I didn't have it in me. Because as much as I wanted to hate him for refusing to save my friend, I knew he was right. Still, it didn't hurt any less.

CHAPTER
FOURTEEN

R *ansom*

I carried the broken little wolf all the way back to the penthouse, the trudge excruciatingly slow since I couldn't use vamp-speed with Red trailing behind me. She hadn't spoken a word to me since Seline died. Her eyes were vacant, unfocused.

But I didn't regret my choice, not for one second.

This wasn't about her; it wasn't about us. It was about condemning another life to a torturous existence. Even if she never forgave me, I wouldn't regret it. For once in my miserable life, I'd made the right decision.

Red's pain surged through the bond, its intensity so cutting it tore at my insides. I hated seeing her like this. I hated that there was nothing I could do to make it better. The woods finally receded, giving way to the dilapidated city center. Just a few blocks away, the remains of the building we now called home shot up into the night sky.

Now came the hard part, facing the rest of the Scooby team. The guilt that swirled through the bond between us was nearly as strong as the pain. She truly believed she'd let her team down, and now she'd have to confront that truth.

"Almost there," I muttered over my shoulder.

She didn't even look up. She just kept marching, her eyes trained to the crumbling asphalt. It was a good thing I'd felt the fear through the bond when I was finishing up my visit with the queen. Her panic had been so all-consuming, I'd shot out of there before Carmen Rosa could finish her sentence. For a terrible moment, I feared the worst, that Ronin had captured her again. The blinding panic had been the most hellish torture, something I never wanted to feel again.

I hated to admit it, but when I found her in the woods with Seline in her arms, I'd been relieved. And now, Red couldn't even look at me.

When we finally reached the abandoned building, I sped up the stairs no longer able to continue my slow pace. Thirty-some floors at normal human speed was where I drew the line. At least inside the building, I knew Red was safe.

I waited for her at the top of the stairwell, contemplating my immortal existence as she raced up the steps two at a time. Despite everything going on, I knew she hated that I was faster than her. With the little wolf slung lifeless across my arms, it was inevitable for my thoughts to race back to my own dead lupine half. My eyes skimmed over her frail form, the soft gray fur so similar to my wolf's.

Sometimes I longed to shift so badly every bone in my body ached. It was like missing a limb, the phantom remains niggling at my insides. This poor girl would never shift again, but at least she was at peace. I mumbled a quick prayer to the gods for a speedy passage. Though I didn't know Seline well, all souls deserved the peace of eternal rest.

The rapid slap of approaching footfalls drew me back to the present. I gazed over the bannister to see the top of Red's head as she raced up the last floor. She'd made it up in record time. I pushed the door with my elbow, balancing Seline's body in my arms, and held it open for her. Red barreled by without sparing me a glance.

I'd let her hold onto the anger for now because I knew deep down, it was the only thing that was keeping her from crumbling. Anger was an easier emotion for her than pain or fear. I couldn't blame her for it either. I'd often fought solace in the fury instead of facing the ugly truth.

When Red reached the penthouse door, she pivoted toward me, her brow furrowed. "Let me take her in."

I nodded and carefully handed the girl over.

A pang streaked through the bond as she stared down at her friend. Red cradled her against her chest before ticking her head at the door. "Can you get that?"

Drawing in a breath, I opened it wide and prepared to meet the firing squad. The moment Red crossed the threshold, a cry rang out across the vast great room. Vera raced from the kitchen with Cal on her heels, then the snooty Fae appeared, and it wasn't long before Spark materialized in the doorway of his bedroom.

Vera peppered Red with questions as she trudged into the living room, cradling their fallen friend, and gently placed the little wolf down on the couch.

"What the hell happened?" Spark shouted as he took her in. His eyes darted from Red to me, accusation lining the amber depths.

I'd let their leader handle this. I sat on the edge of the

couch, arms crossed tightly over my chest as the team huddled together.

"We ran into the horde while we were out on our run," Red began. "Ronin's got an abandoned building out at the edge of the forest where he's keeping the serviles."

"So you thought you'd take them on by yourselves?" Spark cried. He'd dropped to the floor, kneeling in front of the wolf's body. Slowly, he ran a hand over her matted fur.

"No," Red hissed, wiping away the tears. "I'm not that reckless, Rhydian." She wrapped her arms around her middle, and another wave of guilt pummeled through the bond. "We were on our way back to find you guys, to get back-up, when we were ambushed." She shook her head, gnawing on her lower lip. "They came out of nowhere. I—I don't know what happened."

Vera moved to her friend and wrapped her slim arm around Red's shoulders.

"I tried to help her, but it was too late." Red's gaze flicked to mine, but I refused to meet her accusatory glare.

"Where the hell were you, fanger?" Spark barked.

"I was at Carmen Rosa's if you recall." I kept my voice measured, trying to keep my cool. I wouldn't take dragon boy's accusations today. "I felt something and returned as quickly as I could. I tracked Red down in the woods, but by the time I arrived, it was too late to help her."

"Couldn't you do something with your blood?"

"It was too late."

"Ransom refused to turn her." Red's puffy eyes turned to Spark and awaited with bated breath for the dragon's response. Surely, he'd agree with me. Out of everyone here, he loathed me the most. He couldn't possibly have wanted the same for his girlfriend.

"Why?" Spark rose and stalked toward me. "Why wouldn't you save her if you could?"

I let out a string of curses. Must I have this conversation again? "That's funny coming from you, dragon boy. You really wanted me to turn your girl into a *fanger*?"

His head dipped, lips pressing together. *Liar.*

"Isn't that what you all do?" I shouted. "Kill fangers? Why would you ever have wanted that for your friend?"

"Enough." Vera moved between us. "Seline wouldn't want us fighting about this."

"And she wouldn't have wanted to become a vampire," Archer interjected.

All eyes darted to his.

He shrugged and ran a hand through his hair. "We talked about it once a long time ago. She said she'd never want to be a vampire. Said she'd rather die fighting than be forced to live forever."

A strangled, choking sound erupted from Red's lips, and she wrapped her arms tighter around herself.

Vera took her hand and tugged her to the couch. "None of that matters right now. Our friend is gone, and we have to mourn her loss, not bicker about it. She wouldn't want that."

The five of them huddled around the sofa, around the body of their fallen friend. Vera's lips began to flutter, and a calming quiet descended over the room. Each of them placed a hand on the wolf, eyes closed. Begrudgingly, I unraveled my arms from my chest and joined them.

"We have loved her dearly during life," Vera began, then the others answered, "Let us not abandon her until she's been welcomed into the house of eternal peace."

Three times they repeated the chant and by the fourth one, I found myself joining in. When the prayer concluded, Vera rose. "I'll prepare her body for the burial ceremony."

"What about her family?" Red murmured.

"We'll bring her body to them once it's complete. Those were her final wishes."

Everyone nodded and remained kneeling as their witchy friend solemnly walked away and returned a moment later with a bag of mystical supplies. I watched as she poured powders and tonics into a bowl, muttering the words of an incantation. The air thickened, the charred scent of magic blanketing the somber atmosphere.

Though I couldn't understand her words, there was something beautiful about them. The twenty-minute cere-mony whizzed by as each member of the team said their final goodbyes. As I watched, my thoughts flickered to the past. Had I had a funeral? Had anyone mourned my loss in the traditional way of the wolves? I'd never even thought to ask.

"Ransom?"

I blinked rapidly to find the Nephilim in front of me snapping his fingers. "You have to let go."

I glanced down to find my hand still resting on Seline's gray fur. Releasing her, I noticed the half-angel's wings were spread out behind his shoulders.

"It's time for me to take her home."

I nodded numbly.

Everyone gathered around the fallen wolf in a tight circle one more time before Cal turned toward the door and marched out. The thick timber closed behind him, and that heavy silence pervaded.

Spark was the first to move, his shoulders heaving as he marched back to his room and slammed the door. Vera let out a sigh and wrapped an arm around Red.

"This is all my fault," Red murmured.

"It's not." The little witch hugged her tight. "It's no one's fault, Nix. It was just her time."

I pressed my lips together into a tight line as Ronin's claims flitted to the surface. If he succeeded in bringing back the god of death, could he really resurrect those we'd lost? I buried the pointless thoughts. We'd never find out because we couldn't let it happen.

I hazarded a glance toward Red and Vera and let out a sigh. If only I'd left the queen earlier. If only she hadn't forced me to renew my pledge about Azara and her mother. If only I'd made it in time to really save the girl. I shook my head out. Tomorrow would be a new day, hopefully a better one because if we didn't find a way to stop Ronin, I would have to eliminate the only two living female warlocks to save Red and keep the rebel king from breaking the shadow curse.

P *hoenix*

MY HEART HURT. A gaping hole had opened up in my chest, and I felt hollow. Most of it was because of the loss of my teammate, but a small part was because of Ransom. Because of how unfair I'd been to him. My logical mind knew it but holding onto the anger was so much easier than facing the pain. I'd lost it back there. Seeing Seline's wolf like that had pushed me over the edge. If I'd been in my right mind, I never would've suggested turning her. I needed someone to blame for Seline and if it wasn't Ransom, then it was me. And I already felt guilty enough.

I crept into the dark bedroom I shared with my vampire mate clutching my wet towel and squinted to make out the bed through the shadows. Ransom had long since gone to sleep, but despite the exhaustion I couldn't get my brain to stop spinning. Not even the hot shower had helped. Seline had become like family over the past three years, my entire team had. Teammates were lost, it was inevitable in our line of work, and still, I never expected it to happen to us.

Tiptoeing to the closet, I grabbed a black t-shirt from Ransom's side and slipped it over my head. His musky, wolfy scent immediately calmed the turmoil within. I hugged the soft fabric to my body and inhaled. Even angry, I needed him, I desired him. Damned mate bond. Tomorrow, I'd apologize for my irrational behavior. I just hoped he'd understand. Deep down I knew he would. Just like I'd forgive him over and over again, despite the awful things he'd do. We were prisoners of the blossoming mate bond, bound together for eternity—or at least for as long as I lived.

Seline's lifeless body zipped across my vision, and I squeezed my eyes shut to chase away the image. She was all I saw now when I closed my eyes. *Sleep, Nix, you have to sleep.* I forced my legs to move toward the bed, to the empty side of the mattress. A small smile crept across my face at the big lump on the opposite end. At least he'd slept in our bed, which meant he couldn't be that mad at me.

I crawled in and tugged the comforter up to my chest. *Sleep, Nix.* Forcing my lids closed, I inhaled and exhaled slowly. If I just laid here long enough, the sleepiness would come. Ransom's soft breaths filled the silence, and I focused on the faint sound, compelling my mind to slow down. Now that Seline had been sent home for burial in Moon Valley, all I could think about was exacting my revenge on Ronin. He may not have killed her himself, but it was his servile army who'd been responsible. I vowed to make him pay.

I rolled over to one side then the other, kicked off the comforter and then drew it back over my head. *Ugh.* It was no use.

"Would you stop that? You're disturbing my beauty rest." Ransom's rough voice sent my heart catapulting up my throat.

"Sorry," I muttered. "I thought you were sleeping."

He rolled over and propped his elbow up, leaning his head in his palm. "Well, I was until you came in here and started rolling around the bed like a beached mer-whale." A hint of mischief lit up his dark irises. "And why are you wearing my shirt?"

I tugged the comforter up higher as if somehow that would hide the evidence. "It was the first one I found," I shot back lamely.

"I thought you hated me."

I blew out a breath. "Fine, I guess we're doing this now."

"Doing what?"

"I'm apologizing."

"Oh, is that what this is?" He arched a playful brow. "Because in my dreams your apologies are *much* better than this."

I shook my head at the insufferable fanger. "You aren't going to make this easy, are you?"

"Of course not."

"I was wrong, and you were right. Turning Seline without her approval would've been wrong. I was totally out of my mind with grief and guilt and... It doesn't matter. I guess I should've believed that you knew what you were talking about."

"Umhmm."

"I don't understand what it means to be immortal or anything else that you're struggling with and so, I'm sorry. I just didn't want to lose my friend, especially not so soon after we'd finally cleared the air between us."

His eyes darkened, and he nodded slowly. "What hurts the most Red is that you still don't trust me."

"I do trust you."

He shook his head. "Not when it really matters."

"I trust you with my life. I just might not fully trust your decision-making skills."

The hint of a smile made his lip twitch.

"Besides, you should be looking at this as a good thing. I wanted you to turn my teammate, someone I cared about, into a vampire. That must mean I don't hate all you fangers as much anymore, right?"

A rueful chuckle slid through his lips. "I think you were desperate."

I shot him a good eyeroll.

"And sometimes I think you simply don't know what you want." He reached for my cheek, and I leaned into his touch, his thumb softly grazing my skin. A flicker of heat lit up down below.

"I know what I want right now."

"Is that so?" Amusement danced across his obsidian orbs.

"You." I snaked my hand behind his neck and drew him closer.

His eyes met mine, but he leaned his head back, our lips a hairsbreadth away. "Are you sure?"

"Yes." I tugged on his head, but he stiffened, keeping his lips at a distance. "Ransom," I whined.

A wicked laugh tumbled from his lips before his mouth finally claimed mine. As he ravaged my lips, he tugged me closer until I was flush against his body. Heated memories of the last time we'd been together rushed to the surface as his arousal pressed against me. I wanted him so badly, needed him after the day we'd had. I needed to connect, to feel alive like only he made me feel.

Losing Seline made something so clear. Ransom was immortal, but I wasn't. That could've just as easily been me. And maybe that was why I'd been so upset. If I'd been on the brink of death, would he have turned me? Did I want him to?

"Red... it's not fun if you're not paying attention," he mumbled against my mouth.

"Sorry."

He rolled onto his side, dark eyes scrutinizing. "What could possibly be more interesting than this?"

"I was just thinking about Seline." I paused and snagged my lower lip between my teeth. "If that had been me dying, would you have turned me?"

A tornado of unease streaked through the bond as he regarded me for an impossibly long minute. The tendon in his jaw fluttered, and the grinding of his teeth reached my sensitive ears. The silence grew thicker with each passing moment.

"I don't know," he finally said. He pressed his lips together and scowled. "No, that's a lie. I would've turned you because despite knowing how wrong it is, I'm selfish and I couldn't live without you."

I watched him for another long moment, could feel the battle surging within him as he wrestled with the decision.

"Would you have wanted me to?" he asked when the silence between us continued to linger.

"No." The answer popped out before I could consider. But I was fairly certain the answer would always be the same.

"Then I guess it's a good thing we can't complete this bond between us." His eyes darkened, and another wave of pain streaked through our connection. "Because from what I've heard, for a wolf, losing your mate is equivalent to a death sentence, and I'm not sure how that would work for an immortal."

I cupped his cheek, drawing him closer. "I'm sorry. I wish I felt differently about it, but after everything that's happened, I couldn't imagine myself as a vampire."

He slowly shook his head. "Don't be sorry. I understand, I do. It's a life I wouldn't wish on you either. If the time ever comes, I only hope I'm strong enough to make the right decision."

"You will be. I'm sure of it."

His scowl faded, lips slowly parting into a smile. "Can we continue now? It's going to be morning soon, and I'd like to ravage you before then."

"Ravage away." I pulled him closer, and he rolled on top of me, fitting his thighs between mine. With only his tight boxer briefs, I felt all of him between my legs.

His tongue tangled with mine, and I closed my eyes letting everything else slip away. These moments of pure bliss with Ransom were the only cure to my raging thoughts. All the fear, all the sadness just melted away as his hands explored my body, his mouth worshipping my lips.

My palms drifted over the smooth planes of his back, over the finely sculpted muscle before moving down his behind. I gave it a squeeze, and I could feel his smile against my lips. "Naughty little wolf," he whispered.

"I meant what I said earlier. I want you tonight."

His eyes chased to mine, a mischievous twinkle lighting up the dark abyss.

"All of you," I added.

"Oh Red, you know you can have me whenever you want. You had me at killing murderous bloodsuckers."

A smile split my lips as memories of the first time we met on the Isle of Mordis flickered to the front of my mind. It was the first thing I'd said to him when I found him hiding in the immense kapok trees.

I slid my hands beneath the waistband of his boxers and tugged them off. I could feel the weight of his arousal against my upper thigh, and a swirl of heat exploded below my belly button.

Ransom's palms skated below my t-shirt—well, his t-shirt, and he drew it up over my head. He tossed it to the floor, and those penetrating irises seared over me. He hadn't laid a finger on me, but I squirmed from the intensity of his gaze. It was more raw, more filled with promise than any touch could ever be.

"Gods, you're beautiful, Red. If Thanatos struck me down right now, my life would've been complete."

"Don't say that." A pang of fear lanced through my insides at the thought of losing him. Was it hypocritical of me to be happy he was a vampire in this case? Immortality did have its perks after all.

He lowered his body and braced his arms on either side of my head, caging me in. His arousal pressed against my center as he moved over me, and I let out a groan. Only my panties stood between us now. And it was too much.

He fluttered kisses down my neck and paused, lingering at my collarbone. He swept his tongue over the sensitive skin where he usually fed from me. Thanks to his healing blood, not a single mark remained.

"Do you want to...?" I ticked my head toward the spot.

"No, not yet." The roughness in his voice sent another wave of heat crashing over me. He shot me a smirk as he moved down my torso, kissing and licking as he went. I arched against him as goose bumps exploded across my skin.

He paused at my panties, then ran his tongue across the

waistline. My hips bucked as the brewing heat hit uncomfortable levels.

"Ransom..." I moaned.

"Don't be so impatient, Red." He clucked his teeth and continued his relentless teasing. That hot, moist tongue glided across the sensitive skin at my pelvis before moving lower between the crease at my upper thigh and my center.

I tried to sit up, but his hand came between my breasts and pushed me back down to the mattress. With a sigh, I chomped down on my lower lip as his fingers found my nipple. A storm of heat brewed between my legs, and I suppressed a whimper. My wolf clawed at my insides, the intensity of the moment drawing her to the surface.

Mate. Mate. Mate.

The chant echoed across my mind. My eyes found Ransom's, and he gave me a tight smile. He must've heard it too. Now, it just seemed like a cruel reminder. Squeezing my eyes shut, I willed the sound away, focusing instead on the raging emotions spiraling between us.

Ransom's fingers finally slid to my panties, and he moved devastatingly slowly as he drew them down my legs. A pleased grin spread his lips, revealing that elusive dimple, and my heart staggered on a beat.

Good gods, I was done for. I'd completely fallen in love with this vampire. Despite everything he'd done and in spite of everything he'd likely still do, I loved him. Maybe it was just the bond or maybe it was something else entirely.

As he positioned himself at my entrance, my insides coiled in anticipation. *Just tell him, Nix. Tell him you love him.* I opened my mouth to say the words as he thrust inside me. Pleasure exploded through my core, and only a moan spilled out. My fingers dug into his back as his hips rolled against mine.

I could barely catch my breath as each thrust pushed me closer and closer to the edge. I wanted to speak, but my addled brain couldn't string together words. So instead, I held him tighter against me throwing my spiraling emotions through the bond and hoping he'd understand what I was too much of a coward to say.

Ransom glanced down at me, those eyes so full of emotion they stole the remaining air from my lungs. "Are you okay?"

"Mmhmm," I mumbled.

He paused, and a twinge of crimson rosied his cheeks. "Do you mind if I take you up on your earlier offer?"

My brows furrowed, and his gaze dropped to my neck.

"Ohhh..." I nodded quickly as his hips met mine once again.

Still inside me, he bent his head to my throat. My insides clenched as the tips of his incisors scraped my over-heated flesh. His fangs sank into my skin, and at the same instant he plunged inside me.

I cried out his name as he filled me. The venom raced through my veins, and the heady sensations rocketed me over the precipice. My insides clenched around him, and I let out another moan as I fell.

My breath came in ragged spurts as Ransom continued to devour me for a few more seconds before his own release came. Once he'd caught his breath, he bent his forehead to mine, my blood on his lips and another drop staining his chin. "I lied earlier, Red. *Now* I could die a happy man." He swept his thumb beneath his lip and popped his finger into his mouth.

Despite the high of the mind-blowing release I was still coming off of, I wanted more. I captured his lips, the coppery scent of my blood still on his tongue and kissed him again. I couldn't imagine what it would be like if we'd actually been able to complete the mate bond. As it was, I could barely keep my hands off him. It seemed that the more physical we got, the more it demanded.

Maybe that was how it worked.

All I knew was that after losing Seline today, I needed to be lost in him. I wrapped my legs around his hips and tugged him down against me. He cocked a mischievous brow. "Again already?"

"I'm ready if you are."

"Oh Red, I'm always ready for you." His mouth claimed mine before his hands gripped my hips, and he flipped me over so I straddled him. I barely escaped the wrath of whiplash. "Only this time, I want you on top," he rasped against my lips. "So I can see all of you."

And that was how we spent the rest of the night because losing myself in Ransom was much easier than dealing with what was to come.

CHAPTER
SIXTEEN

R*ansom*

THE QUEEN EYED Red and me from across the training room, and the hair on the back of my neck bristled. Perhaps the two of us had become too openly friendly in the past few days. The last thing I wanted was Carmen Rosa catching wind of this thing between us. Nothing like giving your frenemies something to use against you.

The blade of the medieval axe whipped over my head, and I barely ducked in time. "Geez, Red, that was disturbingly close."

She smirked. "Then stop daydreaming and focus."

I grabbed her arm and jerked her toward me. My lips brushed the shell of her ear, and I whispered, "I can't when you're this close to me and smelling like that." My nostrils flared at her scent. "You're incredibly sexy when you're murderous."

She laughed before pushing me away. I staggered back a few steps, giving the queen a show. Red and I were playing a dangerous game, but gods it felt so good I couldn't stop. The more I made love to her the more I wanted her and the closer to the surface my wolf surged. His growl had been so loud the other night we'd stopped mid-orgasm.

Every day that passed I cursed myself for not telling her the truth about the mate bond, but after our conversation a few nights ago, I couldn't find it in me to tell her. She didn't want to become a vampire, and I was immortal. If by some twisted will of fate, we actually succeeded in completing the bond and I lost her, I'd be forced to live an eternity of torment without her.

A niggling voice in my head told me I was being an idiot. Maybe it was my wolf. Even without completing the bond, if anything happened to her, I'd likely put an early end to my torturous existence.

I loosed a frustrated breath. Sometimes it felt like Red and I were destined to endlessly orbit one another, the moon and sun, without ever quite meeting for the rest of our days.

Red's boot grazed my chin, and I leapt back. "Naughty little sicari," I huffed out.

"Why aren't you fighting me?"

"Because I can't stop thinking about fanging you." My fangs dropped, and I threw her a cheeky smile.

"Maybe we should switch sparring partners."

While I loathed the idea, she was probably right. If the Scooby gang had any hope of surviving what was to come, they needed to train with the best. Me. "Anyone but Spa—"

Red whistled at the dragon, cutting me off. "Sparky, come train with Ransom."

Identical groans erupted from both our lips.

"Do I really have to?" Spark whined.

"Yes." Red slid him a sidelong glare. "We're not losing anyone else from this team, and who better to practice with than the enemy himself?"

The dragon's nostrils flared as his eyes darted between us. "I think you've been getting enough practice with him for all of us."

Crimson blossomed across Red's cheeks as her jaw dropped, forming a capital O.

"Watch your mouth, dragon boy," I hissed. He'd taken Seline's death the hardest, understandably, and he'd been unbearable the past few days. I'd given him an out because of his grief, but there were limits to my patience.

He shrugged and gripped the stake tighter in his hand. "Whatever, let's just do this."

Red marched toward me, brushing by my shoulder on her way to spar with the winter Fae. "Please don't kill him. He's been through a lot lately," she whispered.

"We all have," I countered.

Shaking her head, she retreated to the other side of the training room. It was all an act though, she'd have her eyes on us the whole time. She'd never let anything happen to her precious Sparky.

"Are we doing this or what?" The dragon stalked closer.

Oh, it's on, dragon boy. My wolf surged to the surface, a deep rumble stirring within my core. I froze for an instant, the sensations so surreal. It was the first time my lupine half had made such an overt appearance when not in the throes of passion.

Sparky lunged and I was so frazzled by my ghostly wolf, his stake ripped into my shirt and pierced the flesh of my left shoulder. I let out a hiss.

127

"What's the matter, fanger, off your game?"

Another growl escaped, but this one was not of the lupine variety. My fangs dropped, and I leapt at the cocky idiot. His stake clattered to the ground as our bodies collided. He smacked onto the mat, and I landed on top of him with a clear opening to his jugular.

The little devil on my shoulder taunted me. *Just one little bite. Just to show the arrogant dragon who's the top dog around here.* Ah, what the hell? My incisors lengthened, and I chomped down on his neck. The sissy dragon let out a shriek as I took a long pull. A little too tart for my tastes.

A familiar presence hovered over me before slender but strong fingers closed around my shoulders. After another quick sip, I retracted my fangs as Red dragged me off the irritating dragon.

"What the hell is wrong with you?" she shouted.

Cal and Archer helped the whiny dragon up as he pressed his hand to his neck. It was barely a flesh wound, and he was being much too dramatic. "I barely nicked the artery," I muttered.

"Ransom!"

"I thought you wanted me to train them, Red? I was teaching him a lesson." I couldn't help the smirk from tugging at my lips. "He left himself exposed, and I made sure he wouldn't make the same mistake again."

A circle of sicari had formed around us now. The remaining slayers had been training together for the past three days and to be perfectly honest I didn't have high hopes for the future of Nocturnis. If the queen returning to her throne relied on this lot, we were all fanged.

Carmen Rosa sauntered over, her eyes narrowing on me. "Ransom is right. While I may not approve of his methods, perhaps we have been going about training wrong." She turned to Red. "On the island you trained with real live vampires and perhaps that's exactly what is missing here." The queen curled her finger, beckoning a few of her guards over. The three burly vampires circled Carmen Rosa. "Ransom, I'd like you to oversee the vampires and make sure that each sicari trains with one for a few hours daily."

"Of course, my queen." I dipped into an elaborate bow.

Carmen Rosa pivoted her gaze to the assembled sicari. "With our numbers down, taking the castle back will prove difficult. You'll all be facing more than just sickly serviles, and it's important that you are prepared. We take Royal Castle back by the end of the week. I won't have that usurper sitting on my throne for one moment longer."

Red's eyes chased to mine, and I attempted a reassuring smile. But the bond didn't lie. A twinge of unease zipped back and forth between us. It was going to be a bloodbath.

MUSCLES I DIDN'T EVEN KNOW I had hurt. So much for the perks of immortality. I stretched out across the bed of the small bedroom I'd found to hide in and sipped on the blood bag the queen had provided. After a quick exploration of Carmen Rosa's new secret hideout, I'd determined this house must belong to Lucíano. It reeked of the Spaniard.

After an entire day of sparring with sicari, I needed a break. Somehow, Red still fought on, encouraging her faltering teammates as well as the whole crew. Or what was left of them. River and his team were the only ones worth anything. The rest that had survived were the newbs. They'd likely only made it this far because they hid or ran away during the last battle. That did not bode well for any of us.

If this siege on the castle failed, it would be up to the

Etrian Assembly to dethrone Ronin and the likelihood of that happening was slim. Getting those eight leaders to agree to anything would be a miracle.

The door of my little hideout whipped open, and I jolted upright. The queen sauntered in, by herself surprisingly.

"There you are." She crossed her arms over her chest as she eyed me disapprovingly. It was worse than the looks my mother used to throw.

Tossing the empty blood bag on the side table, I slid to the edge of the bed. "Just needed a snack break."

She nodded, her gaze heavy on me. "Besides that little show with the dragon, how are your urges to feed?"

I shrugged. "Not too bad." For once, it wasn't a lie. With Red allowing me to drink from her, I felt sated most days. If I didn't have her, I wasn't sure what would happen though.

"Good." She sauntered closer, and tiny fingers brushed at my subconscious. They pried and pressed their way in.

Gritting my teeth, I fought her influence. "Whatever you want to know, just ask, my queen. No need to compel it out of me."

A saccharine smile split her crimson lips. "I need to confirm you'll do what you have to if everything goes wrong when we siege the castle."

"I already told you I would."

"Things are different now between you and Phoenix. I'm not blind to matters of the heart, my son."

I willed my thoughts to blank, not to think of Red, of how she felt, of her tantalizing scent. "I don't know what you're talking about."

"I was wrong before. It's more than the blood bond between you; I'm certain of that. Now, what does exist between you, I'm not entirely sure of." Her dark brows knitted together as she scrutinized me.

Had she heard my wolf earlier? Would she make the connection?

"Just remember that whatever you feel for Phoenix will die along with her if Ronin gets what he wants. I've gotten word that the warlock Drakin is dangerously close to returning Thanatos to corporeal form. If that happens, we'll have another set of problems on our hands. Taking out Azara and her mother, Luna, is the easiest option. If you can't do that, I'll have no choice but to eliminate Phoenix—"

A growl tore from my clenched teeth, and I leapt up. Before I could stop myself, my hands curled around the queen's throat. "You won't touch her," I snarled.

A wicked grin twisted her lips. "That's what I thought." *Now let go of me.* Her words echoed through my mind, and a blinding pain pounded through my skull.

My fingers fell away from her throat, and I staggered back, pressing my palms to my temples.

"Don't mistake my kindness for weakness, Ransom. While I am fond of you and your father, don't think for a minute I wouldn't kill you if I had to."

I snorted. "I never doubted it for a moment, my queen." I took a measured step closer. "And I ask you not to underestimate me either. I'll follow through with our deal as promised, but if you ever threaten Red again—" I let my words fall away before I revealed too much. The queen was smart, and it was only a matter of time before she figured out the truth. "You know she's my favorite food source."

"Hmm." Her lips pressed together. "So you say, Ransom." She turned on her heel and marched to the door. The moment it slammed shut, I slumped down on the mattress. Ronin had to be stopped. If not, I'd be forced to kill Azara and her mother, and Red would never forgive me.

CHAPTER
SEVENTEEN

P *hoenix*

"I STILL BELIEVE it's highly unlikely. Impossible really."

I stared at the archangel in an immaculate white tunic whose alabaster wings took up the majority of the kitchen. Cal's wings were pretty and all, but compared to the male before us, they looked puny. The archangel's feathery appendages were blinding, like the light of heaven itself radiated from them.

"But the fact that you came means there's a tiny chance?" I asked.

Cillian glanced over at Cal. "I came because Callan asked me a favor, but no, I don't truly believe it's possible. I've lived for many centuries, Phoenix, and I've never heard of a vampire with a soul. The very phrase is a paradox."

"But it's written in the spell...," said Vera. She still held the slip of paper tight in her fist.

He shrugged, his silky blonde locks bouncing on his shoulders. "I don't know what to make of that."

I squeezed my eyes shut and pictured the dark scrawling on the parchment.

...the blood of the wolf with the mortal bite...

...the blood of a faery born without elemental magic...

...the blood of a one-winged angel...

...the blood of a female warlock...

...the blood of a vampire with a soul...

"HAVE any one-winged angels gone missing by chance?" I blurted.

Cillian nodded slowly, darkness settling over his brilliant azure irises. "The queen had contacted me a few weeks ago about the situation. Unfortunately, one of the Sons of Heaven, Gabrielle, who lost his wing in battle over a century ago had gone missing just a few days prior. Generally, angels can self-heal so the fact that his appendage never returned has always been a mystery. There are likely less than a handful of one-winged angels in existence." He shook his head. "Anyway, legions of angels have searched for him, but we've come up empty-handed."

I pressed my lips into a thin line. Why hadn't Carmen Rosa told us? I made a mental note to have Archer contact his father to see what he could find out about faeries born without elemental magic. Archer's father, Julias Darkhen, was one of the most influential Fae in the Winter Court. As cousin to the king, his family wielded a good amount of power. Hopefully, he'd be able to give us a head's up since the queen was keeping us in the dark about it. The thought made the hair on the back of my neck prickle. What else was she keeping from us?

"You believe this vampire could be the one to break the curse?" he asked, his light brows furrowing.

"Maybe." I still wasn't sure if I should be hoping for or against it.

"Well, I'll certainly be able to give you an answer either way. It's a fairly simple procedure for an archangel." He glanced between Vera and me. "Where is this Ransom fellow?"

"He should be back any minute. He just went out for some supplies." I paused and chewed on my lip. "He didn't know you were coming. He's not exactly on board with this."

Cillian quirked a brow. "On board with having a soul?"

"No, he just doesn't believe it's true. He thinks he would know, would feel something."

"Ah, I see." He wrapped his big arms across his chest.

The hair on the back of my neck rose, and every nerve-ending in my body stood at attention. Which meant one thing. Ransom was near. With the daily blood exchanges and nightly romps in bed, our connection grew stronger by the minute. I was starting to think we were fanged whether we completed the mating bond or not. Pushing the swirling thoughts to the side for now, I focused on the archangel. "Do you think you could wait in the other room so I can talk to him when he comes in?" The last thing I needed was Ransom making a scene in front of one of the top-ranking angels in all of Celestia.

"Of course."

Cal ticked his head at the bedroom he and Vera shared. "Come on, Cillian, we can wait in here."

"Fine, and then perhaps you can tell me more about this situation with Thanatos you mentioned."

I shot Cal a thumb's up as he led the archangel away. We needed as many influential leaders on our side if everything went sideways with Ronin.

A few seconds after the bedroom door closed behind Vera, the familiar whoosh of Ransom's vamp-speed echoed down the corridor. The door whipped open, and he filled the threshold, holding grocery bags in each hand.

"Honey, I'm home." The sight of him brought an unexpected smile to my lips. It all seemed so normal. "What are you smiling about?" He sauntered closer, a roguish grin flashing across his handsome face.

"I guess I like this domestic side of you."

His gaze flickered to Cal and Vera's bedroom, and his brows slammed together. "Who's here?"

Damned vampire hearing.

"Don't freak out." I held my hands up. "Just put the stuff down, and I'll explain."

He side-eyed me, but surprisingly did as instructed. Once the groceries were safe on the counter, I took his hand and led him to the barstools, forcing him to sit.

"It's the Archangel Cillian. I asked him here to find out about your soul."

A surge of anger flooded our bond, the onslaught so powerful it was like a punch to the gut. "Red, I told you it wasn't me." His words came out eerily calm and much too quiet for the amount of fury that raced between us.

"I think you're wrong." I held my ground, refusing to let fear ruin this for him. I placed my hand on his chest, and the angry flutters of his heart smacked against my palm. "There's something there, I know it."

He slowly shook his head. "I said no."

"Please, Ransom. Cillian came all this way. He said it's a quick test, and we'll finally be able to put it to rest."

"No," he growled and shot up.

My hand slid from his chest, frustration gnawing at my insides. "Why are you acting like this? Why don't you want to know the truth?"

"I already told you I don't need a holier than thou archangel telling me I'm a soulless demon. I already know what I am, and I'm trying to accept it. Why can't you?"

"You're not accepting it. You're just giving up!"

"Don't you see there's nothing to give up, Red? It was lost a long time ago. This is all a waste of time." He raked his hand through his hair tugging at the ends.

"You're just scared. I know it. But it won't change anything, I swear."

His head whipped back and forth. "It already has." He turned on his heel and zipped out the door before I could get another word out.

My knee bounced up and down as I sat on the edge of the couch, waiting. Ransom had been gone for hours, and all the terrible things he could be doing raced across my mind. I should've gone after him.

I knew he was scared, but I still didn't understand why he was being so stubborn about this. I huffed out a breath and raked my hands over my face. I'd give the infuriating fanger another hour and if he wasn't back by then, I was going after him. With everything going on right now, the last thing I needed was my vampire mate going on a blood bender.

The click of a lock sent my heart catapulting up my throat. My eyes darted to the entrance, but the door didn't open. Instead, the shuffle of approaching footsteps came from the other side of the penthouse.

Spark appeared around the corner, his hair disheveled and a sleepy look on his face. He yawned and leaned against the kitchen counter. "What are you doing still up?"

"Ransom's not back yet," I muttered. "You?"

He trudged over and folded down beside me. "I haven't been sleeping so well lately."

I curled in beside him, wrapping my arm around his broad shoulders. I'd been a super crappy friend to Spark. With all my drama, I hadn't stopped for a second to check in on him. "How are you?"

He shrugged. "As okay as I can be, I guess."

I tightened my hold around him, and he released a sharp sigh.

"Seline wasn't you, Nix, but I cared for her."

I nodded slowly, my pulse ratcheting up. "And she loved you."

"I know, and I probably would've loved her too in time. Once I'd gotten over you."

I caught the sheepish smile from the corner of my eye.

"But I'm not stupid. I know there's no fighting a wolf mate bond, even a dead one, apparently."

I pivoted toward him and took his hand, squeezing. "I'm sorry I didn't tell you sooner. I should've, it was just... I couldn't even wrap my own head around it. I still can't. Ransom died and yet somehow, I feel his wolf as clearly as I feel your fingers around my hand."

His head dipped slowly.

"Sorry, do you not want to hear about this?"

A rueful chuckle slipped out. "Nah, it's okay. We might as well be miserable together, right?"

I leaned my forehead to his. "We'll get through this; I know we will."

"I hope so." He gave me a weak smile, and a tiny crack raced across my heart.

I missed my friend, and I only hoped that the one good thing to come from Seline's passing would be to bring us closer again.

The front door whipped open, and Ransom zipped in. His onyx eyes lanced over me, then Spark and our intertwined fingers. "Well, that didn't take long." He staggered in, narrowly missing the kitchen island.

My nostrils flared at the smokey scent of bourbon in the air. "Are you drunk?"

"I don't know, Mom, am I?" He leaned against the granite countertop, his eyes puffy and unfocused.

Spark stood, releasing my hand. "I'll leave you two to hash this out."

"Oh, how noble of you." Ransom dipped into a mock bow. "The great dragon alpha heir bowing out. Finally realized you have no chance with her?"

"Ransom!" I hissed.

Spark closed the distance between them and loomed over my drunk mate, jabbing a finger into his shirt. My pulse spiked. "I'll give you a pass this time since you're wasted, but if you plan on sticking around, you better get used to this. Nix is my team leader, but more than that she's my friend, and I love her. Get your shit together, fanger, because I'm more than willing to step in if you can't make her happy."

Ransom's cocky smirk fell away, his eyes darkening. I glanced at bardy across the room in case I had to step in. There was no way I was letting those two go at it. "Fair enough." Ransom turned on his heel and sauntered to the bedroom.

That was unexpected.

Spark and I exchanged a look of surprise before he shook his head and turned toward his own room. "Night, Nix. Get some rest," he called out over his shoulder.

"Right." Rest? Not when I had to deal with a drunk vampire. Curling my hands into fists, I stomped to the bedroom. If Ransom had ravaged the nearest blood brothel, I needed to know so I could do some damage control.

I marched in and found him splayed across the bed in only boxers. Even annoyed as all hell, I couldn't keep my eyes from raking over his impressive form. That sculpted chest and those perfectly carved abs. My fingers ached to touch him, to have him pressed against my body.

I cleared my throat, and he glanced up at me beneath dark, sooty lashes. "So where have you been all night?"

"Isn't that obvious?" The scent of bourbon lingered in the air between us.

"A bar?"

"Better than a blood brothel, right?"

A smile tugged at the corner of my lip, and a wave of relief splashed over me. Sure, he'd gotten drunk, but it was monumentally better than a blood bender. Was he actually making progress? I schooled my lips back into a thin line. I was supposed to be mad at him for refusing to meet with Cillian and then storming out like a child.

"Yes," I finally answered. I crept toward the bed and perched on the edge of the mattress. "So that's all you did?"

He sat up and inched closer. "That was all I did, Red. I swear it on this gods' damned bond between us."

The smile I'd tried to force away finally split my lips. "I'm proud of you."

A deep chuckle vibrated his chest. "What does it say

about me if getting drunk at a bar is something to be proud of?"

Nothing good. I kept the thought to myself. As much as I wanted to be mad I couldn't. I understood how much his wolf meant to him, and I knew that was why he'd run off earlier. He couldn't face the possibility or more importantly, the disappointment.

"I needed to let off some steam," he continued. His fingers danced across the mattress until they entangled with mine. "My first impulse was to eat a whole village of innocents." He shrugged. "But then you popped into my head, and I couldn't do it. I'm not sure if you're my salvation or eternal damnation."

I reached for his face with my free hand and cupped his cheek. "How about your redemption?"

His mouth moved to my palm and fluttered kisses across my skin. "I don't care what you are, as long as you're mine." He pushed me back onto the mattress, and I let myself get lost in his heated kisses and tantalizing touch.

CHAPTER
EIGHTEEN

R*ansom*

My DEAD HEART rapped out a ragged beat as I watched Red
sleep for another moment. I hated leaving her like this, but if
I didn't do it now, I'd lose my nerve. The bourbon binge last
night had provided surprising clarity. Or maybe it was what
that arrogant dragon had said when I'd returned.

Either way, I needed to know the truth. If not for me,
then for Red. Because if I truly was the vampire with a soul,
that meant Ronin and Thanatos needed me just as badly as
they needed her. I could use that to my advantage.

I silently slipped into my clothes and forced myself to the
door. With one hand wrapped around the handle, I hazarded
another look back. Red was radiant as she slept, her deep
auburn hair splayed out over the pillow like a crimson halo.

If I had a soul, we could complete the bond. And if I didn't...

I shook my head, chasing away the dismal thoughts. I had to be strong like her, be brave for her. I whipped the door open and marched out. Now all I needed was Vera's sun-blocking potion.

THE PORTAL DEPOSITED me on the lush earthly grounds of Celestia, the realm of the Sons of Heaven. I stared up at the soaring tower where the angels resided, Turrem Angelus. The unearthly edifice was said to reach all the way to the heavens. No way I belonged up there.

With the sun warm on my shoulders, I marched toward the angelic sentinels stationed in front of a golden arch. Both stood at the ready, their angel blades aglow in azure flames.

"What is your business here?" the blonde male asked.

"Ransom De La Sangue here. I'd like to see the Archangel Cillian."

"Is he expecting you?" the woman interjected.

"Not exactly. I was supposed to meet with him yesterday, but I missed the appointment."

The male narrowed his crystal blue eyes at me.

I gave him my best smile in return. "If you could just let him know I'm here, I'd be forever grateful."

The female's wings unfolded, the silvery feathers spanning across her shoulders and way beyond. Without a word, she leapt into the cloudless blue sky.

"So this Cillian's a good guy, huh?"

The angel glared down at me, light brows furrowed.

"Tough crowd." The sentinel and I remained in silence until the female returned a few moments later.

A tight smile replaced the scowl she'd greeted me with as she spoke. "The Archangel will see you now."

My silly heart gave a little leap of joy. Why was I doing this to myself again? Oh, right, for the girl. It was always about the girl in the end, wasn't it? She was a damned good one though.

"Come with me." The angel stretched out her arms, and I eyed her skeptically.

"Excuse me?"

Before I could get another word in, the woman curled her arms under my shoulders and legs and cradled me against her chest. Her massive wings flapped, and we shot up into the sky. *Well, this is oddly strange yet magical.*

I watched as the lush green below receded, and the warm breeze caressed my skin. I thanked the gods for Vera's potion as we flew higher. I expected to feel nervous or anxious or uncomfortable at least, but instead an odd sense of calm washed over me as we soared up to the tower. She must have been using her angel healing power. Was it on purpose or did it just happen naturally?

Too soon, the angel's wings began to slow, and she descended onto a cottony cloud at the foot of the angelic compound. Two more guards stood in front of a gilded gate, the pair of males even more intimidating than the ones I'd encountered below.

She lowered me onto my feet, and my boots sank into the soft fluffy cloud. I'd only been to Celestia on a few occasions, so I still found the whole thing startling. I was certain I'd fall through the cloud at any moment and descend into the darkest pits of hell, where all demons belonged.

The female ticked her head at the guards, and they parted, opening the immense golden gate. Beyond it stood the alabaster tower, stretching high into the sky. I wasn't sure if it actually reached heaven, but I sure as hell couldn't see the top.

As soon as we entered, another angel appeared, his wings dwarfing all the others. The male gave me a faint smile as he approached, and my escort dipped her head. "Archangel Cillian, your visitor, the vampire Ransom De La Sangue."

"Thank you, Felicity. I'll take it from here."

She dipped her head again and turning on her heel, jumped off the cloud and descended back to earth.

"You're just about the last person I expected to see here." The archangel's lips twisted as they scoured over me.

"That makes two of us."

He ticked his head toward a small bubbling brook adjacent to the entrance of the tower. A few white marble slabs had been fashioned into chairs and placed around it. "Please, tell me what's brought you today."

I settled onto the chair, the cold stone digging into my back. *Not the most comfortable seat ever.* Perhaps it was on purpose so that visitors wouldn't get too comfy in the angel realm.

Cillian regarded me for a long moment, his light cerulean eyes nearly the same color as the perfect sky. "Well?"

Ah, yes, now it was my turn to speak. "I apologize for missing our appointment yesterday, but you see, I was caught a bit off guard."

"Yes, Phoenix explained your reluctance."

"Did she now?"

He nodded. "I understand your doubts, and I don't fault you for them, which is why I'm sitting here with you now. I also have my own selfish reasons. This Ronin fellow has presumably captured one of my brothers as well. I'd like to see him safely returned. If you are indeed the vampire with a soul that the spell speaks of, it is in all our best interests to know."

My head dipped slowly. "Exactly why I'm here."

"Good. I'm pleased you've reconsidered." He rubbed his hands together. "Let's get started then."

A wave of anxiety shot through my insides as the archangel stood and hovered over me, still rubbing his palms together. A brilliant blue light began to glow between his hands, and a surge of warmth emanated in my direction.

"Close your eyes and relax," he whispered, his melodic voice soothing the rising panic.

I released a breath and allowed my lids to drift closed. The warmth rolled over me, surrounding me in a bright cocoon. Even with my eyes shut, the blinding light seeped in through the cracks.

A swell of energy permeated my skin and burrowed its way into my veins, my very bones. It circled my body, seeping into each and every nook and cranny until it settled in my chest. I drew in a breath as my lungs grew heavy, and every inhale became an effort.

"Almost there," Cillian murmured.

The soothing warmth encircled my heart, encompassing it in a soft feathery pillow. Its steady thrumming picked up as if jolted back to life by magic. I sucked in a breath as the beats became thunderous, each palpitation ramming into my ribcage. My heart felt so full I was certain it would burst.

Then all of a sudden, everything went dark. The warmth dissipated, and my eyes snapped open.

Cillian stood over me, lips screwed into a pout.

"Well?" I blurted.

"It's... not possible." He shook his head, light brows scrunched together.

"Spit it out for me, angel. I'm on the edge of my seat over here."

"I felt something," he mumbled, more to himself than me. "But it can't be..."

"My soul?" I cried.

"It was only a flicker, extremely faint, but something of your soul still remains."

All the air whooshed from my lungs, and I slumped back on the unyielding marble chair. "You're sure?"

His head dipped slowly. "I'd like to try it one more time to confirm, but I'm certain I felt something." The angel's forehead was creased, the lines only deepening as he regarded me. "I simply can't understand how it could be possible."

"That makes two of us." I chewed on the inside of my cheek as the million-dollar question zipped across my mind. Would the angel have any insight into lupine mating bonds?

"Whenever you're ready." Cillian pressed his hands together again, and the blue light burst from his palms. He repeated the procedure, but this time moved even slower. My entire body felt as if it would go up in flames by the time he finished.

He nodded again. "It's confirmed. You must be the vampire with the soul the spell speaks of."

The swirl of emotions that rocketed through my insides was too much, too powerful. I shoved everything back to the dark corners to deal with later. I had to ask the question still poised on my tongue. "Let's say my soul really did remain intact, for wolves, the mate bond is a sort of soulmate bond, so would that mean that I'd be able to complete that connection with another wolf?"

Cillian released a breath before shrugging. "I'm not entirely sure, Ransom. As I said, little remains of your soul, it's more of a tiny spark. I'm not certain that enough is there to sustain the bond." He shook his head, eyes settling on mine. "But I've never seen anything like this, so I'm not discouraging you from trying. It certainly wouldn't hurt."

"Hmm." He was wrong of course because hope did hurt, could kill even. I had a soul... a tiny flicker but still something. I couldn't believe it. A smile split my lips unbidden. Did that mean my wolf still lived too? It would explain everything I'd been feeling from him lately.

"Ransom, you understand what this means, right?"

I nodded absentmindedly.

"When Ronin finds out you're the one, he'll come after you too."

Oh, right, Ronin. The other reason why I'd come. "No one has to know, Cillian." I narrowed my eyes at the archangel. "We must keep this between us."

His lips twisted. "This is a matter that could affect the entire realm of Azar. We cannot keep it a secret when so much is at risk."

"Just give me some time to sort this out myself. If I cannot handle it, then I'll agree to inform every one of the truth. I'll do it myself even."

"I'll give you a week, or until things escalate with Ronin. If the queen cannot succeed in vanquishing him, I'll be forced to go to the Etrian Assembly. We cannot let the shadow curse be broken, or the peace we've fought for all these years will shatter."

Well, at least we had someone on our side. It was a shame the archangel didn't sit on the assembly and thus had no vote. From what I'd heard, Cillian was second to Amanadiel, the head archangel who presided over the Sons of Heaven and held the seat on the Etrian Assembly. He was an influential friend to have.

I extended my hand and was pleased when Cillian shook it. "One week then. And thank you for your assistance and discretion in the matter."

"You're welcome. I only hope I've made the right choice." A smile parted his lips, escalating the angel's beauty to astronomical levels. "I'm happy for you, Ransom. The gods must have plans for you if they've bestowed such an honor. For you and your mate. I wish you both well."

I nodded quickly and released his hand as heat burned my cheeks. Good gods, the angel had succeeded in making me blush. Now the important question remained: would I tell Red the truth now or wait until I confronted Ronin?

CHAPTER
NINETEEN

P *hoenix*

THE CLANG of weapons rang out through the training room, a mix of grunts and battle cries filling in the space between. I watched Ransom from across the vast chamber as he fought yet another sicari recruit. The girl was young, only seventeen. She'd been jerked out of training on the Isle of Mordis to battle the rebel king and a fanging god. A pit of dread formed in my gut. Did we really even stand a chance? My fingers tightened around bardy, the feel of the worn shaft oddly comforting amid the chaos.

Ransom took it easy on the girl, moving at a quarter of his normal speed and still it was clear she was no match. My heart ached for her as I watched them. I couldn't help my gaze from constantly drifting to Ransom. Even training in slow-mo, he was a thrill to observe. He was as graceful as a gazelle, and as deadly as the fiercest wild cat. I focused on him for a few more seconds before turning my attention to the other sicari training.

Ransom had been acting strangely since yesterday. He'd been gone when I awoke and returned with a lame excuse of scouring the Darklands for more sicari in hiding. I just hoped he hadn't been out hunting for blood again. He seemed to have his cravings under control lately. I ran my fingers over the matching pin pricks on my neck—or rather where they should've been. Ransom was adamant he'd heal me after every feed, and he swore I was more than enough for him. Still, I couldn't help the twinge of doubt.

Another sicari newbie caught my attention from the corner of my eye. The young girl sparred with one of the queen's men. The vampire had her pinned to the floor, her stake just beyond her reach. She wriggled beneath him, but she was no match against his strength. His fangs descended, and he snapped at her neck. In real life, she would've been dead.

I marched over, unable to stop myself and crouched down beside her. "Never give up," I cried. "If you can't find your weapon, you have to be smart. Use any and all advantages. Strength, speed, agility-- fangers have the upper hand in all those things, but there's one thing in which even you can go toe-to-toe with them."

"What?" she gasped.

I pointed at my temple, then eyed her free leg. The vamp had trapped her torso to the floor, but her knee had just enough room to cause some damage to the guy's family jewels. "Use *whatever* you can."

It was like a lightbulb went off in her brain. She jerked her knee up, landing a solid hit to his crotch. He rolled off her, squealing.

The girl leapt up and grabbed her weapon, rewarding me with a smile. "Thanks."

"When a vampire gets kicked in the balls, it hurts just as bad as for a human." I shot her a wink. "There's no such thing as cheating when you're fighting for your life, got it?"

She nodded quickly.

As the vampire muttered curses in my direction, I returned to my spot at the head of the room where I could see all the action. My whole team was here, helping the young ones train and getting pointers from the few senior sicari remaining. Even Carmen Rosa's inner circle members had joined in on the fun, Lucíano included. I was just waiting my turn to get a swing at him with bardy.

"Attention, attention!" One of the queen's guards appeared at the front of the room, clapping his hands. "The queen has urgent news." The vampire stepped to the side and Carmen Rosa coalesced behind him, wearing all black from head to toe. Black leather pants and chunky heeled boots along with a black tee and cargo jacket completed her look. It reminded me of an upscale version of our trainee uniforms back on the island. My gaze drifted to her waist and the range of weapons strapped to her belt.

That pit of dread amplified to boulder-sized proportions.

Ransom must have felt it because he appeared beside me a moment later. "What do you think this is about?" he muttered.

"Nothing good."

"To what do we owe this pleasure, my queen?" Ransom asked.

"I've just received word from one of my men that the warehouse that Nix and the recently departed Seline stumbled upon has been taken by River and his team. The entirety of Ronin's servile army has been either killed or captured."

A wave of whoops broke out across the space.

"In light of this news, I've decided to move up the time-line. We take back the castle this evening before Ronin has time to bolster his defenses."

My jaw dropped. My mind flitted back to the young sicari training with Ransom just a moment ago. We weren't anywhere close to being ready.

Ransom must have read my mind because he blurted, "Are you sure that is wise, my queen?"

"If I hadn't thought it wise, I wouldn't have suggested it." She shot him a scathing glare, then she turned to her Royal guards. "We've waited long enough, and between my guards, my Royal followers, and you, my faithful sicari, I'm certain we will take back our home."

This made no sense. Even if River and his team did manage to take out the horde at the warehouse, we had no idea how many were at the castle. Plus, he and his team must've been worn out after the fight. They were our strongest assets and leading our sorry team into battle with our best players weak was a *bad* idea.

"Can't we wait until tomorrow?" The words burst from my mouth before I could stop them. "So we have time to plan?"

She shook her head, jaw clenched tight. "We attack tonight, at midnight. We will catch them unaware before Ronin can replenish his forces." The queen's dark gaze lanced across the room. "We *will* fight, and we *will* win. Is everyone ready?"

Muttered yeses filled the room, nowhere near the excited whoops of a few seconds ago.

This was a bad idea. I could feel it deep within my bones.

THE MOOD in the penthouse was abysmal. A heavy silence pervaded, and even Ransom's normal light banter was MIA as we collected our weapons and gear for tonight. Everyone moved around the space quietly, tiptoeing and whispering as if anyone made a sound, the battle would erupt.

Vera and Cal sat on the couch, the Nephilim helping to gather all her witchy supplies into a bag. They exchanged whispered words and the occasional lingering touch, and it had my insides in knots. The same dismal thoughts must have been racing through their minds too. What if we lost someone else tonight?

Worse, what if we lost everyone?

Archer dropped a bagful of weapons by the door, the loud thump and clatter drawing everyone's attention. "Sorry," he mumbled as he strode back into the kitchen.

Spark was perched on the island, sharpening a stake. He'd been at it for hours. He'd whittled down the wooden ones to saplings.

"Okay, guys, I think it's time for a pep talk." I marched to the middle of the room and waited until all eyes were on me. Even Ransom emerged from the bedroom he'd disappeared into a few minutes ago.

"Please go ahead, oh fearless leader." Ransom shot me a smirk as he moved into step beside me.

"I know this seems like a brash move—"

"More like suicidal," Spark interjected.

I shushed him with a narrowed glare. "But let's be honest, how much of a difference would a few more days have made with the new recruits?"

"Nothing, because they're useless," said Archer.

"So ultimately it's going to come down to us, River and his team, and the vampires fighting on our side. We've got to go in this like any other battle. Success is never guaranteed, right?"

"It is if you're Phoenix Morana." Spark shot me a smile.

"True..." I waggled my brows at him. "That's the attitude we need for this fight, guys." I steeled my nerves and spat out the next words before I lost my nerve. My team deserved to know the truth about my past with Ronin. "There's something I need to tell you. I've known Ronin for a long time. I vowed to take him down ten years ago, and tonight, I'm going to do everything I can to make sure that no other little girl goes through what I went through all those years ago."

Five pairs of eyes bored into me, the one at my side the heaviest of all. "Ronin and his men killed my parents when I was just a kid. I watched them die." I paused and drew in a strengthening breath. "We were living with the tigers back then, in a small camp on the border. He decimated the village, and somehow by divine intervention, my sister and I survived. It's a long story, and I promise I'll get into it one day, but the details aren't important. I vowed to get my revenge and years later, when I was given the opportunity to become a sicari, I took it for one reason only: to kill Ronin."

I released a breath, the confession loosening the tightness in my chest. I should've told my team the truth long ago. Somehow, I thought it would make me look weak, but I realized now that my past made me strong, made me the person I was today.

"I'm sorry I didn't tell you sooner, but I wanted you all to know now. This isn't just the queen's vendetta to get her castle back. Taking Ronin down is personal. So despite the odds, I need each of you fighting with all you've got."

"Always do, boss." Spark's eyes lit up.

"We'll make you proud tonight, Nix." Vera leapt up and wrapped her arms around me. "And I'm proud of *you*."

Hot tears pricked at the back of my eyes, but I blinked quickly forcing them away. Tonight, I had to be strong. There was no room for weakness. Tonight, we took Ronin down.

CHAPTER
TWENTY

R*ansom*

RED HELD it together for her team, despite the onslaught of emotions I felt pummeling her insides. I watched her, completely enthralled, as she delivered that speech to her team. Though I'd already heard the story, listening to her tell it again awakened some inner need to protect her, to keep her from such tragedy ever befalling her again.

Thanatos, I loved her. She was fierce, determined and so gorgeous I could barely keep from touching her. I wanted to complete the mate bond; we had to at least try. But what would she say when she found out I'd kept the truth from her this whole time?

It didn't matter. I had to tell her.

My gaze remained focused on my mate and her team as they exchanged hugs and high fives. I only hoped the happiness would last. After tonight, everything could change.

Once the Scooby gang began to disband, I strode over to Red and nuzzled her ear. "Have I ever told you how incredibly sexy you are when you boss the others around?"

She arched a brow, her lips puckering. "I was not bossing them around. I was trying to be inspirational."

A chuckle escaped my lips, and I drew her into my arms. "You said exactly what they needed to hear. It's no wonder you were chosen to lead."

A deep blush blossomed across her cheeks, and my heart fluttered faster. Two big secrets on the eve of war. My soul and our bond. Should I tell her now or wait? What if it was too late then? The dismal thought crushed the air from my lungs. Losing Red wasn't an option. I'd kill Ronin or even Thanatos himself before I let them touch a single hair on her head.

"What?" She eyed me, brows knitting.

I inhaled a deep breath and blew it out. "Let's talk." Wrapping my hand around her forearm, I led her to our bedroom. *Our.* I enjoyed the sound of that way too much.

"What's going on?" She wiggled free of me and crossed her arms over her chest. "Is this about where you disappeared to yesterday?"

Busted. "I didn't disappear. I left a note and told you exactly where I'd be."

She shot me a good eyeroll.

"I—"

Red raised her hand cutting me off. "Wait, before you ruin everything by telling me you were off raiding blood brothels, there's something I need to tell you."

My head snapped back. "I wasn't—"

She cleared her throat. "Just listen."

I nodded and flopped down on the edge of the bed. "I'm listening..."

"There's something I didn't tell you about that night— the night Ronin attacked the tiger camp. At first, it was because I didn't believe it had been real, but now with all this god of death stuff, I think it's worth mentioning." She snagged her lower lip between her teeth and paced a tight circle. "The goddess Luna appeared to me that night. She saved me from dying in that fire, and she's the one that summoned my wolf to emerge. Everyone keeps calling me Luna blessed and the truth is, I think I actually was."

I listened quietly despite the wheels spinning in my head. I couldn't help but compare Red's story with Sierra's. She too had been visited by the goddess. I supposed it made sense since they were both Lunar pack wolves, direct descendants of the goddess herself.

"Well? Aren't you going to say something? That I must have hit my head in the fire or imagined the whole thing due to oxygen deprivation?"

A faint smile tugged at my lips, and I took Red's hands in mine, stopping her manic pacing. "No, because it makes absolute sense. I've always known there was something special about you, Phoenix Morana. The goddess blessed you with the kiss of death, made you what you are today. You rose from the ashes to save us all."

Red's lips twisted, and her eyes grew shiny. A swell of emotions surged through our bond, one of them far more intense than I'd ever felt before.

Her arms came around my neck, and mine instinctively laced around her waist. Her emerald eyes met mine, the sparkle taking my breath away. "I love you, Ransom."

All the air expelled from my lungs. If she'd jabbed a stake

in my heart, I would've been less surprised. I stared at her gaping like an idiot.

"The typical response is I love you too." Red smirked. "Or thank you, at least."

A laugh tumbled out as I cupped her cheeks and drew her lips to mine. My heart felt so full, I was certain it would reanimate and start pumping on its own instead of the dark magic that allowed me to thrive. Our tongues danced together, and she tasted even sweeter than normal, if that was even possible. I wanted to devour her, claim her as mine in every way possible. This woman that loved me.

"Can you say it again?" I whispered against her lips. "It's hard to focus with all the blood rushing to my lower half."

She laughed against my mouth, even as her hands moved down to the waistband of my jeans. "I love you, Ransom De La Sangue." Her lips brushed mine as she said the words, and my tongue darted out to greet them. "I've probably loved you for a lot longer than I care to admit."

A rueful chuckle slid out. "As long as you got there somehow."

Her fingers began to work on the button of my jeans, then the zipper. I groaned as she slid my pants off my hips. "Wait, wait—" Gods, I wanted to shoot myself for stopping this.

Red's finger on my lips halted the next words. "I don't care what you did yesterday. We can talk about it after the battle. Right now, I just want to be with you."

"But it's kind of about th—"

She shook her head and slid her hand beneath my boxers. Her fingers closed around me, and I let out a hiss. "Later," she whispered. "Now, make love to me."

Thanatos, have mercy. How could I argue with that? My

jaw snapped shut, and I tugged her shirt off with such enthusiasm a sharp rip echoed between us. "Oops."

"I'll get another one," she rasped out as I began to work on her bra.

The black lacey thing fell to the floor and her head tipped back, long waves of crimson curtaining her breasts. Gods, she was beautiful. *And mine.* My wolf's voice echoed in the back of my mind.

I only startled at the sound for a second before my mouth captured hers again. I'd deal with my wolf and my soul later. Right now, Red was right. This moment was ours and ours alone.

My fingers made quick work of her pants, and they sloughed onto the floor a moment later. I drew her nearly naked form against mine and backed up a step, then another, until we reached the bed.

I lay back, stretching across the mattress and pulled her onto my lap so she straddled me. My arousal brushed against her panties as she settled over me, and the mere touch sent a wave of desire barreling through my lower half.

She lowered her body against mine, those perfect breasts brushing my chest and I captured her lips, wrapping my hand around the back of her neck. I could do this with her for all of eternity. The fleeting thought froze my thundering heart. I'd be alive for eternity, but Red wouldn't be.

"What's wrong?" Red's voice jerked me from my dark musings. She must have felt a twinge of my panic through the bond.

"Nothing," I whispered, closing my eyes and chasing the dismal thoughts away. "Say it again."

A broad smile parted her lips as she gazed down at me. "I love you."

"Again." I tugged at her panties, then pulled my boxers down and lifted her over me.

"I. Love. You. Ransom." She drew out the words and as she said my name, I brought her down on my arousal. She let out a hiss as I filled her, my name still on her lips.

"I love you, Red. More than anything in this world or the next." I thrust my hips slowly, and she met my every move. "I will love you forever, and nothing will ever keep us apart again. I promise."

She grinned down at me, her smile more brilliant than the sun. "Forever," she echoed as our hips moved in perfect rhythm.

As soon as this battle was won, I'd tell her we still had a chance. And then gods' willing, we'd complete the mate bond, and I'd truly make her mine forever.

A NERVOUS ENERGY hummed through my veins as the portal blinked to life on the quiet streets. On the other side of the swirling vortex, war awaited. I tightened my hold on Red's hand and searched the bond between us for signs of my mate's fear. Nothing. A calm stillness pervaded through her half of our connection.

Red was born for this.

She glanced up at me from the corner of her eye and offered me a tight smile, her free hand clenching that ungodly weapon. The unguarded girl gripping the sheets as she cried out my name from an hour ago was gone. She was in battle mode now.

I only hoped it would be enough to face what was to come.

The rest of the team surrounded us, and that quietness

descended over each and every one of them. Vera, Callan, Archer and even Spark. I'd never given them the credit they deserved. They were all fierce and determined, just like their leader. They had a courage I doubted I'd ever possess to take on enemies far stronger and more powerful than they were.

"Everyone ready?" Red's voice broke the icy stillness.

"Ready, boss," they shouted in unison.

"Ronin dies tonight, and we put an end to this."

They all nodded, and I found my head bobbing with theirs.

"For Seline." Red stretched out her arm and the others followed suit, hands joined in the center. She glanced up at me, and I placed my palm on top of the pile.

After a quick pause in remembrance of their fallen friend, the team disbanded.

"After you, Nix." Spark smirked at Red and motioned toward the abyss of swirling lights.

Her fingers tightened around bardy, and she dipped her head. "Let's do this." She leapt into the portal with her weapon held high, and I jumped in behind her. I'd follow her to hell and back, and I had a feeling today we'd get a chance to test out that vow.

CHAPTER
TWENTY-ONE

P*hoenix*

MY BOOTS SLAMMED into hard stone when the portal spat us out at the edge of the Royal compound. Chaos exploded around me, the cries and clatter of weapons jerking me from the calmness that took over before the fight. Serviles spilled out in all directions, at least a dozen for each one of us.

Ransom landed beside me a moment later, hissing out a curse as his eyes razed over the scene. "Where the hades did all these serviles come from if River and his team took out the warehouse?"

"That's exactly what I was wondering."

Thanatos. The god of death's name lingered between us. He was the only one who could've resurrected an entire army of fangers so quickly.

"Doesn't matter," I muttered, my fingers tightening around bardy's shaft. "We'll just have to kill them all."

"Oh Red, you sure know how to make slaughter sound sexy." Ransom shot me a wink, and despite the tension in the air, I couldn't help the smile that flashed across my face.

At least I'd told him the truth today. If everything went to hell, at least he knew I loved him. Because I did, with every fiber of my being. I refused to go into battle today with something so important being left unsaid.

Cal and Vera dropped from the portal next, then Archer and Spark. They formed a tight circle around us. The battle raged on from the peak of the hill, down the valley and up to the gates of Royal Castle. The queen's legion hadn't managed to breach the newly resurrected gates yet, which wasn't a good sign.

The Royal guards, inner circle vamps and the queen's other supporters battled at the front of the line. They were the best fighters and were most likely to break through the line of serviles. I squinted, trying to make out the fangers on Ronin's side. Along with his generals, there were dozens of Royals. How many had deserted their queen?

"Team one!" River's voice through the com jerked my attention toward the hill. The sicari teams' leader stood at the center of the skirmish with the serviles, directing the recruits.

"Copy," I answered. "What's the plan?" We'd gone over a few possible scenarios just hours ago, but with everything moving so fast, we hadn't nailed anything down.

"I need you and your team in the front. If we have any hopes of winning this, we've got to get those gates down. They're heavily warded, but if we can take down the guards, we can move our witches in to break through them."

"Done." I caught River's gaze from across the sea of

serviles and nodded. This was it. I turned to my team. "You heard River. We're going to the front of the lines."

"Right behind you, Nix." Spark moved in step beside me.

"No, not you."

His brows furrowed.

"I need you in the sky. You're one of the last dragons here and your aim is the most accurate. We need to roast the fangers without hitting our people."

"That's going to be tough, Nix." He scanned the battlefield. Most of the sicari were surrounded by rings of serviles.

I squeezed his shoulder and gave him a reassuring smile. "Do what you can. We need to take out as many of these bastards as we can."

He nodded quickly, and emerald scales began to ripple over his arms. "Be careful."

"You too, Sparky."

My eyes trailed his broad back as he headed up the hill, a golden mist beginning to encircle his human form. I turned back to the others before he'd completed the shift. "Archer, Cal, and Vera you're with me. We'll move along the outer perimeter taking out as many serviles as we can without slowing down. Ronin's generals are our targets."

My friends nodded, tightening the circle around me. I turned to Ransom, my insides roiling at what I had to say next. "I need you to go ahead. You're faster than all of us, and they need you at the front."

His head whipped back and forth. "No way, Red. I go where you go."

"Ransom, please. We'll only slow you down. The longer it takes for us to get the gates down, the longer the fight will last and the less our chances for survival."

He gritted his teeth, head still shaking.

"I'll be fine. I've got my team, and I've got bardy." I smirked as I fondled my favorite weapon.

"Red... don't make me do this."

I fixed my eyes to the tumultuous sea of darkness churning in his irises and intertwined my fingers through his. Steeling my voice, I leaned in and whispered, "I'll be right behind you."

He hissed out a curse, then brushed his nose against the shell of my ear. "I only just got you, Red. If you die on me, I'm bringing you back as punishment, got it?"

As always, his humor dispelled the rising tension, and my lips cracked into a smile. "I love you too," I murmured against his cheek as I brushed my lips against the fine stubble.

He finally released me and turned to the rest of the team, flashing his pearly white incisors. "Watch her back. If anything happens to her, I'll bite you."

"She was our friend long before she was *yours*," said Vera. "We will always have her back."

With a reluctant nod, he pivoted to face me once again. "I love you," he mouthed, and a swell of goose bumps puckered my flesh.

Everything would be fine. I'd be right behind him.

With one heated lingering gaze that had my heartrate skyrocketing, he spun on his heel and disappeared into the chaos. I released a shallow breath, my shoulders slumping forward the moment he was gone. For gods' stakes, what was he doing to me?

My fingers clenched firmly around bardy and I forced myself back to warrior mode, despite the ache in my chest. I scanned my team, the determination written in Archer, Cal and Vera's faces reinforcing my crumbling resolve. "We stay tight, and we stay together, got it?"

"You got it, Nix." Vera's hand reached for mine, giving it a firm squeeze.

Raising bardy up high, I leapt into the fray, the blade glistening in the moonlight. I sliced my way through the horde, sticking to the edges to make our way to the front as quickly as possible. My team fought around me, Archer shooting blades of ice and impaling the approaching fangers, while Cal cut through the crowd with his angel sword. Vera used a fatal combination of weapons and magic, cutting down more serviles than the males combined.

A spine-tingling shriek rang out through the commotion, and the stench of burning flesh reached my nostrils. Spark. I hazarded a quick glance up to the sky as the dragon soared across the darkness, spewing flames. As I cutdown vamp after vamp, I could feel the sicari marks burning into my skin with each kill. How many more would I have after this battle?

The only one that really mattered was Ronin's.

If we could take him down this would all be over. A servile leapt in front of me, and I spun bardy in my palm and thrust the pointy end into the fanger's chest. He exploded into a cloud of dust and ash. Barreling through the murky fog of gray powder, I kept my eyes trained ahead, to the wrought iron gate encircling the Royal compound.

Where was Ronin? Was he hiding in the castle or was he out here fighting?

He didn't strike me as a coward. I scanned the masses, searching for that shiny bald head. *Where are you?*

Next, I searched our connection for Ransom. I'd had one eye on the field and the other checking for any signs of distress. So far so good. He was near, I could feel him, but I couldn't make him out through the dense crowd.

"Almost there!" Cal shouted as he brought his flaming sword across the neck of another servile.

The massive gate stood about thirty yards away. The horde of serviles thickened the closer we got. Worse, I started to recognize some of Ronin's generals from my time in captivity.

Screams and shouts, growls and snarls echoed all around us as we moved through the mess. I winced every time I passed a fallen sicari, but thank the gods, there hadn't been many. The serviles were easy-peasy compared to the Royals we were approaching, the ones who'd abandoned the queen to follow the rebel king.

A shrill voice caught my attention, and I whirled toward the familiar blonde as she shouted orders to the servile mob from atop the gate. Dinah. My eyes locked on vampire Barbie, and I barreled through the other fangers and made a beeline for Ronin's general.

A growl vibrated through my core as my wolf's jealousy surged to the surface. She hated her almost as much as I did. We'd been forced to watch her ogle our mate one too many times. Fur sprouted over my arms, and I could feel the change coming. Before I lost control, I tossed bardy to Vera for safe keeping.

I dropped down to all fours as a wave of heat raced across my flesh. Crimson flames danced atop my fur, an unearthly hellish glow tingeing my wolf. Serviles raced out of the way as I cut a path through the center, straight for Dinah.

Her eyes landed on me, and her jaw dropped, mouth curving into a capital O. My own lupine lips curled into a smile. I'd been forced to watch as she'd kissed Ransom, and now, she would experience one final kiss: my kiss of death.

I reached the gate and lunged at her. She scrambled up the wrought iron railing as I snapped at her heels.

"Not today, wolf bitch!" she shouted as she climbed over the gate and landed on the other side. She waggled her fingers at me, and a burst of anger ignited in my core. I rammed the gate, but an explosion of sparkling purple energy shoved me back. I flew into the air and barely got my feet out from under me as I landed. *Mother fanger!*

I had to get on the other side. Another one of Ronin's generals leapt in front of me. I vaguely recognized him from the warehouse. He circled me, keeping a wide berth as I snarled and howled.

My flaming fur made for the perfect armor. None of the fangers dared to come close. I sat back on my haunches as he twirled around me, waiting for the perfect moment. The muscles in my hind legs coiled, primed and ready. A servile stumbled between us, and I took the opening. I jumped on top of the starving fanger and used him as a trampoline to leap on top of Ronin's man. My teeth sank into his shoulder before he knew what was happening.

With a shriek, he sank to the floor as dark veins began to spiral across his arms. The circle of serviles around me staggered back, eyes going wide. Time sped up as I moved across the front line, setting fangers ablaze until only a few of Ronin's generals remained. Seconds, then minutes raced by until the path to the gate was nearly clear, piles of ash blanketing the entrance.

When the job was done, I focused on the thread of magic that lived deep within my core and willed my human form back. I insta-shifted once again, my stark-naked female form emerging through the commotion. Luckily, my witchy best friend appeared beside me with clothes and bardy. I wasn't sure which I was more relieved to see.

I clicked on the com and called out for River. He answered in seconds. "The gate's almost clear. I've got Vera up here, and she can start on the wards. Send the rest of the witches up."

"Will do. Nice job, Phoenix."

A portal blinked to life, and two witches and a warlock jumped through. They were all that remained of our magical brethren on the sicari force.

"You got this, Vera." I shot my friend a reassuring smile as her lips began to flutter. The four of them joined hands and soon the smokey scent of magic swirled in the air, battling the noxious odors of war.

Movement caught my eye just over her shoulder, and the connection between Ransom and me began to hum. I snuck around the witches and pressed my face between the iron bars. My stomach plummeted as my gaze settled on a bald head. Then Ransom.

TWENTY-TWO

Phoenix

I REACHED FOR THE BARS, but that damned electricity raced through my palms the moment I made contact. With a curse, I staggered back. Ransom and Ronin stood at the end of the bridge into Royal Castle, engaged in... conversation?

I strained to listen, but I was too far to make out what they were saying.

"I need to get in there now, Vera!" I cried.

She followed my line of sight, her lips fluttering all the while. Nodding quickly, her chants picked up in intensity.

"What the hell are you doing?" I hissed, knowing full well Ransom couldn't actually hear me. Vamp senses or not, the overpowering sounds of battle drained everything else out. I focused on the tie that connected us and shot through some nasty vibes. *Come on, come on, Ransom.*

More dark forms appeared around the arguing pair, and my chest tightened. "Get out of there, Ransom!" I shouted.

This time Ransom's head twisted to mine, and Ronin's followed. A sinister smile curled the rebel king's lips, and ice spilled through my veins. The circle of Ronin's generals closed in around them.

"Vera, I need to get in there right now!"

She held up her hand, eyes shut tight.

I paced in front of the gate, anxiety eating at my insides. What were they talking about? What was going on in there?

From afar I recognized Ronin's general, Stark, and that familiar blonde head bobbed among them. Dammit, Dinah. Why wouldn't she just die already? The only male I didn't see was Drakin, but for some reason the warlock's absence didn't lessen my anxiety, only amplified it.

A sharp crack rang out and a pungent, charred odor blanketed the air.

Vera's eyes snapped open. "It's done; the wards are down."

I reached for the bars of the gate, and my fingers easily wrapped around them. I hauled myself up and glanced back over my shoulder at my friend. "Thank you!" I called out as I climbed up and over.

Behind me, I could just make out the remaining sicari teams racing for the gate and Dragon-Spark banking toward us. He'd take down the gate, and this would be over.

A swell of hope lit up my insides as I raced across the compound. Ronin and Ransom still stood face to face, neither moving. The stiller they stood, the more my nerves flared.

I raced the last few yards as Ronin's Children closed in around Ransom. The king's dark eyes met mine over his circle of followers. "So nice to see you again, Phoenix. I was beginning to think you wouldn't come today."

Two vampires flanked Ransom, each one taking an arm. Panic's sharp claws dug into my heart. "Let go of him!" I cried.

"I'm afraid that's not possible, Phoenix. You see, despite my generous offer to return your family from the shadows of death, it's become alarmingly evident that you've chosen not to join me, and therefore I must now take away that choice." He narrowed his eyes and for a second, smoke and screams clouded my vision. I was back at the tiger camp, a weak nine-year-old girl. My ribcage tightened around my lungs as I struggled to draw in a breath. "Join me or Ransom dies."

My throat tightened, all the air evacuating my lungs. What was Ransom doing? Why wasn't he fighting?

"Don't listen to him, Red. He won't do it. He needs me alive."

"For now," Ronin snapped.

One of the vampires pulled a stake from his pocket and trained it at Ransom's heart. My knees wobbled, but I forced my expression to remain calm.

"Tick-tock, Phoenix, join me, and you and your vampire lover can spend your last few days together, or watch him die." He inched closer, and the hair on the back of my neck stood on end. "Just remember I offered you everything—a chance to stand beside me as we usher in a new era, a chance to have your parents back, a chance to live. You have brought this upon yourself."

"I'd never be on your side, you delusional fanger!" I cried out, my insides shattering. I glared at Ransom. *Do something!*

"Then he dies."

"No!" A sob wrenched free.

"Don't listen to him, Red, he's bluffing. He can't kill me, I promise you. Go now!"

"I won't leave you," I hissed.

A dark chuckle slithered from Ronin's lips, his cold gaze bouncing back and forth between us. "I understand now." His eyes narrowed. "I always wondered what there was between you, and now it all makes sense."

My heart rammed against my ribs, desperate to get to Ransom. Was that what they'd been whispering about earlier—the mate bond?

"Take her," Ronin shouted, and his generals moved in.

I don't think so, mother fangers. Ransom's shout barely registered as I dropped to the ground, instantly in wolf form. Brilliant crimson flames reflected across Ronin's irises, the echoes of my fiery red wolf. He backed up a step as he urged his generals forward.

Stark lunged at me first, one of my captors from my imprisonment at Ronin's old warehouse. He tried to grab at me, but scorching flames blanketed my fur, and each attempt was followed by a satisfying squeal as the fire burned his skin.

Another member of Ronin's Children I didn't recognize moved in behind me. I spun around as the female attacked. She got her long fingers around my neck, her face contorted in pain and a snarl on her lips as flames licked up her arms. I wiggled out of her grasp and chomped down on her forearm. She let out a shriek and darted away as fire and black veins crawled across her body.

Sucker.

"Red, watch out!" Ransom's cry sent my head spinning toward him.

Drakin and another man raced at me. I barely spared the cloaked figure a second glance, my attention focused on the neon green energy crackling from the warlock's splayed hands.

Oh, shift! I darted out of the way, the magical bolts whizzing just over my head. I raced around the circle of Children as the energy shot out from the warlock's fingers, hitting some of the other vamps. I darted behind Ransom and the two males holding him and let out a howl. Ransom let out a curse and shook free of his captors.

What the hell? Why had he waited so long?

I cocked my lupine head at him, but there was no time for explanations. His dark eyes were set on the cloaked figure beside Ronin. There was something familiar about the way Ransom looked at him. His eyes had glazed over, and the hard set of his jaw had gone slack.

I let out a yip. He didn't move. *Ransom!* I called out to him in my head to no avail. His eyes were still locked on the dark figure. I risked a quick nudge to his thigh, hoping the scorching flames wouldn't jump up his pant leg. Nothing. No reaction whatsoever.

I wanted to scream. This time, I wasn't so gentle. I butted my head straight into his thigh, and Ransom let out a curse as my fiery fur seeped through his jeans. His eyes widened, and he blinked quickly. His gaze bounced from me, to the male beside Ronin, then back to me. "Run!"

I shook my wolfy head, but Ransom ignored me, grabbing me by the scruff of the neck.

From the corner of my eye, I vaguely noticed all movement had stopped around me. All the fangers' gazes had shifted. I followed their line of sight as Ransom continued dragging me away. The cloaked male lowered the dark cowl over his head, and the breath caught in my throat.

Long, midnight hair framed an angelic face with high cheek bones, a perfectly straight Roman nose, and a wide, sculpted jaw. The male was gorgeous, with an otherworldly glow. He was so beautiful he was almost painful to look at. He sloughed off his cloak, and massive onyx wings stretched out behind him. *Oh gods, no. Thanatos.* Drakin had done it. The god of death stood before us in corporeal form.

My jaw dropped, my mouth forming a capital O. The male's sapphire irises found mine, their intensity like cut diamonds. He snapped his fingers, and a gleaming scythe appeared in his palm. Damn, where was bardy when I needed him?

Thanatos pointed a long finger at me, and ice zipped through my fiery veins. "Bring her to me."

Ronin signaled at his men, but the god of death shook his head. "Not them, you, Ronin."

The rebel king's face blanched. "But my lord..."

"I've been watching your men for the past ten minutes trying to capture her. They've been unsuccessful. Now it's your turn. Prove to me that you are worthy to lead my rebellion."

"Now would be a good time to run, Red," Ransom hissed beside me.

The familiar sound of his voice loosened the invisible clamps around my chest. At least he'd been freed of the god's superpowered compulsion.

Ronin stalked toward me, sweat beading on his bald head, and a swirl of satisfaction lit up my insides. He was scared of me. The king of the Children of the Night was terrified.

"Red..." Ransom growled.

I dug my claws into the dirt, holding my ground. This was it. Just me and Ronin. My chance to avenge my parents' death.

From my peripheral vision, I caught Drakin lifting his arms. Thanatos slapped his hands down, narrowing his eyes. "You are not to help Ronin," he hissed. "That goes for all of you." The circle of vampires staggered back as if their feet moved by the god's command.

Even Ransom took a step back.

Steeling my nerves, I bared my teeth at the approaching fanger, and a growl ripped free. The arrogant smile that was typically etched into Ronin's face faltered. Confidence blossomed in my chest, and I almost missed him reaching into his jacket. He moved so fast, the dagger was nothing but a blur as it split the air between us. A dark shadow sped in front of it, and all the air squeezed from my lungs at the squelch of a blade cutting through flesh followed by a familiar groan. Ransom landed on the ground just a few feet in front of me with Ronin's dagger protruding from his gut. His belly, not his heart. I forced my lungs to continue pumping. He'd be okay. He was immortal. It was no more than a flesh wound.

Fiery rage surged through my veins. I fought the instinct to lie down beside my mate to ensure his safety and instead, compelled myself on. The muscles in my haunches coiled tight before exploding forward. I leapt up and slammed into Ronin.

He fell back, and I dug my claws into his shoulders as we hit the ground. Flames jumped off my fur as I snapped and snarled in his face. He rolled over, tossing me off but I landed in a crouch and attacked again. His clothes were torn to shreds, patches of blistering skin revealed beneath. He darted to the edge of the circle of fangers, but they closed in around us, keeping him inside.

"Fight her!" Thanatos shouted.

Ronin's face was twisted in agony, the odor of burning flesh making my nose twitch.

"Are you so unworthy of the task?" the god of death called out. "She's only a girl."

Another wave of anger burned low in my core. Only a girl? I galloped toward Ronin as he backed into the wall of vamps. He revealed another dagger and threw it. It zipped end over end, but I easily avoided it this time, darting to the left.

"Protect me, I am your king," Ronin cried at the generals behind him.

No one moved.

I wasn't sure if Thanatos had compelled them or if they were just that scared to disobey the god of death. I wasn't going to lie, he was scary AF.

Ronin tried to shove his way through the vamps, but they held steady. I stopped a few feet away from him, enjoying the sight. He finally spun around to face me, sweat and dirt covering his forehead and cheeks, claw marks and angry welts blanketing his body. This. This was the man who'd stolen everything from me.

A deep growl vibrated my chest. I crept closer and his eyes widened, pupils nearly blown out. A surge of confidence zipped through the bond, and I hazarded a quick glance over my shoulder. Ransom sat on the floor, a few yards away, his eyes intent on mine. He nodded slowly, and I lunged.

Ronin toppled against the ring of vamps, and this time I didn't hesitate. Flashing my fangs, I bit down on his neck as we hit the floor. He let out a scream, and warm blood filled my mouth. I didn't let go, despite the urge to spit it out.

From the corner of my eye, I could already see the dark veins spiderwebbing up his neck, but still, I didn't release him. Instead, I bit down harder and whipped my head back and forth. The snap of bones sent a chill up my spine, but I didn't falter.

With one last spine-tingling crunch, Ronin's head came free. It tumbled to the floor at the feet of his Children. I glanced down at the vacant eyes, the expression of fear carved into his face for eternity, and relief flooded my system.

Ronin was dead.

"Drakin, bring her to me now." Thanatos' words sucked all the fun out of my triumphant moment.

Before I could move, familiar arms scooped me into a firm chest. Ransom. Squeezing my eyes shut, I searched my core and willed the flames to extinguish. When my lids opened, I was back in human form. Okay, I needed to work on that. Now was not the time to be naked and exposed while the god of death was trying to capture me.

A sharp crack rang out, and thundering shouts echoed across the compound. The gate. Sicari flooded the castle complex, and a dark shadow appeared overhead. Tipping my head up, I immediately recognized the huge dragon. Sparky. His cry resounded through the chaos, his enormous wings blotting out the night sky.

"There!" I pointed to a small clearing in front of the remains of building one.

"On it, Red." Ransom raced through the horde of battling serviles and sicari. I scanned the crowd for the rest of my team.

"We're right behind you!" Vera's voice jerked my attention to her and Cal who were flying toward us. Archer raced just behind. Another swell of relief surged through my chest.

Dragon-Spark landed in the middle of the commotion, and Ransom climbed up his massive leg, holding my naked form tight against his chest. Archer followed us up a second later, while Cal hovered next to us with Vera in his arms, his angel wings flapping like mad to remain suspended above the battle.

"Now what, boss?" Vera asked.

I opened my mouth to answer, but Ransom cut in. "We retreat." I stared up at him, frowning. He pressed his finger to my lips, stilling my objections. "The actual god of death is down there, Red, and he wants you. It was a good fight; now let's not ruin it. The queen and her men have gotten into the compound. They'll take the castle, and we'll finish this another day."

I hated to admit it, but he was right. Slowly, I nodded. "Let's go home."

CHAPTER
TWENTY-THREE

R *ansom*

I WAS BECOMING A CREEPY STALKER, in Red's words. I couldn't tear my eyes away from her as she slept. After coming so close to losing her again yesterday, I couldn't risk sleep. What if Thanatos decided to take her from me? He was the god of death after all. No one knew how far his reach extended. Could he simply snap his fingers and take her life?

A chill skirted up my spine at the thought. *He won't do it. He needs her to break the shadow curse.* The truth stilled the building panic. The truth was that he needed us both. Had Thanatos not made an impromptu appearance yesterday, I may have convinced Ronin to back off on Red for a little longer. I'd admitted the truth to him—that I was the vampire with the soul. One of the last pieces of the puzzle he needed to finally rid the immortals of permanent darkness.

I'd only been trying to buy Red some time, but now that Ronin was dead and Thanatos was here, I wasn't sure what else I could do to stall the inevitable. My mind flickered back to my discussions with the queen. Now that the god of death was all corporeal, she'd surely expect me to move forward with the plan to eliminate Azara and her mother, Luna.

I huffed out a breath and glanced at Red. So peaceful as she slept. I longed for that peace if only for a few minutes. And I'd never get that while she was in danger. I knew Red would never forgive me if I went through with my deal with the queen. But she'd be alive, so wasn't it worth it? I chewed on my lower lip as I considered.

I had no desire to take Azara or her mother's life. I liked the dark lord and Luna had never done me any harm. In fact, I'd heard nothing but incredible things about the female warlock. How could I save them all? I wasn't the hero... I was barely a good guy.

Red stirred, and my heart immediately picked up its sluggish pace. Since discovering the truth about my soul, my ghostly wolf seemed even more restless, as if confirming his presence made him all the more real. I longed to complete the mate bond, to at least attempt it. But first I had to tell her the truth. A few truths actually.

"Are you watching me sleep again?" Her lids fluttered open, that sleepy look oddly attractive on her. Hell, I found every look attractive I was so damned smitten.

"I couldn't help it," I countered and lay down beside her.

She stretched out, revealing bare skin between her t-shirt and the waistband of her panties. My gaze immediately darted to the bit of exposed flesh. I was like a starving animal around her, no better than the serviles. Only now it wasn't her blood I craved, it was so much more.

I ran my finger across the strip of bare skin, and she

squirmed at my touch. A laugh tumbled out, and I was instantly transported to one of our first undercover missions. "That's right, I forgot how ticklish you are." That night at Ronin's VIP club was the first time I'd ever gotten an honest laugh out of her. Looking back, perhaps that had been the moment she'd realized she could actually have fun with a fanger.

I dug my fingers into her sides, and a peal of laughter bubbled out. "Ransom!" She squirmed on the bed, trying to fight me off, but we needed this, this moment of abandon before what was to come. Red went on the offensive, digging her nails into me. I rolled over and she jumped on top of me, pinning me to the mattress as her fingers ravaged my soft spots.

A few moments later, we were both breathless and panting hard. Another part of me was pretty hard too from her straddling me, but I forced back the lusty sensations. If we started that, I'd never get out what I needed to say. I'd procrastinated for long enough.

Begrudgingly, I sat up and drew her with me. Her curious eyes lanced over me as I organized my thoughts. "You know, I suppose I owe you a thank you for yesterday."

She nodded, the sleepiness from a moment ago all but vanished. "Well, I couldn't let Ronin take you again. Then I would've had to save your sorry vampire butt again."

I let out a rueful laugh.

"You know, when I saw Thanatos, a tiny part of me thought about my parents, of what Ronin had said about bringing them back. I even thought about Tyrien…"

I shook my head, my expression sobering. "Don't waste a single second thinking about that bastard. As for your parents, there's no telling if Ronin spoke the truth. Who knows what they would come back as."

She nodded grimly. "I know. I just can't help it." Her eyes narrowed, and she cocked her head at me as if she'd found a lost train of thought. "Why weren't you fighting them yesterday?"

"I was trying to make a deal with Ronin, for your life."

"Why would you do something so stupid?"

I grunted. "I try to be the hero just once and look where it gets me."

"You know he wants—*wanted* to break that curse more than anything. He'd never let me go."

"Not unless I had something he needed just as badly."

Her brows furrowed, then her eyes widened. I could almost see her putting the pieces together. "You didn't. You didn't hurt Azara, did you?"

Okay, she had *not* gone in the right direction. "No." *Not yet.* I huffed out a breath. "Remember what I was trying to tell you yesterday? About where I went."

Her lips drew together, and she nodded slowly.

"I know you didn't want to hear it then, but I need to tell you now. Ronin may be dead, but after the show Thanatos put on last night, I fear our troubles have only multiplied."

"Yeah..." She chewed on her lower lip, her eyes on the new kill marks across her shoulder. One of those belonged to the rebel king. "You know, killing Ronin wasn't anything like I'd expected it to be. I keep waiting for the weight of my parents' death that's been boring down on me all these years to disappear, but it's still there. He's gone, but it's *still* there. All these years, I imagined what it would be like, but I just feel empty now. Like my life's purpose is over."

I took her hands in mine and fixed my eyes to hers. "I will be your life's purpose, like you are mine. I can't live without you. There are still so many battles to fight, Red. Let me fill that emptiness for you as you've done for me." My mouth captured hers, tugging those pouty lips between my teeth. With a gentle nibble, she melted into me. It would be so easy to get lost in her, to forget about everything else, but that wasn't in the cards for us today.

I forced my lips to release hers, and they screwed into an irresistible pout as she regarded me. "I have to tell you..."

She clasped her hands together, twisting the sheets between her fingers. "I don't think I want to know. Ransom, it's taken me so long to admit to loving you and what if what you're about to tell me ruins everything?"

A stake to the heart would've hurt less. Wasn't love meant to be forever? Shouldn't she be able to forgive me for whatever I may do if her love was real? I tossed the useless thoughts aside and squared my shoulders. "I didn't do anything bad, Red." *This time.*

"Then what is it?"

"I went to see the Archangel Cillian," I finally spat.

Her eyes widened, two pools of impossibly brilliant emerald. "And?"

All the words stuck at the back of my throat as a surge of hope pummeled through me. Gods, she wanted this so badly for me. "You were right," I mumbled. "I'm the vampire with a soul."

A shriek of happiness exploded from her lips, and she wrapped her arms around my neck as she plowed into me. I fell back against the mattress, her joy infectious. A beaming smile parted my own lips, a mirror of hers.

"Guess you're not doomed to be mated to a soulless fanger anymore."

"I knew it," she mumbled against my lips as she pressed her mouth to mine. After a few glorious seconds, she pulled back. Her brows slammed together, and unease replaced the thrill from a moment ago. "Wait a second, this means Thanatos is going to come after you."

"Assuming he knows." I shrugged. "I'd only just told Ronin, and I don't believe he had time to fill the Reaper in on the good news."

She straightened, looming over me. "But he's the god of death, couldn't he figure out that sort of thing?"

"It's likely, but there are also thousands upon thousands of immortals out there. Assuming his power is similar to the Archangel's, he'd have to test a hell of a lot of vampires before finding the right one."

"And what if it's not like the angel's? He *is* a god, Ransom."

"Well, he's already coming after you, and I'll be wherever you are so he's going to get a two-for-one deal anyway."

She crossed her arms over her chest, frowning. "Now, I'm not sure if this is a good thing or a bad one."

Kneeling, I pulled her into my arms. "It's a good thing, Red. I have a soul, a tiny flicker of one apparently, but one all the same."

She hesitated for a moment before her lips began moving. "What does that mean for your wolf?"

"I'm not sure yet." I paused and swept an errant lock of hair behind her ear. "Maybe nothing." Or maybe something I didn't dare consider yet.

"I don't think it's nothing." She pressed her palm to my chest. "That tiny soul is the reason I feel him, the reason I'm so connected to you."

"Or maybe it's just because I'm so irresistible." I shot her a smirk.

She cupped my cheek, giving it a little slap. "Definitely not that."

"Let's test that theory, shall we?" I snaked my arm

around her waist and tossed her down on the bed. Pressing her into the mattress, my lips descended on hers. Maybe just one more time before I told her I hadn't been one hundred percent forthcoming about the mate bond.

Sharp knocks at the door had me muttering a curse against Red's luscious lips. "We're busy, come back later!" I shouted.

"You have a visitor," Cal hissed back. "A very impatient one."

"Get your hands off my sister, Ransom, or I'll break this door down." I jerked up as my old alpha's power slammed into me.

Red and I exchanged a panicked glance as we blurted in unison, "What's Hunter doing here?"

"Just a second," she called out as she scrambled out from under me.

"I'm not sure I like this sibling blood bond thing, Red. There's no escaping him now."

"I heard that," Hunter muttered through the door.

Red ran into the closet, and I couldn't help my lingering gaze from drifting to the doorway as she stripped down. Gods, I'd never get enough of her. If we lived an eternity, it would never be enough. *Ha!* Sad thing was, I would live forever and be forced to survive only from her memories once she was gone. A biting pain raced across my chest, burying itself deep in my heart.

Red tugged the shirt over her head, and her hand clapped over her own heart. Her gaze jumped to mine. She'd felt that. The searing pain her loss would cause me—be it tomorrow or sixty years from now. "You okay?" she asked, massaging the left side of her chest.

"Yes, don't mind me and my dark musings." I forced a smile.

She darted out of the closet and grabbed my hand. "Let's not make the supreme alpha wait, huh?"

I trailed her out the door, the easy light-hearted feeling from a few seconds ago dwindling. The moment my gaze focused on Hunter's scowl and the tense set of his jaw, they disappeared completely. "What's happened?"

"Azara's been taken."

P*hoenix*

"No, no, no!" I growled. Ronin was finally dead, and we couldn't even get a second of peace. "When did it happen?"

"Just last night." Hunter dragged a hand through his hair. "The assembly is in an uproar, given the shadow curse situation and as you both know, Azara hails from a rather influential family. Both her grandfathers, Lucifer, and Garrix, the high warlock of Maginaria, are furious."

"It had to be Thanatos," Ransom muttered.

"Excuse me?" A vivid gold eclipsed my half-brother's green eyes, which I now realized happened when his wolf was close to the surface.

"Oh, you didn't hear about the arrival of our new friend?" Ransom shook his head. "I thought the Etrian Assembly was supposed to be aware of all that went on in Azar."

189

"When?" he barked.

"Last night."

"So you mean to tell me the god of death has kidnapped the dark lord of the Underworld?"

"Looks that way, doesn't it?"

Hunter buried his face in his hands and muttered a curse. "And Ronin?"

"Red killed him." Ransom threw my brother a satisfied smirk.

The supreme alpha's eyes darted to mine, and a slow smile crept across his face. "Well done, Nix." Something like pride glimmered through those golden orbs.

"No time to celebrate now since someone way worse has stepped into his shoes."

He paced a quick circle then turned his attention back to us. "So the two of you saw him last night?"

We nodded in unison.

"Anything you can tell us that could help get Azara back?"

"I don't know how much it'll help," I offered, "but whenever he's around, Ransom and all the vamps go all googly eyed around him."

"Great."

"It's like the super amped up version of all compulsion," Ransom added. "As our creator, he seems to have this effect on all his children."

"But Ransom can break through it." I inched closer beside him without realizing.

"It's not me, it's you, Red. Your pull on me is stronger than even the god of death's."

I couldn't help a smile from parting my lips.

Hunter eyed me then Ransom, and heat flooded my

cheeks. "Has anything happened here that I need to be aware of?"

Oh, for gods' stakes this was embarrassing. The warmth intensified, climbing all the way to my ears. I tossed my head to the side, hiding behind the auburn curtain of hair. "No," I blurted at the same time Ransom said, "Well actually—"

I elbowed him in the gut. I did not need him telling my half-brother all the intimate details of our love life. "Ransom has a soul," I interjected.

"Red..." he growled.

"Sorry." I shot him a wicked smirk. "I thought we were sharing things now."

"So he is the one from the spell..."

"I am."

"That's why you can still feel your wolf, and we can communicate, and you and Nix can—" His words fell away as Ransom shot him a narrowed glare.

"We don't know anything for sure." He waved a dismissive hand before clearing his throat. "Anyway, we've gotten off topic. We have to get Azara back before Thanatos can harvest her blood or whatever he has to do to break the shadow curse. The dark lord's well-being is intricately tied to Red's."

"And yours," Hunter added. "Which reminds me, before I leave, I'd like to have a word with you in private, Ransom."

"Of course, my supreme alpha." He dipped into a dramatic bow, and my brother rolled his eyes.

Brother. The word still felt weird even in my head.

"Where's Talon?" My thoughts flitted back to Azara's mate. He must've been going crazy.

"He's been hunting for her since last night. He assumed Ronin had her, but now that we know about Thanatos—"

191

"I'll join him," Ransom interjected. "I'll tell him what's happened and help him find her."

I stiffened beside my vampire mate. The worst had happened; Azara had been taken. Would he be forced to follow through on his deal with the queen?

"While that's very selfless of you, Ransom, I don't think you should be anywhere near Thanatos. If he manages to capture you, he'll only be missing the final piece of the puzzle: my sister."

"And I go where he goes." I crossed my arms firmly over my chest. There was no way I was letting these two fight my battles for me.

"No point arguing with her, trust me I've tried." Ransom nudged Hunter in the shoulder.

"Fine, then I'll go too."

Ransom waggled his finger at his former alpha. "I don't think so, old friend. Sierra would have my balls if something happened to you, and I'm quite fond of them." His mischievous gaze slanted toward me. "Especially now."

Mother fanger, why couldn't he keep his mouth shut?

His brows suddenly drew together and something unreadable flashed across his expression, erasing the typical smirk.

"What?" I asked.

Ransom shook his head, dark brows still drawn together. "Nothing. Nothing important. We can talk about it later."

"I see the bond between you seems to be growing." Hunter's lips curled into a half-smile half-grimace as if he could imagine what had been bringing us closer together. Since he too was mated, he likely knew the cause very well.

"By the day," I finally answered with a dramatic eyeroll.

"Oh stop, you love me, and you know it."

I did, but that was beside the point. Knowing he had a

soul changed things. The unbelievable relief I'd felt when he'd told me the truth was incredible. My feelings for him seemed so much clearer now. It all finally made sense.

"So where do we find Talon?" I asked Hunter, returning my attention to the problem at hand. And more importantly, could we find Lucifer? Hadn't Azara said she was sure he'd step in if things got bad? This would definitely qualify.

"Last I heard, Talon requested a meeting with the Etrian Assembly. Your best bet would be to meet up with him there."

"Sounds good. You'll let us know when it's happening?"

Hunter glanced up at the clock in the kitchen. "It's happening in an hour."

"Then we'll see you there."

"And while we're at it," said Ransom, "perhaps we can get an audience with the assembly, regarding the good god Thanatos."

"I'll see what I can do." Hunter's smoldering irises scanned over me before turning to Ransom. "You better keep an eye on her. Azara is no easy target, and Talon is no fool. If Thanatos was able to snatch her without leaving a trace, there's no saying what could happen."

I swallowed hard. I'd heard of Azara's powers, and they made mine look like amateur hour. If Thanatos really wanted me, it was only a matter of time.

"I'll guard her with my life, brother." Ransom moved closer, his shoulder and hip brushing mine.

"Good." He ticked his head toward the door. "Can I talk to you now, Ransom, before I go?"

"Of course."

Hunter crept closer, a sheepish smile on his face. "Be careful," he mumbled before stretching his arms out.

Oh. I awkwardly walked into his embrace. His big arms

wrapped around me and surprisingly, the stiffness dissipated. I hugged him back, and his strength seeped into me.

Ransom cleared his throat. "Ahem. I think that's enough for now." He tugged me away from my half-brother, and a faint smile pulled at my lips as I watched the pair march out the door.

I'd never wanted a brother growing up, but I never knew how badly I'd needed one. Guess the same was true for my vampire mate.

P *hoenix*

THE MAD FLUTTER of wings battered my insides as I climbed the mountain of steps up to the Etrian Hall. The gigantic monument was encircled by towering columns and crafted from gleaming white marble. It was the seat of the leaders of Azar, a tiny plot of neutral land between the Fae realm and Maginaria.

This was my first time here as the area was heavily warded. It was an invitation-only type deal. Ransom and I had only gotten in because of my half-brother, the supreme alpha. Hunter had gone in ahead of us, and now it was our turn to join. The last part of the schedule was when the assembly heard special requests.

That was where we'd find Talon.

I'd hoped to get a word in myself. The idea of taking on a

god was just a *little* bit daunting. We reached the top of the sprawling staircase, and the two guards at the doors eyed us. The bigger one, a dragon by the looks of him, revealed a small tablet from beneath his jacket. "State your names and business with the Etrian Assembly."

Ransom nudged me in the side, and I cleared my throat. "Phoenix Morana. I'm here to request assistance from the assembly. I was invited by the supreme alpha Hunter Silverstalker."

"Same," said my vampire buddy. "Only the name's Ransom De La Sangue."

The guard scanned his tablet, tapped a few buttons and the double doors slid open. Another guard stood at the entrance of the grand hall in a meticulous white uniform, arms crossed behind his back.

"Chester will escort you back." The guard ticked his head at the other male.

"Thanks," I mumbled.

As we stepped into the foyer, I couldn't help my head from tipping back to admire the soaring ceilings. Magnificent colorful frescoes were painted across the circular cupola, depicting the seven houses of Azar along with a small section reserved for the demons of the Underworld.

Lowering my gaze, I followed the guard down a corridor that shot off the main rotunda. The slap, slap of our boots on the marble echoed through the vast space, and my heartrate began to escalate, beating in time with our footfalls.

An eerie silence pervaded.

The guard finally stopped at a pair of gilded doors where two more sentinels stood. They too wore the same pristine all-white uniforms. Our escort turned to us with a tight smile. "When the doors open, you may enter. It should only be another minute or two."

"Perfect." Ransom crossed his arms over his chest and leaned against the immaculate alabaster wall.

The guard glowered at him and sharply cleared his throat.

"Sorry about that." Ransom straightened, a teasing grin spreading his lips. Then he bent his head to mine and whispered, "You ready?"

"For what exactly?"

"To plead our cause."

"But we don't even have a real appointment." The official plan was to corner Talon and offer our help to find Azara.

"Let's not miss this opportunity, Red. To have the ears of the entire Etrian Assembly is a once in a lifetime event. It's time they knew the truth of what occurs in Nocturnis."

Ransom's speech to the team from the other day came to mind. The serviles and the other starving vamps didn't choose to be the bad guys. They'd been condemned to this life. Even if we did win this fight with Thanatos, their predicament would remain the same. Not enough Blud.

"You should tell them," I whispered. "Your speech the other day was really moving. Everyone on the team saw you differently from that day forward. You're the one with the gift, Ransom. There's something about you that makes others follow. Maybe it's the alpha thing or maybe it's just you and your charming ways." I shot him a smirk. "You tell the assembly and force them to listen."

He nodded slowly, and a hint of anxiety crept through the bond between us. I wrapped my fingers through his and squeezed. He was a born leader, and I'd only realized that recently. Maybe Carmen Rosa had seen it all along. She'd wanted him for her inner circle, hadn't she? Perhaps she wanted him for even more...

The doors creaked open, and my wandering thoughts

stilled as my eyes landed on the assembly room and the seven pairs of eyes piercing into me. I couldn't help my gaze from drifting to the empty seat. The one that belonged to Azara.

I finally forced my focus onto the raised dais and avoiding the curious stares, I fixed my eyes on Hunter then the other familiar face, Spark's dad, Fenix, the dragon alpha. Carmen Rosa was next, the final face I recognized. Had Azara been here I would've been acquainted with four members. Not bad out of eight. I'd made friends with some pretty influential people in the last year.

The four assemblymen I'd never met were the high warlock of the Coven Council, Garrix, also Azara's grandfather, an elderly man with graying hair and piercing blue eyes; the representative from the Ocean realm, a strapping male with a golden trident clenched in his fist; the Fae king of Winter Court, Elrian Wintersbee, who I knew only by name; and finally, the archangel Amanadiel, his deep ebony skin in sharp contrast to the massive white wings spread out behind him.

The room was thick with power, the combined effect of their magic and mystical abilities making it hard to breathe. The slap of approaching footsteps drew my attention to the center of the room, to a familiar hulking dragon shifter.

Talon dipped his head as he stood at the foot of the dais. "Thank you for taking the time to meet with me today, leaders of the assembly."

Ransom tugged on my hand and steered me to a chair at the back of the room. He folded down beside me, and I watched as Talon recounted the events of Azara's capture.

Throughout the explanation, the leaders peppered him with questions, most he didn't have answers to. It was as if

Azara had disappeared into thin air. Which did not bode well for us. What kind of powers did Thanatos really have?

"I've searched the Underworld," said Talon, returning my attention to his speech. "And have been unsuccessful. So now I'm here to ask for access to Nocturnis as I've recently been informed of the appearance of the god of death, Thanatos. He was seen there last night, and perhaps that is where he's taken my mate."

A wave of murmurs rang out through the assembly.

"Has anyone actually seen Thanatos?" the old warlock asked.

Hunter's gaze chased to mine, and he slowly nodded. "Phoenix Morana, one of the queen's Royal sicari encountered him last night." He ticked his head at me, and all eyes pivoted in my direction once again.

"Please, Phoenix, come forward." The high warlock, Garrix, stood and crooked a finger at me.

Ransom shot up. "I was there as well, Ransom De La Sangue, formerly of the Royal Pack of wolves, now of the Royal vampires."

"Fine, both of you then." The gray-haired male slanted a look at Carmen Rosa.

The queen straightened in her chair. Where had she been when the assault on the castle went down?

"Now, tell us what transpired," said Garrix.

My gaze flickered to the queen, unbidden. With a barely perceptible nod, she scooted to the edge of her seat. I drew in a breath and began, "As you may know, the vampire rebel, Ronin, had taken the castle, and it was our mission to take it back for the queen. While we were battling with the Children of the Night, Ronin's warlock, Drakin appeared with Thanatos." I paused, not knowing exactly how much of a backstory they needed.

"Drakin, under Ronin's instruction, had been attempting to summon Thanatos for some time now," Ransom interjected. "During my time in captivity under the rebel king, he frequently told stories of his master plan to bring back the god of death and return vampires to their former glory."

Another rush of murmurs zipped around the room.

"I took it as the ravings of a madman until I witnessed the god take over the form of the warlock, Drakin."

"And you are both certain that the male you saw is the actual god of death?"

Ransom nodded quickly. "As a vampire, I have no doubt. I could feel his power all the way to my very bones."

"He seems to have some sort of compulsion ability over the vampires," I added.

"Just wonderful," Garrix growled before turning to Carmen Rosa. "This is all your fault, dear queen. Had the rebellion been vanquished at the start, none of this would've come to pass. Now we have to deal with resurrected gods and quests to break shadow curses. That spell was placed for a reason. Undoing it will throw Azar into turmoil once more."

"I am handling it, Garrix," the queen snarled.

"Are you though?" The warlock eyed me. "It seems to me that the fate of Nocturnis rests in the hands of these two young people, the captured dark lord and their unique blood."

I gasped. How did he know about our blood?

Ransom stepped forward. "If I may, allow us some time to recuperate the dark lord Azara. Without her and without us, Thanatos won't be able to accomplish anything."

"Or we just kill them all now." King Elrian rose, and a chill seeped up my spine. "It seems to me the answer is clear."

P*hoenix*

SHOUTS BROKE out across the room as Talon whirled at the king of the Fae. "That's my mate you're talking about," he growled. Two guards appeared from nowhere and restrained the shifter as he lunged for the high Fae.

"We will not be killing anyone," Hunter snarled, leaping up.

Garrix clapped his hands. "Enough, enough!" he shouted. Then he turned to the queen, light brows knitted. "Do you honestly believe you can handle this? Or will it require the assembly to step in?" He paused. "Before you answer that, understand that should our assistance be required, you will lose your throne for your inability to rein in your own citizens."

Carmen Rosa nodded, her lips pressed in a tight line. "As I said before, we will handle it."

"The queen is right," said Ransom. "We will handle our own war just as we always have. Thanatos will be returned to the ether or gods' knows where he resides, the curse will remain unbroken, and all will return to how it once was. We simply need time. I make this vow not for the queen but for my mate." He turned to me and squeezed my hand. "Because I will never let any harm come to her, I swear that to all of you. If any of you even think about harming a hair on her head, I promise you a lifetime of unending hell and torture." His fangs dropped. "I know it well because I have lived it." He paused, and a thick silence descended over the room. "The only thing I ask in return when all of this is over, is that you consider the lives of the immortals in Nocturnis who wanted no part in this, who had no part in a civil war long ago where we were all condemned to live in eternal darkness and forced to drink meager rations of Blud. If the vampires were treated more equitably, matters such as these would not rise again in the future."

I squeezed Ransom's hand as pride swelled in my chest. In that moment, I knew without a doubt that he was destined for so much more. That one day, Ransom would occupy the seat now filled by Carmen Rosa. *He* would one day be the vampire king.

The queen's eyes met mine, an unreadable expression on her face. Regret? Pride? She knew it too. Ransom, the vampire with a soul, was the future of the immortals.

"Ransom De La Sangue," Garrix crooned, "if you manage to avert an all-out war in Azar, I'll give you whatever you want."

Ransom nodded, a smile splitting his lips and highlighting that elusive dimple. "I'll hold you to that, Garrix."

"Fine then, if there's nothing else..." The old warlock's eyes scanned the room. "We shall reassemble in a week, and Carmen Rosa will provide us with an update."

The thick tension in the air dissipated, and I let out a breath. The leaders of Azar rose, descending from the raised platform. Hunter and Carmen Rosa headed straight for us. From the corner of my eye, I could just make out Spark's father with Talon. The dragon alpha was having a hard time getting the guards to release him after that outburst. Totally justified in my opinion.

"Nicely done, you two." Hunter squeezed my shoulder with a warm smile. "Who knew you had a diplomatic flare, Ransom? Where have you been hiding it all this time?"

He shrugged, a smirk playing on his lips. "Maybe I just never needed to unearth it before."

Carmen Rosa remained oddly silent, her penetrating eyes raking over us as we talked. I focused on bolstering my mental walls just in case she went in for a sneak attack. No way the queen was going to stand by and do nothing. First, Ronin took her castle and now Thanatos was making her look like a fool who couldn't handle her own people. And Ransom's speech... well, I couldn't have been the only one moved by it.

Ransom dipped his head to the queen as if he'd made the same connections I had. "My queen, how may I serve you today?"

A rueful laugh slid from her crimson lips. "Put an end to this disaster as soon as possible."

"Ransom and I are going to talk to Talon as soon as Fenix pries the guards off him. We'll go with him to find Azara, if he'll let us."

The queen's dark gaze flitted to Ransom. "Make sure that he does."

The icy tone sent a shudder up my spine. She couldn't still want Ransom to kill her, could she? Azara was a prisoner. We had to save her.

Carmen Rosa took a step toward Ransom and motioned to the back of the vast hall. "I'd like a moment in private, my son."

His jaw clenched, the tendon twitching as he slowly dipped his head.

She moved in front of him, and like an obedient little pup Ransom trailed behind. The pit of dread that had taken root in my gut amplified ten-fold. I followed their movements across the room, anxiety eating at my insides. He wouldn't. He wouldn't agree to kill Azara.

"You okay?" Hunter's voice averted my gaze.

"Yeah, fine." I chewed on my lower lip as my half-brother gave me a you're-full-of-BS look. "Okay, I'm not. I'm worried about what they're talking about." I ticked my head at Ransom and the queen huddled in the corner.

He followed my line of sight, brows furrowing. "Why?"

I picked at an invisible hangnail as I considered telling him Ransom's dirty little secret. What he'd agreed to in a misguided attempt to protect me.

Hunter bent his head, so we were eyelevel. "What's going on, Nix?"

"Ransom struck a deal with the queen a few weeks ago." I shook my head, lips pressed tight. "In exchange for my safety, he promised he'd kill Azara and her mother, Luna, if things got bad. It was the only way to prevent the curse from being broken."

He muttered an expletive, a streak of gold surging through his irises as he turned his gaze toward the pair still talking in the corner. By the tense set of Ransom's jaw and the flutter of emotions surging through our bond, it was nothing good. "You don't think he'd actually go through with it, do you?"

"I don't know. You've known him a lot longer than I have." The moment I spat out the words, I felt the lie. Of course, I knew. He'd kill them. He'd kill anyone to save me. *Oh gods, I'm going to be sick.* I clutched at my stomach as a wave of nausea crashed over me.

"This isn't good, Nix."

"No, *shift.*"

He cracked a reluctant smile. "You need to make sure he doesn't do anything that stupid. A move like that could start a war. Another war."

"I'd never let him do it. I'd take him down if I had to." And that was the truth. Would I kill him? No. Would I snap his neck and put him in a much-deserved timeout? Absolutely.

As if Ransom could feel my heavy gaze on him, his eyes darted in my direction. His lips curled into a tight smile, and my insides roiled. The queen still expected him to follow through with the deal. I was sure of it.

"Nice to see you alive and well, Nix." A familiar deep voice averted my attention from my scheming mate and his queen. Fenix Skyraider towered over me with Talon at his side.

"Thanks, it's good to be here."

The males shook hands then Talon turned to me. "I heard you were looking for me."

"We want to help you find Azara. Thanatos must have her, and Ransom thinks he might be able to find him with Vera's help and some mystical scrying."

The hard set of his jaw relaxed a fraction. My heart went out to the dragon. Being torn apart from his mate was wrecking him. The anguish was so clearly carved into his face.

He finally nodded. "I'll take whatever help I can get. I have my friends in the SIA scouring the lands, and I hope they come up with something soon. I haven't told her parents yet. They're in the human world, and I don't want to scare them until I've tried everything I can to get her back. She's my mate. My responsibility."

"I get that. We'll get her back, I promise."

The slap of approaching footsteps turned my attention to my mate. Carmen Rosa had disappeared, but Ransom strode toward us, a blank expression on his face.

"What was that about?" I whispered as he moved beside me.

"Nothing important." He slid on the mask, the typical smirk and arched brow firmly in place. He was not getting away that easily. As soon as I had him alone, I'd get the truth out of him.

Ransom turned his attention to the big dragon. "What about Lucifer?"

Talon rolled his eyes. "He'll be my last resort. You remember how helpful he was last time."

My vampire mate snorted. The devil sure was an interesting guy.

"At least if what you told me about breaking the curse is true, I know Thanatos won't kill her." Talon huffed out a breath, his massive chest rising and falling. "It's the only thing keeping me sane right now."

I didn't want to finish his sentence. The god of death wouldn't kill her *yet*. Not until he had all the pieces of the puzzle. Ransom and I were the final missing parts. I gulped. I longed for bardy, for the feel of the worn wooden staff and the confidence it instilled. We'd been stripped of all our weapons before our arrival.

"I'd like to go immediately," said Talon. "The sooner Azara is back in my arms, the better."

"Of course. You can come back with us to Nocturnis, and we'll get Vera on the locator spell."

"What makes you think it'll work?" Talon ticked his head at Garrix. "The high warlock is Azara's grandfather and arguably one of the most powerful magic users in all of Azar. He tried searching for her this morning as soon as I told him."

"Because Ransom is a vampire, and he has a direct blood link to Thanatos. The god of death created them all, right?"

Talon nodded.

"Well, I wish you all luck," said Fenix. The dragon alpha had remained silent during the exchange. "Don't hesitate to contact me if you need anything; Azara is family after all. The Brotherhood of Dragons prefers not to get involved in conflicts of neighboring realms, but in this case, I'd force the council to make an exception."

My brows knitted as I tried to piece it together. I'd completely forgotten that Fenix's wife, Kimmie-Jayne was Azara's mom's half-sister. Yikes, just thinking about that made my head hurt.

"Thank you." Talon's head dipped toward his alpha.

With a quick wave, the dragon marched out.

Talon pivoted back to us, dark shadows encircling his eyes. "Thanks for your offer to help too. I just hope you're right about the blood tie to Thanatos."

"It's always about the blood, isn't it?" Ransom shot Hunter a smirk, and again I felt like I was missing out on some inside joke. It happened a lot when I was with those two, and I was starting to get annoyed.

Hunter turned to me and squeezed my hand. "Let me know if I can help with anything. Especially if you need me to knock some sense into someone..." He narrowed his eyes at Ransom who shrugged innocently.

"Let's get this show on the road." Ransom's hand slid to the small of my back, and we turned toward the exit of the assembly room.

I, for one, was thrilled to get out of here. So much power packed into one place had been suffocating. I only hoped our appearance had made a difference.

R*ansom*

I POPPED the cap off the bottle of malta, the dragon version of beer, thanks to my oversized reptilian roommate and eyed Talon over my shoulder. He sat at the edge of the seat, his knee bouncing like mad. I couldn't help the surge of empathy from tightening my ribcage. If someone had taken Red, I would've ripped both the human and supernatural worlds apart in search for her.

I shook off the thought, burying the unwanted emotion. I had to be clearheaded for what was to come. Carmen Rosa still expected me to follow through on my promise. My gaze chased to Talon's huddled form. The mate bond for dragons, like wolves, ran so deep, the pair so intimately connected that the death of one typically meant the end of the other. Could I really condemn this man to such a fate?

The scary thing was that to save Red, I would. I'd do anything for her. Sure, I'd feel like shit about it, but if it came down to Phoenix or Azara, the choice was clear.

And still, I felt conflicted. Damned remnants of a soul.

I popped the lid off another bottle and took a long pull. I'd need this today. I marched over to the couch and placed the two maltas on the table.

"Thanks," Talon uttered. His body may have been here, but his thoughts were with his mate.

"Don't you share a mate link with Azara? A way to communicate telepathically?"

His head dipped. "I should be able to. I haven't felt anything from her since I woke up, and she was gone."

"Drakin," I murmured.

"Excuse me?"

"He's Ronin's—well, I guess he's Thanatos' warlock now."

"I figured someone was blocking us from communicating through our bond." He reached for the bottle and swallowed down about half of the amber liquid. Slamming it back on the table, he raked his hands over his face. "It's like half of me is missing."

I nodded slowly, not sure what words of comfort I could offer the man. Red and Archer were off searching for Vera as she and Cal hadn't been in the penthouse when we'd returned. They were likely off fornicating. I smirked. I couldn't blame them. I'd be doing the same thing if I could. The world as we knew it was about to be destroyed by the god of death, if not now then when?

"You and Nix..." Talon's words fell away as he regarded me.

"We haven't completed the bond," I answered. *Yet.* The

looming word echoed across my mind in a familiar gruff, lupine voice.

"What are you waiting for?"

My jaw dropped, mouth floundering. What *was* I waiting for? For Thanatos to come in the night and steal her away from me? I couldn't admit to this male that I was petrified. So frozen with fear that we wouldn't be able to complete the bond that I preferred to live in ignorant bliss.

"It's complicated," I finally responded.

"It always is." A rueful grin flashed across his face before it returned to its more sullen version. "The mate bond... there's nothing like it. You think you feel a lot now, just wait. The intensity is staggering." His palm rubbed a circle around his chest. I recognized the gesture, the constant ache when your mate wasn't at your side. "And it's also the most real thing you'll ever feel in your life." He sat back, exhaling slowly. "Don't wait, Ransom. Life's too short, and the gods are too cruel."

I handed him the malta and picked up my own. "Cheers to that." I forced a smile. "Let's just hope this god is cruel but stupid."

Talon chuckled.

"Since you're the one with all the connections," I continued, "you think you can find out from Lucifer or Garrix how one exactly goes about banishing a god?"

"GG's already on it. If anyone can figure it out, it's Azara's grandfather."

"Good." I didn't want to kill Azara, and I'd try to exhaust all other methods first. I'd much rather send Thanatos back to the ether.

The invisible bands around my heart tightened, and the front door whipped open a moment later. Red strode in with a disheveled Vera and Cal at her heels. Archer marched behind them, the eternal pissed-off expression still carved into his face.

"About time." I winked at the little witch. "I hope your little romp was worth it."

"Oh, it was." A satisfied smile stretched across Cal's face before Vera jabbed her elbow into his side.

"Sorry, we didn't think you'd be back so soon." She glanced over my shoulder at Talon. "Just give me a minute to gather my supplies."

The dragon nodded before finishing off the malta.

"Let me get you another one," I offered. As I scooted into the kitchen, Red trailed behind me.

"We need to talk. Now," she growled.

"Whoa, whoa." I raised my hands in surrender. "What's gotten you all feisty?"

"Not here." She wrapped her fingers around my forearm and dragged me out of the kitchen. "We'll be right back, Talon," she called out.

I dropped the bottle of malta on the living room table before Red hauled me to the back bedroom. As soon as the door closed, I shot her a wicked grin and unbuckled my jeans. "While I could never deny you, do you really think we should do this now with Talon just outside waiting?"

"Ransom!" she hissed. "That is *not* why I dragged you in here." She stuck her fingers under the waistband of my jeans and refastened the button. The faint touch spiraled down my core.

Gods, I was so inappropriate. "You're no fun, Red," I whined.

"Stop trying to distract me."

Dammit, the girl knew me too well.

"What did Carmen Rosa say to you at the assembly?" My arms came across my chest, a flesh and blood barrier against her assault. She knew me *much* too well.

I contemplated lying, but that would only get me into more trouble. "What do you think?" I countered.

"She still wants you to kill Azara, doesn't she?"

My teeth ground together. "Yes," I hissed.

Red closed the distance between us and fisted the collar of my shirt between her hands. "Tell her you refuse, Ransom. Tell her or I will!"

"It's not that simple, Red. You can't afford another enemy right now. If I refuse her, she'll try to kill *you!*"

"I'd rather die than let you murder that girl."

"No!" I growled. "I won't let anyone take you from me. I don't care about the consequences."

Those emerald eyes seared into me, her emotions ravaging the bond between us. "Listen to me, Ransom. If you kill her, I'll never forgive you. I don't care what your reasons are. I don't choose to live over her. My life is no more valuable than hers."

"It is to me," I roared.

"Then get over it!" She released my collar and shoved me back.

I staggered a few steps, the back of my calves hitting the bed. "I can't..." The words trickled out, a whispered confession. "I'm so in love with you I can't breathe when you're not beside me. Every waking thought centers around you, your eyes, the feel of your skin against mine, the breadth of emotions that I thought were long lost when I'm inside you. You brought me back to life, Phoenix. I was dead and gone. I only live for you."

The fury etched into her features waned, the tight set of

her jaw softening. She stepped closer, all the fight draining from the pulsating bond between us. "You can't only live for me, Ransom. You have to live for you." She jabbed her finger into my chest.

"How about for us, then?" The ghost of a smile crept across her lips as I closed my hand around her finger and brought our hands between us. "I don't want to kill Azara. It's the last thing I want to do, but for now, the queen can't know that. I'll play along and if the worst happens, I'll figure it out."

"You'll just wing it?" she squeaked.

"Yes, I'm pretty good at that."

She trapped my chin with her thumb and index finger, forcing my eyes to hers. "Swear to me, Ransom, that you won't kill her. Swear it on the love you claim to have for me."

"Claim?" I scoffed. I'd never felt anything more real, more intense in my life.

"Do it." She stared up at me, those emerald eyes more brilliant than a thousand suns.

"I swear," I mumbled.

Red tugged on my chin. "You swear on what?"

"I swear on my undying love for you that I won't kill Azara." I leaned in capturing her lips before she could stop me and sealed the promise with a kiss.

She pulled back too soon, eyeing me suspiciously. "Good. And remember, if you break your word, you'll have bardy to deal with."

I glanced over her shoulder at her favorite weapon-slash-obsession which leaned against the doorframe. Sometimes I was certain it was magically spelled to follow her wherever she went. It always appeared at the most inopportune moments.

"I'm shaking in my fangs, Red." I tossed her a mischievous smile.

"Oh, bite me."

My incisors lengthened, and a wicked grin split my lips. "Don't tempt me. It's been a while since I've fed."

Her face fell, and a pang of guilt jabbed at my insides. "I'm sorry, with everything going on I totally forgot about it."

I raised a hand, shaking my head. "Red, you're not my private juice box. There's no reason to apologize. I've made do. I just miss your sparkly unicorn blood." I licked my lips, and a shot of desire darted through the bond—from Red's end. "Unless *you* want to?"

She eyed the door then her gaze darted back to mine.

I stepped closer, and my hands closed around her hips. My thumb grazed the bare skin between her top and jeans. "I can be quick... and quiet." Her pulse quickened, the flutter of her jugular catching my eye. Gods, she *did* want this. Which made it about ten times hotter.

"Are we still talking about blood, or something else?" She winked, and it was just adorable when she tried to be funny.

"If we're fast, we can do both."

She tugged at the hem of her shirt and pulled it over her head. All the blood rushed to my lower half as I took her in, jaw slightly unhinged. Gods, she was beautiful, and she was mine.

"I didn't think you'd take me up on the offer," I breathed as I got to work on her jeans. My heart raced, my arousal already pressing at the zipper of my pants.

"That speech today at the assembly, Ransom, it got to me. I would've jumped you right then and there if I'd had the chance." Her lips pressed against mine as she fumbled with the buttons of my shirt. "I was so proud of you," she mumbled against my mouth.

Despite every lusty bone in my body screaming at me not to, I stopped undressing her and held her out to arm's length. "You were?"

She nodded quickly, lower lip snagged between her teeth. "You don't even realize it, but you were born to lead. And one day, you will." She cupped my cheek, and a tornado of emotions whipped around my ribcage.

Even before I died, I never thought I'd amount to much. Sure, I was the alpha heir of the Royal Pack, but my father was nowhere near giving up his seat. It could've been decades before I assumed that role.

I stared at the woman in front of me, my mate, the person that meant more to me than anyone in this world. When she looked at me like that, I wanted to believe her. I wanted to become the man she saw.

Red moved closer, lacing her arms around the back of my neck. "I love you, Ransom, now drink. We're supposed to be fast, remember? You've got five minutes. Talon and Vera are out there waiting for us."

"Ugh, buzzkill."

She smiled and tilted her head to bare her neck. Her pulse fluttered, and my fangs lengthened to sharp points. Wrapping my arms around her waist, I drew her body flush against mine. Then I dipped my head and ran my tongue across her puckered flesh. She let out a sigh, arching against me.

As much as I wanted to draw out the moment and the intense pleasure, now was not the time. I bit down and her heady, warm blood filled my mouth. As if I hadn't been aroused before, my manly parts were throbbing now. She tasted like salvation, like life in a bottle. Energy hummed through my veins, seeping into all the dark crevices. It was impossible, but the more of her I consumed, the more alive I felt. The more my wolf surged to the surface. As if confirming my speculations, a low rumble vibrated my chest.

Red's breath hitched, and after one long pull, I carefully retracted my fangs. She stared up at me from beneath hooded lids.

"You heard that?"

"Umhmm," she mumbled, her eyes glassy and unfocused. Gods, she was as affected by me as I was by her.

Mate. Mate. Mate. My wolf picked up his feverish chant as I sloughed off my pants. I bit into my wrist and offered her my blood before I got too carried away. She drank from me greedily, every suck intensifying the spiraling heat in my core.

When she finally released me, her eyes met mine, and she pressed her forehead to my own. "Even if we can't complete the bond, you are my mate. I feel the truth of it deep within my bones, engraved in my very DNA. I want you to know that."

I willed the words out, to tell her maybe there was still a chance. But her hand found its way inside my boxers, and I let out a hiss as her fingers closed around me. All logical thought abandoned me as her hand began to move up and down my hard length.

Hunter, Sierra, Talon, they were all right. I needed to tell her. We needed to try, even if it meant failing. Once we found Azara, I'd admit the truth. Right now, we needed this. With so much uncertainty around us, this was the only thing that was certain. My love for her, my desire for her.

Wrapping my fingers around the back of her neck, I brought her mouth to mine and kissed her deeply. My blood was still on her lips, the metallic tang swirling between us. We'd exchanged blood so many times, and the bond had never been completed. How would it be different if we did it while making love?

I tossed the thoughts aside for now and walked Red back until she hit the bed. Lowering her down gently, I crept over her, bracing my arms on either side of her head. "I love you," I whispered as I claimed her mouth, then all of her.

CHAPTER
TWENTY-EIGHT

P *hoenix*

"THAT WAS A LONG *TALK*." Vera shot me a conspiratorial grin as she arranged her witchy supplies across the coffee table.

"You know how Red is, she's insatiable. Once she gets started—"

I jabbed my elbow into the infuriating fanger's side. The misery carved into Talon's face made me regret the quickie, big time. How could I have been so careless? To enjoy that moment with my mate when Talon was enduring so much pain at the loss of his. Ransom was such a bad influence.

"I'm sorry," I blurted to Talon. "I hope you weren't waiting for too long."

Vera shook her head. "Nope, we're just getting started. I was about to go in there and drag you guys out." She

219

unsheathed a small dagger and crooked a finger at Ransom. "I'll need your blood now, please."

He strutted toward my friend and offered his wrist. "It's a good thing I just had a refill."

Vera's brows knitted as she pressed the dagger across his milky white flesh. His skin parted, and she turned his wrist, so the blood dribbled into a large urn.

"So how is this going to work exactly?" Talon asked, scooting to the edge of the couch cushion.

"My guess is that Drakin is cloaking Azara, which is why we can't track her. What I'm hoping is that he's not also hiding Thanatos. Why would a god have to hide, right? Using Ransom's blood, we should be able to get a lock on him." She paused and chewed on the inside of her cheek. "This is all conjecture of course. I've never tried a locator spell on an actual god before, but if it truly is Thanatos' bloodline from which all vampires descend, it would make sense."

Talon nodded slowly. "I'm willing to try anything at this point."

Vera added a vial of a deep purple sludge that smelled like tar, and the concoction in the urn began to fizzle. Then she sprinkled some white powder across the top, muttering the words to an incantation that sounded vaguely familiar. The blood mixed with the other ingredients, popped, and churned, and a dark, smokey cloud drifted above the old urn. "Okay, it should be ready now." She lifted the ancient vase and set it down in the middle of the room. Then revealing a stick of what looked like chalk from her pocket, she began to scrawl markings across the floor. I recognized some of the runes, old symbols for life, death and rebirth. That was the extent of my knowledge of the witchy pictograms.

"This isn't like your typical locator spell. Since Thanatos is a god, he doesn't have a human form I can latch onto, only an essence. Instead, I'm going to try to conjure a picture of where he is. Then I'm hoping we'll be able to put the pieces together to determine his location."

We all nodded as Vera finished up. When had my friend gotten so good at this stuff? I'd been so wrapped up in my own fanger-killing prowess, I'd never considered how powerful she'd become.

She swept her hands together and sat back on her knees, her picture complete. A white circle surrounded the urn with dozens of runes scrawled along the outside ring. "Okay, I'm going to give it a go." She turned to Talon and offered him a reassuring smile. "Like I said, I've never done this before so it might take a few tries. I'll get it eventually."

"Thank you, for all you're doing."

Vera adjusted her position, so she sat cross-legged just outside the circle. Pressing her palms together, she began to chant. The smoky, charred scent of magic filled the room, making my nose twitch. I kept perfectly still, eyes intent on my friend.

Ransom and Talon sat on either side of me, both males' gazes equally as transfixed as my own.

A crack formed in the center of the circle, and light seeped through the fissure. An image began to coalesce. I sucked in a breath. Before the excitement reached a fevered pitch, the light blinked out of existence.

"Dammit," Vera muttered.

"What's wrong?" Talon shouted.

"Nothing, the hold is too tenuous. Let me try something else." She turned to Ransom and held out her hand. "Come, sit with me. I need to bolster the connection."

He slid down onto the floor beside her. "What should I do?"

"Just think of Thanatos and how he made you feel when

you were in his presence. Nix said he seemed to have some sort of power over you? Focus on that."

He nodded, pressing his lips into a tight line.

My teammate repeated the procedure, this time her fingers wrapped tightly around Ransom's. Sparks ignited between their palms as she chanted, the echoes of the powerful magic coursing through my mate rushing across the bond.

It was like tiny zaps of lightning puckering my skin. I wondered how intense it must have been for Ransom if I felt the aftershocks so clearly. Again, the burst of light appeared, only to fizzle out a few seconds later.

"What's wrong?" I asked.

Vera's brows knitted as she stared into the urn, the dark maroon fizzing and popping. "Did you guys just bloodshare?"

Heat flared along my cheeks at our dirty little secret. Only it wasn't a secret, and I knew my friends didn't judge me for it. I judged myself. After everything, I hated how much I wanted *his* blood, not the other way around.

"Of course," Ransom replied when I kept quiet. He stood and moved beside me, weaving his arm around my waist.

"Hmm." Her lips puckered. "It could be that. Nix's blood is diluting the connection to Thanatos." She turned to Talon and frowned. "I'm sorry, but we might have to wait a day to try again."

Guilt ravaged my insides as I took in the disappointment in Talon's face. This was all my fault. If I hadn't given into a moment of pleasure with Ransom, I wouldn't have put Azara's life in more risk. "I'm so sorry," I blurted. "I had no idea—"

The big dragon shook his head. "It's not your fault." But the scowl carved into his jaw said otherwise.

"We can go with you today to search on foot, anywhere. Thanatos has to be in the Darklands. Maybe Ransom can find him somehow." I nudged my vampire in the side. "Right?"

"I can certainly try."

Talon rose, exhaling a ragged breath. "No, it's fine. I can cover more ground in the sky anyway."

I shot up and moved in front of the burly shifter. "We'll trail behind you on foot. We won't slow you down." I glanced over at my vampire mate who could probably run as fast as the dragon could fly. "Well, at least I'll try not to. I can give you a com, and we can stay in touch that way. If Ransom or I come across anything, we'll let you know."

He nodded slowly. "Okay."

"And I'll draw more of Ransom's blood tomorrow after Nix's has cleared his system," said Vera. She wagged a finger at him. "No more sexy times until then."

Oh, for gods' stakes just stab me now.

With a quick wave, Talon trudged toward the door, and I trailed after him. "Wait, let me get you that com." I rifled through the bag of supplies in my go bag by the door and handed him the small, sleek device. "We'll find Azara. I promise."

That grim expression was still etched into his wide jaw as he placed the silver disc behind his ear. "I know. We have to. I won't let my daughter grow up without her mom."

Another pang of guilt streaked across my chest, jabbing at my heart. My life wasn't worth Azara's. She was a mother, had a child that needed her. When we found Thanatos, I'd do anything to save her, even if it meant offering myself up instead.

"We'll be right behind you."

Talon nodded solemnly, and I couldn't help my gaze from following the big shifter as he trudged down the hallway. As soon as I closed the door behind him, I plodded back into the living room, lead weights replacing my shoes. "I can't believe we messed this up so badly."

Ransom curled his arm around my shoulders and gave me a weak smile. "Aw, come on, Red, we'll fix it tomorrow. And don't listen to Vera, we can still have sexy times, just no blood sharing." He flashed me a wicked grin, highlighting those pointy fangs.

"That's not what I was worried about, you insufferable fanger," I gritted out and wriggled out of his embrace.

"To be honest," Vera said, drawing my attention back to her, "You two have been bloodsharing for a long time. I don't know how much a day off will really help, but I didn't want to completely crush Talon's hope."

"Thanks, Vera," I muttered. "We'll find another way then." Turning to Ransom, I jabbed a finger into his chest. "Get dressed, we're going hunting."

As it turned out, hunting for a god wasn't as easy as I'd imagined it to be. Even with Dragon-Talon and Dragon-Spark, who'd been a last-minute addition to the tracking party, coasting overhead, Ransom zipping all around the Darklands and me in fur trying to sniff out the dark deity, we'd gotten nowhere.

My muscles burned, and the pads of my paws were tender, each step worse than the last. I wasn't used to remaining in my wolf form for so long and the fatigue was real. We'd searched all of Ronin's old hideouts and come up empty. We hadn't even run into a single servile on the street. That had been my other brilliant plan: to force a fanger to take us back to its leader.

But it was like they'd all disappeared. Which did nothing to ease the brewing storm of nerves in my gut. What was Thanatos waiting for? He had to know I was the wolf with the mortal bite. Why hadn't he come for me yet?

And Ransom—he was the final piece of the puzzle. Had Ronin had time to tell Thanatos about the vampire with a soul before I killed him?

As if my wolfy vampire mate had heard my thoughts, a gust of air zipped by me, and Ransom appeared.

"No good, Red. I've searched up and down the river, along the borders and all Ronin's usual haunts and I've come up empty. Drakin must have new, bolstered wards up."

I sat down on my haunches and cocked my head.

"Come on, little wolf, come on out. We can't carry on a conversation this way." He grinned mischievously. "And the thought of you naked has been the only thing that's kept me going all these hours."

I snorted and stretched out my legs. As much as I hated giving him the pleasure, I was itching to be back in skin. Searching the dark depths where my shifter magic resided, I called to the flicker of light and a moment later, I stood in front of my mate, fully naked.

His roving eyes raked over me, his gaze so intent I could practically feel him touching me. A stream of desire raced through our bond, blanketing my bare skin in a heated caress. He finally tore his gaze away and tugged his t-shirt over his head. "You better put this on because I'm about two seconds away from taking you against that tree and giving Talon and Spark the show of a lifetime."

A shudder surged up my spine as an obscene amount of heat flared below my bellybutton. Mother fanger, would I ever get enough of him?

His fingers brushed mine as I reached for the shirt, and

tiny sparks lit up between our flesh. I paused as a pair of obsidian orbs drilled into me. The depth of emotion stole my breath, and my fingers froze, still clenching the shirt.

Ransom's arms came around my waist, and he dragged me against his bare chest. His lips hovered only a hairsbreadth from my mine. "Can I take you on a date tonight?"

My head snapped back, eyes widening. "What?" A laugh tumbled out. Of all the things I expected in that moment, that had been the last.

"I want to woo you, Red. I want to enjoy what could be our final days together."

"Don't say that." I shook my head as I glanced up at him.

He shrugged. "Fine, even if they're not, can we just pretend to be normal for the rest of the evening? We won't find Azara tonight."

I chewed on my lip, pausing to consider. The idea of a date with Ransom had a weird giddiness bubbling up in my chest. I'd never had an actual date in my life. Which was pretty sad. There was no time or place for that on the Isle of Mordis. But I couldn't get Talon's look of anguish out of my mind. How could I be so selfish? He and Azara had been so welcoming. I should've spent the night searching for her.

Ransom's arm tightened around me, and he cupped my cheek with his free hand. "Please, Red. Do you want me to beg?"

My thoughts flitted back to the dungeons, to when Ronin had us imprisoned. Ransom had offered the same back then, and I'd been too pissed off to take him up on it. "Okay."

He grinned.

"I want you to beg." I shot him a smirk.

A burst of laughter escaped through his kissable lips. "You're nothing if not unpredictable, Red." He dropped down to his knees and glanced up at me. "And that's why I love you." He cleared his throat and took my hands in his. "Red, will you please do me the honor and allow me to escort you for a night out on the Rive Gauche?"

My nose crinkled. "You had me until that last part."

He huffed out a breath, rolling his eyes. "Where would you like to go then?"

I shrugged. "I don't know, surprise me."

His eyes lit up in amusement. "Very well. Your wish is my command." He dipped his head and brushed his lips against my knuckles. "Is there anything else you'd like while I'm down here?" His gaze flitted to my bare thighs. His shirt barely skimmed my upper legs, and I was completely naked underneath.

Heat unraveled, and I pressed my thighs together. "Not right now," I breathed out.

Ransom chuckled darkly before rising. He brushed his lips against my mouth and inhaled, as if he were breathing me in. "Let's tell the boys we're calling it quits for the night."

I reluctantly nodded. He was right; we wouldn't find Azara tonight, but I still hated admitting defeat.

After speaking to Talon and Spark on the com, we headed back toward the penthouse. "Where is everyone by the way? When was the last time the Darklands were this quiet?" A prickle of unease lifted the hair at the back of my neck.

"Something is brewing, that's for sure." He moved instep beside me and laced his fingers through mine. "Whatever it is, we'll be ready. But tonight, it's all about you and me."

I couldn't help a silly smile from stretching across my face.

R*ansom*

RED HAD BEEN RIGHT; the date thing was slightly out of the blue given the situation, but the more I thought about it the more right it felt. Red loved me, that alone was a reason to celebrate. And Ronin was dead so bonus point. Besides that, my old friend Sierra had also been right; if I wanted to tell Red the truth about the bond, we needed to do it with our clothes on.

After weeks of going back and forth about it, I had to tell her our wolves might still have a chance. That phantom presence in my chest stirred. *Come out, come out, wherever you are*! Sometimes I was certain my wolf was just screwing with me. Maybe he hadn't died at all, and instead he'd only been in hiding as a way to torture me, punishment for my misdeeds when I'd first turned.

"Are you done primping yet?" Red's voice seeped through the door. I could hear her smile, and it felt *good*. She could deny it all she wanted, but she was actually excited for this date. The date I had in no way prepared for.

"Be right out, don't be so impatient, my little sicari."

The slap of her heels as she paced in front of the bathroom door sent my own heart accelerating. *Thanatos, was I actually nervous too?* With one last glance in the mirror, I tugged at my shirt collar and smoothed back an errant strand of dark hair. *Perfect.*

I opened the door, fairly confident, until I saw her. All the air whooshed from my lungs, and my jaw dropped. She turned toward me and for a second, my heart staggered. For the longest minute of my life, I just stared, dumbstruck, awestruck, at the beautiful, mesmerizing woman who'd chosen me. Despite all my flaws, despite what I was.

A tight black silky dress caressed her curves, the low-cut halter top revealing the perfect swell of her breasts. I swallowed thickly as my gaze roamed her body, from the sparkling emerald of her lively irises to the shapely pucker of her lips, the exquisite column of her throat and all the way down to her long, sexy legs. Gods, she was heavenly, and she was *mine*. I wanted her, needed her so badly it hurt. I desired every part of her, wanted to spend all of eternity wrapped in her arms. I not only wanted to be her mate, but her husband, the father of her children. The thought sent a fiery poker through my soul. If I had a soul, did that mean...? I shook off the thought, unable to focus on that right now.

My heart finally stuttered on, until my lungs began to function once again. I closed my mouth and forced my brain to string together a sentence. "You, you are captivating, Red."

A sheepish smile curved her pink lips, a look I didn't often get from the mighty sicari. She seemed as affected by me as I was by her. She inhaled a sharp breath and finally breathed, "You too."

I stepped forward and took her hand, oblivious to our roommates who milled around the kitchen and living room. They could just as easily have been ants for all I noticed them. Tugging Red toward the door, we made our escape.

THE PORTAL SPAT us out onto the spongy soil, and my free hand shot out to steady us. My arm was wrapped around Red as she teetered on those high heels. When I'd seen the stilettos back at the penthouse, I'd almost told her to opt for a more comfortable shoe, but the ruby red strappy things were just too sexy to deny.

"Is the blindfold really necessary?" Red grumbled.

"One hundred percent necessary." My gaze raked over her, her full lips screwed into a pout. The full moon danced across her deep auburn hair setting it aflame.

"When can I take it off?" Her nose crinkled as she inhaled a breath of moist air.

The jungle was alive at nighttime, the chirp of crickets and rustle of leaves providing a soothing backdrop to the silence. After spending three years here, I was surprised she hadn't already figured out where we'd landed.

"Soon," I whispered, leaning in close. A wave of goose-bumps cascaded down her arm, and a smile split my lips unbidden.

The nerves from earlier began to dissipate as I led Red deeper into the jungle. I just hoped I could find the right place before she got tired of waiting and ripped the blindfold off.

She walked hesitantly across the leaves and scattered

foliage, the crunch, crunch echoing in time with my heart-beats. My hand tightened around hers as I guided her over a fallen branch.

"Are you luring me out into the woods to kill me?" She smirked.

"Never, Red. I would simply devour you in the comfort of our home."

Leaves rustled in the distance, the towering kapok trees home to dozens of wild birds as I recollected from my brief stay on the Isle of Mordis. Some would say my choice for our first date was in poor taste, seeing as it was an island dedicated to the hunting and murdering of vampires, but it was also where we'd first met. Where I'd felt that irresistible connection I then spent the next few weeks denying until it was impossible. I could still see her so clearly as I hunkered down within the sprawling branches of the old kapok.

Sɪᴄᴀʀɪ. Dammit. I poked my head out from behind the thick bark, and a pair of emerald eyes lanced into mine. My lifeless heart flipflopped and for a second, I felt alive again. What in all the realms? I stared down at the attractive girl, her deep auburn hair cascading down her slim shoulders. In her right hand, she held a medieval battle axe of some sort, reaching nearly her height. I'd never seen a female wield anything like it. Gods, it was kind of hot. She reached for something behind her back but came up empty-handed. She scowled up at me, and I shot her a smirk.

There was something so tempting about her...

"What's the matter, Red? You can't climb?" I called out.

She glared up at me for a long moment before she shuddered, like something had spooked her. With her eyes averted, I forced my gaze away from hers and leapt out of the tree, despite every bone in my body willing me to stay.

In a moment of weakness, I turned back and found her eyes still trained on me. My blood hummed, energy crackling through my veins. I needed to get closer, to touch her, to taste her. I fixed my eyes to hers, and crimson flooded my irises as power swelled through me. If I could just compel her, I could get a closer look.

Come here, little sicari. I willed her forward with my compulsion.

Moonbeams glinted through the canopy of leaves, calling my attention to her eyes. They were as clear as before, sparkling beneath the pale blue light. Definitely not compelled. How was that possible? I shook my head out, breaking my non-existent hold over her, and a smirk curled the corner of my lip. How was she blocking me?

I waggled a finger at the girl and clucked my tongue. "No closer, Red. I haven't fed today, and you're much too pretty to waste for a snack."

"Charming," she bit back.

"I'm glad you think so." I shot her another smirk, flashing my pearly-white incisors. "I was hoping we could be friends. The name's Ransom by the way, rhymes with handsome." I sketched a bow, keeping my eyes pinned to hers.

She laughed, and the sound sent my heart racing. More than that, a presence I hadn't felt since the day I'd died stirred within my core. I sucked in a breath and clapped my hand over my chest. No, it couldn't be.

Her lips twisted, and a look of horror contorted her features, as if finding me amusing was the most ghastly thing in this gods' forsaken world.

"What's a gorgeous girl like you doing in a place like this?" I lifted a flirty brow.

"Oh, you know, killing murderous bloodsuckers." She clutched something behind her back, another weapon no doubt.

"Bloodsuckers? So trite, little sicari." I straightened, trying to

get a better look at her. I knew I should run and yet for some ungodly reason my feet were rooted to the spot. "You see," I continued, "I don't belong here with these animals, or bloodsuckers, to use your colorful terminology. Perhaps you could tell me the quickest way back to Nocturnis?"

"Unlikely." She casually leaned against the axe. "Because you see, Ransom, you're the only thing standing in the way of me graduating with a perfect score."

"Ah, you sicari are all the same. Murder, stake, kill." I rolled my eyes dramatically. "This is quite a conundrum then. It seems as though only one of us is destined to leave this island."

"Damned right," she hissed.

Still, I couldn't get my feet to move, as if an invisible cord had bound me to her. "It's a shame," I forced out. "I would've liked running into you in a dark alley in Nocturnis." I smirked and ran my tongue over the pointy tip of my fang. Move, Ransom. I coaxed my legs to heed my commands. "Another time then, Red." With one last glance, I whirled around and vamp-sped through the encroaching trees.

"RANSOM, can I take this thing off yet?" The annoyance tingeing Red's tone drew me from the past.

I hadn't been able to get her out of my mind since that day. If someone had told me I ever would've returned to this island of my own accord, I would've laughed in their face, but love made one do stupid things.

I scanned the surrounding kapoks, certain this had been the place, and released Red's hand. "Yes, it's time." Moving behind her, I slowly unraveled the double knot. My body pressed against her back, and her breath hitched. Her pulse spiked at my proximity, and a wave of satisfaction lapped over me. For so long, I'd been certain that our connection was only one-sided. Finding out it wasn't, was one of the best days of my life.

The blindfold fell to the ground, and Red squinted as her gaze settled on our surroundings. "The Isle of Mordis..." she whispered. Whirling around, her brows knitted. "Why?"

"Why do you think?"

She glanced over my shoulder, her curious gaze landing on the kapok trees and a spark of understanding lit up her eyes. "This is the spot where we first met." The hint of a smile curled her lips, and it was like my heart had sprouted wings.

"You recognized it." It was supposed to be a question but came out as a statement, as the look in her eyes spoke volumes.

"Like I could ever forget it. You cost me our first-place spot."

A rueful chuckle burst from my lips. "Of course that's what you'd remember."

She gave me a lopsided grin and weaved her arms around the back of my neck. "Okay, okay, it's not the only thing I remember, handsome Ransom."

My lips twitched. "You mock me now, but I definitely made an impression."

"I can't deny that, fanger." She brushed her lips against mine, and those wings fluttered like mad.

As much as I wanted to give into her heated kisses, I couldn't yet. I needed to tell her the truth about the mate bond, but first I had to butter her up, so she didn't make good on her promise all those months ago when we first met on this island.

Reluctantly, I pulled away and drew a small vial from my pocket.

"What's that?" She eyed the deep purple liquid.

"A gift from Vera for our date." I uncorked the ampule and tipped it onto its side. As the liquid dribbled out, a dark cloud of smoke coalesced across the ground. When the fog cleared, a blanket along with a picnic basket and a bottle of wine had appeared on the moist earth. Tiny sparks of light shimmered around us, creating a circle just above our heads.

"Wow." Red's head dipped back to take in the glimmering lights, then her eyes settled on the fancy display complete with lit candles. "Vera really went all out."

"She did." I was very impressed with the little witch and made a mental note to thank her profusely upon our return. I'd asked for romantic, and she'd definitely delivered. I reached for Red's hand and helped her settle down on the blanket. Then I grabbed the bottle of wine. "Shall we?"

"Abso-fangin-lutely. Let's get this date started."

CHAPTER

THIRTY

P *hoenix*

I SNUCK a peak at Ransom from over the edge of my glass as I took a long sip of the Fae wine Archer had provided for our date. The fizzy bubbles went straight to my head, and I felt like I was floating on a cloud. Who knew my faery teammate could be considerate like that? He'd always told us about the stuff back when we were at Camp Kill and so far, every sip lived up to my expectations.

Ransom's eyes chased to mine as if he'd felt my gaze wander to his. He set the glass back on the ground and smirked. "Vamp got your tongue, Red?"

I couldn't help but laugh at his cheesy line and silly grin. Things had been good between us lately, really good. I was trying to enjoy it, but that lingering doubt always remained.

I hated it. It was like living in constant fear for the other shoe to drop.

"What?" He must have sensed my mood change because his dark brows drew together.

"Nothing." I shook my head. I refused to ruin this night. Tomorrow, I could deal with all the uncertainties.

He nodded, but his lips screwed into a pout. An adorable pout that I just wanted to kiss off him. That reminded me of other things I wanted to kiss, and a swell of desire rushed over every inch of me. Could we even do that here? In the middle of the jungle? What if some trainees were out and about or worse, fangers?

"Do you want to eat anything else?" Ransom pointed at the basket of delicacies Vera had conjured up. They tasted even better than the real thing.

I rubbed my tummy and groaned. "I couldn't eat another bite."

He licked his lips and his fangs extended, sending another thrill coursing through my system. "I, on the other hand, could always go for one more bite."

I wagged my finger at him, plastering on a serious face, which was tough when the Fae wine had made me totally giddy. "You heard what Vera said. No biting until after she tries the locator spell again tomorrow."

"Right, right, right." His fangs retracted, and a moment of silence stretched between us. For the past hour, I hadn't thought about Thanatos, the queen, fangers, Azara, anything. And it had been perfect. Now, reality had made its way into our island bubble.

"Nope, don't do it, Red." Ransom poked my nose, drawing a smile. "We're still on our date. No thoughts of gloom and doom, please."

I nodded slowly. "You're right."

He took my hand and tugged me to my feet. I kept my other hand clenched around the faery wine. My new favorite drink. "What are you doing?" I giggled. Yes, actually giggled. This stuff was potent.

"Dance with me." Ransom pried the wine glass from my hand and set it on the ground before wrapping my arms around the back of his neck.

"But there's no music."

"Sure, there is." He ran his nose across the shell of my ear and began to hum a tune. Then he slowly swayed from side to side, guiding my hips along with his.

My body instinctively molded to his, all my soft curves pressing against the hard planes of his form. I leaned my head on his shoulder and breathed him in. My wolf stirred, anxious to be free. As if Ransom's ghost wolf had heard her, a low growl vibrated his chest, resonating against my ear. I glanced up and met those bottomless irises.

"He's been exceedingly restless lately," he mumbled.

"I wonder why."

His lips pressed into a thin line, then the hardness of his expression waned. "It's probably all the sex."

I laughed and leaned my forehead against his. With our mouths only a breath away, my heart began to pound. Emboldened by the intoxicating effects of the Fae wine, I snuck my fingers beneath the waistband of Ransom's pants.

"Oh, Red," he groaned, immediately hardening against me. His lips captured mine, and I danced my fingers further down until they found all of him. I wrapped my fingers around his length, and he moaned in my mouth.

"Wouldn't it be ironic if we had sex in the same place we first met?"

"Ironic...fantastic? Who can keep track?" He leaned into my touch as I began to move up and down. "Oh gods, Red, I can't believe I'm doing this but—" His hand wrapped around my wrist and pushed it away.

My brows knitted as I regarded him.

"You don't know how much I want this... how much I *always* want you, but there's something I need to tell you first."

It was like a bucket of ice water had been tossed over the burning embers in my core. "What?" I panted out. The shoe... it was the other shoe, and it was about to drop.

He kissed my nose, then moved down to my lips brushing his mouth gently against mine.

"Just say it, Ransom," I blurted, taking a step back and putting some much-needed distance between us.

His lips twisted into a scowl, a pained expression sharpening his features.

"Oh gods, Ransom, what have you done?" Fear lanced through my gut, twisting my insides. His anxiety zipped through the bond only amplifying my own.

He moved closer and framed my face with his hands. "It's not like that, Red. Please, calm down."

I drew in a deep breath before wriggling free of his touch. I needed to think clearly for whatever was to come, and I couldn't do that when his hands were on me. "What is it?" I repeated.

He released a sharp breath and dragged his hands through his perfectly gelled hair. "I may have neglected to tell you a fairly important factor in regards to the mate bond."

"The mate bond?" I squealed.

He nodded slowly. "What did you think I'd done, Red?"

"I don't know. Made another deal with Carmen Rosa or worse, Thanatos."

His brows furrowed, and disappointment flashed across his expressive features. "I would never do that."

I wanted to believe him, but I didn't. Because his love for me made him even more reckless. "So what is it about the mate bond that you didn't tell me?"

He inhaled slowly and inched closer. "There may still be a way for us to complete it."

Mind. Blown. That was the *last* thing I'd expected him to say. "What do you mean?" I stammered.

"It may not be a hundred percent necessary for you to bite me, which means we could get around the whole kiss of death thing."

My heart rioted in my chest. We still had a chance. A furry head butted at my insides, and auburn fur rippled over my arms. "How?" I finally blurted.

His arms came around my waist, pulling me into his chest. "I don't want you to get your hopes up, just because it worked for Hunter and Sierra doesn't guarantee it'll work for us."

My brows slammed together as I stared up at him. "I don't understand."

"Hunter and Sierra didn't complete the bond in the normal way. I was actually there for it." He palmed the back of his neck, crimson tinting his cheeks. "Sierra was dying. She was unconscious. They'd made love before, a few times, but Hunter had never bitten her. They'd never exchanged blood. Technically, the bond is supposed to be formed while during *the act*. But somehow it worked. He held her close, skin on skin, then he bit her and *fed her* his blood."

"So she never bit him?"

"Correct."

"And it worked?"

"Correct."

I considered the story, my thoughts whirling back to my half-brother and his mate. Then realization hit me like a runaway freight train. "This isn't new information to you. If you were there, you knew all along that it was possible."

His lips thinned, and he slowly nodded.

"A couple weeks ago when we made love and we were about to... You said it wasn't possible. *You* stopped us." A surge of ice rushed my veins, and I tried to wiggle free of his hold. Hunter and Sierra knew. Now all their covert shared looks made sense.

His arms only tightened around me. "I was stupid. Scared, Red."

"But you've known, all these weeks. We've slept together countless times and never, not once did you mention it. Even after I told you I loved you..." A tiny crack raced across my heart. There were so many things I doubted about Ransom, but his love for me had never been one of them. "You're not sure..." I muttered and finally broke free. Wrapping my arms around myself to keep from falling apart, I clenched my jaw to stop the trembling.

"Of course, I am." Ransom reached for me again, but I staggered back.

"Don't," I growled.

"Phoenix Morana, I have always been sure about us. From the day I first laid eyes on you on this damned island, you were it for me. I knew it with every fiber of my being."

"Then why? Why didn't you tell me the truth?"

"When you first agreed to it, I was scared. That's the gods' honest truth. I wasn't sure of your feelings for me and then later, I didn't think I deserved you. Hell, I still don't. After you rescued me from Ronin's dungeon, I was in a bad place. I vowed to tell you once I'd gotten myself under control, once I was deserving of a mate like you. And then when Seline died, you said you

241

never wanted to be a vampire. I was terrified to tie myself to you and be torn apart when you inevitably passed. When you finally admitted you loved me, the idea of giving you hope for it to only be ripped away if it didn't work was too much. And it wasn't just your hope but mine too. What if what happened with Sierra and Hunter was a fluke? We've exchanged blood so many times, and our connection has never been completed. The more we bloodshared the more my hope shrank."

I released a breath, forcing the anger down. Ransom's points were valid, but his lie didn't sting any less. He still knew all along and kept that from me. "You should've just told me."

"I know. But speaking the words would've made them real, and I wasn't ready at the time." He exhaled sharply, his shoulders slumping forward.

"And now you are?"

"I'm still scared to death, Red, but you deserve the truth. With the chaos that has become our lives, I suppose I realized just because I'm immortal doesn't mean we have forever." He crept closer, and this time I didn't back away. Tentatively, he placed his hands on my shoulders. "I love you, and I'm done being a coward. Even if I'm devastated and spiral out of control when it doesn't work, at least I'll know that I tried to have it all. With you."

"I don't know if I like the sound of that." I narrowed my eyes at him, a grin pulling at my lips. "The spiraling out of control part, not the having it all part."

"Even if I do, you'll be there to bring me back, right?" The depth of hope in his dark eyes shattered my remaining defenses.

"I'll always bring you back, you infuriating fanger."

His lips captured mine, and I melted into his embrace. I

loved this crazy, impulsive, flawed man more than I thought possible. Mated or not, I doubted the connection we shared would ever be severed.

Ransom's hand cradled the back of my neck as he deepened the kiss. Then he slowly walked me backwards to the blanket. He gently eased me down, his lips never leaving mine. He hovered over me, bracing his forearms on either side of my head, and caged me in.

"I love you, Phoenix Morana. Will you do me the honor of being my mate?" His fangs lengthened and he flashed me a beaming smile, highlighting those adorable dimples.

"I love you too, Ransom De La Sangue, and I will. But not tonight."

His eyes widened, and the rush of disappointment surged through the bond.

"Why not?"

"Because if it doesn't work, I can't have you spiraling out of control. I need you right now, Ransom. I need you if we're ever going to save Azara and take down Thanatos. Plus, Vera will kill us if we mess up her spell again by intermingling our blood."

He chewed on the side of his lip, and his fang nicked the skin. I had to tamp down on the desire to lick it. "Perhaps spiral was a bit of an exaggeration..."

"No, it wasn't. I know you, Ransom, and I know as much as you want to complete the bond because of me, another big part is also in the hopes of reclaiming your wolf. Even if I swear to be with you regardless of the outcome, there's nothing I can do to bring back your lupine half. So for now, I think it's best if we wait."

"Damn you and your good logic," he growled.

I wrapped my legs around his hips and drew him flush

against me. "But that doesn't mean we can't practice." A smirk curled my lips as I stared up at him.

"You sure know how to take the sting out of rejection, Red." He grinned as he pressed his lips to mine. His tongue tangled with my own for a feverish second before he drew back.

My wolf let out a growl of displeasure.

"Let's make a deal, Red. I don't want to wait until we take down Thanatos. Who knows what could happen by then? When Azara is safely back in the arms of her mate, we give it a try. I swear I won't go off on a blood bender if it doesn't work. I'll swear it on my undying love for you. Deal?"

I finally nodded. The truth was that I wanted to complete the bond as badly as he did. My wolf longed for it. "Deal."

Ransom's mouth descended on mine, and everything else fell away.

R *ansom*

THE LITTLE WITCH stared at her grimoire, her eyes crossed as her finger swept over the yellowing page. I had a feeling the spell wasn't the problem, but rather the amount of blood Red and I had shared. It would likely take days if not weeks for her blood to fully dilute from my system.

The thought was oddly satisfying. A piece of her always resided within me.

Talon had returned this morning after an unsuccessful night of scouring Nocturnis for Azara with his new dragon bestie, Sparky. I was thrilled with the arrangement as it kept our irritating dragon teammate from the penthouse. He'd become obnoxiously sullen since the loss of Seline. A pang of guilt streaked across my chest and my callous musings. If anything happened to Red, I would be more than just sullen.

My little sicari sat cross-legged beside her friend, encouraging her as she flipped through countless pages. If the blood wasn't the problem, then it was Thanatos. He was a god after all, and no one really knew how magic worked with the divine being.

Despite the tension in the room, I was happy. The date with Red had been a success, even though she'd refused to attempt to complete the bond. I understood her apprehension. In the past, I'd become unhinged at much more trivial issues. If we tried and failed, I couldn't deny a part of me would forever be broken. But if Red remained at my side as my pseudo mate, I was certain I could come back from the devastating loss of my wolf.

I was certain I could accomplish anything with her at my side.

"Ugh!" Vera let out an exasperated grunt. "I don't get it. I'm doing everything right."

"It's not just you," said Talon. "Azara's grandfather has been at it for days as well. I don't know how we're going to find her."

I actually felt bad for the big shifter. He seemed wrecked without his mate. The strong, proud dragon I'd met in the Underworld just a few weeks ago had disappeared, leaving behind this shell of a man.

I'd never let Thanatos take Red away from me. My hands curled into tight fists, and a growl echoed in my chest. Talon's sharp hearing must've caught the sound because his silver irises blazed as he regarded me.

I shrugged nonchalantly. There was no reason to get into my ghost wolf right now.

Red stood and marched over to Talon. "If we can't find Thanatos, then we'll just have to make him come to us."

My ears perked up, and I shot my future mate a sidelong glance. "How do you plan on doing that?"

"Simple. We'll use me as bait."

"Absolutely not," I growled. Somehow, I was already on my feet, glaring down at her. "You will not put yourself at risk like that."

"What other choice do we have?" she gritted out.

Talon cleared his throat. "Ransom's right. It's too risky. Azara would never want you to put your life in danger for hers. Not to mention that if Thanatos gets his hands on you, he's one step closer to breaking the shadow curse."

A sharp crack echoed across the room, and I instinctively reached for Red and shoved her behind my back. She struggled behind me, her fingers reaching out for bardy, which I could just make out leaning against the wall. A brilliant light exploded from a fracture in the ether, and a whirling portal churned to life.

The rest of the Scooby squad spilled out from their rooms, each with weapons in tow. My fangs descended, and another growl tore from my clenched lips. A second later, two figures emerged from the mystical vortex.

"Good gods, my queen, couldn't you have at least announced yourself," I hissed when her familiar form coalesced.

"There was no time." Her eyes scanned the penthouse, scrutinizing each person in the room. "Cozy," she mumbled.

Luciano nodded at me then Red. "We apologize for the intrusion, but an urgent matter has come up."

"Ever heard of a fire message?" I retorted.

"This needs to be discussed in person." The queen narrowed her eyes, and I held back my next rebuttal.

"What's going on?" Red slipped free from my hold and marched toward the queen.

"Lucíano has just gotten word from the Winter Court king, Elrian."

Talon grunted. "What's that bastard want now?"

Apparently, the dragon still wasn't over the fact that the Fae king had thought killing everyone mentioned in the spell was a feasible solution, including his beloved Azara.

"The king had been in the process of rounding up all the high Fae without elemental powers—"

"Let me guess: to kill them?" Talon asked.

Carmen Rosa shrugged. "It's not my place to question what the king does in his realm to his people. All I know is that a family member reported one such Fae missing."

"Great," Red muttered.

"Which means Thanatos is now one step closer to breaking the curse." The queen scowled, wrapping her arms across her chest. "It seems the vampire with the soul is the only missing part of the puzzle, besides the lovely Phoenix of course."

Red's eyes flickered to mine. "How do you know that Thanatos hasn't figured it out yet?"

"Because if he had, there would be nothing stopping him from capturing both of you and breaking the curse."

"Maybe we're just too well hidden," I offered.

The queen snorted on a laugh. "If I could find you, Ransom, I have no doubt the god of death could. You are his offspring after all."

"So it's good that he doesn't know that Ransom is the final piece," said Red, folding her arms over her chest.

"It is, but we can't assume he won't figure it out soon."

"Then what do you suggest, my queen?" I eyed the conniving old monarch. If she'd traveled all this way, there had to be more.

Her dark eyes darted at Red. "I have a proposition for you."

A chill raced down my spine at the wicked gleam in her eye, and I instinctively moved closer to my mate.

"I would like to give you the gift of immortality."

"Over my true death!" I snarled.

"This is her choice, Ransom. Not yours." The queen raised a hand, not even sparing me a glance. Her eyes remained trained on Red. "If you became a vampire, your wolf would cease to exist. There is no other wolf like yours to our knowledge, which would eliminate the problem. Thanatos would be unable to perform the spell to break the curse, and he'd be forced to slither away to whatever dark corner he emerged from."

I whirled at Red, squeezing her hands. "You would have to die, Red. You'd be cursed to an eternity of hunger, of endless torture."

"But you'd be together," said the queen. "Forever."

Something unreadable flickered across Red's expression.

"No, Red. It's not worth it. Trust me."

She swallowed hard, her lips pressed into a tight line.

"I vowed I'd never hurt you again, Phoenix," the queen continued, "and I intend to keep my promise, but this seems like the most advantageous solution for all."

"Don't do it," Spark hissed. "You're much too important to become a fanger."

For once, I agreed with the dragon.

"The life of a vampire is not all bad," said Lucíano. He slanted me a look of disgust. "There are many that are perfectly capable of controlling their dark urges and lead a very respectable life."

"I have to think about it," Red finally said.

"No..." I shook my head and took her hand, fixing my

eyes to hers. "There's nothing to think about. I won't let you do it."

"You don't want to spend forever with me?" A rueful smile twisted her lips.

"Not like this."

She turned to Carmen Rosa and drew in a deep breath. "Give me a day to consider your offer, and I'll get back to you."

The queen nodded, a satisfied smile spreading her crimson lips. "You'd become my greatest sicari yet. As my direct offspring and with the power of my blood running through your veins, you'd be unstoppable."

Conniving little bitch. She knew exactly how to play to Red's desires.

"I'll think about it."

"Very well." She turned to Lucíano. "Have the warlock summon the portal for our return."

"Of course, my queen." He turned on his heel and disappeared into the kitchen.

I darted at Carmen Rosa, wrapping my hand around her forearm. "Don't do this. I beg of you."

"It's her choice, Ransom." She paused, eyes narrowing. "And to be honest, I'm quite surprised. I thought you of all people would be thrilled to have your love at your side forever."

"Not when I know what it'll cost her."

"What it'll cost her or you?" She dug her finger into my chest, and my ghostly wolf let out a growl.

I coughed loudly, but it was a poor effort at hiding the sound.

"He's ready," Lucíano called from the other side of the room.

The queen turned back to Red, ignoring me. "I look forward to your response."

My mate nodded. I searched her gaze, but she was purposely avoiding my eye. She wouldn't be crazy enough to agree to this would she?

CHAPTER
THIRTY-TWO

P*hoenix*

THE MOMENT THE QUEEN LEFT, I slumped down on the couch. Burning gazes bored into the side of my face, none more powerful than Ransom's. I couldn't meet his eyes, not yet. Not when I had no idea what I would say. I knew Carmen Rosa's idea was crazy, but was it though? It would solve all our problems without the bloodshed. Well, except for mine.

"Don't even think about it, Red." Ransom stomped over and knelt in front of me. "I will not let you become the sacrificial lamb."

"Why not? Haven't you always promised me forever? How would we have that if I'm mortal?"

"You can't be serious about this," Spark growled. "You've hated fangers your entire life. I understand how things are different with Ransom because of the mate bond, but to become one?"

Vera nodded. "Spark's right, Nix. You'd be giving up everything."

"To save everyone," I cried.

"They're not worth it!" Ransom jumped up, a whirling tornado of emotions streaking through our bond. He grabbed my hands and jerked me close. "Having you with me forever would be my wildest dream come true, but I would never wish this life on you. If something happened and there was no other way... then maybe, *maybe* I would consider it. But not like this. Not when it's your choice. It's the wrong decision, Red. Don't let Carmen Rosa convince you otherwise."

Scrutinizing eyes still drilled into me, their weight suffocating. Didn't they realize it wasn't an easy choice for me either? But what if it was the only way?

Archer stepped forward, the Fae member of our team making his presence known. He'd remained silent throughout the entire exchange. "Let's be honest, I'm the most pragmatic one here."

"Or cold-hearted," Spark mumbled with a grin.

"I say we leave it as a last resort. If everything else goes to hell, Nix becomes a vamp." He shrugged. "It's not the worst thing in the world." Then he turned to Vera. "And if you can't find Thanatos magically then it's about time we found him the old-fashioned way. By using Nix as bait."

Ransom lunged, and I barely caught his arm before he pummeled into the Fae.

"Stop it!" I hissed. "Archer's right. Any way this goes down, we need to find Thanatos. I'm totally onboard with using me as bait."

"Of course, you are," Ransom snarled.

A wave of murmurs filled the room. I needed a minute by myself to figure this out. I couldn't stand the scathing gazes any longer. Shooting up to my feet, I raced for the door. "I'll be back," I called out over my shoulder.

By the time I hit the second step of the stairwell, I was in fur. Nothing cleared my head better than when I was in wolf form. There was something so freeing about it.

"You'd have to give up your wolf if you became a vampire." Ransom's voice echoed down the staircase.

Dammit. I knew I wouldn't get away that easily.

"No more midnight runs, basking beneath the light of the moon, kiss of death, fiery, flaming, fur..." He paused, and I turned back to face him on the landing. "No more mate bond."

My wolfy head snapped back. I'd been so focused on the idea of finally having forever with Ransom that I hadn't even considered my wolf or the bond. What were the chances I'd be blessed like he was with the remnants of his lupine half *and* a soul? I'd most likely turn into a regular run-of-the-mill Royal vamp.

I slowed my pace and let out a whine as he caught up to me.

"I understand why you want to do this, I do. You've got that selfless, do-gooder blood in you. And I'm honored that you'd even consider spending the rest of eternity with me. I only ask that you think long and hard before you give it all up." His words trailed off again and his hand reached for me, fingers rubbing behind my ears.

I let out another whine and fell back on my haunches. Gods, that felt amazing. I had to suppress the urge to rollover and give him full access to my belly.

"There are other things to consider too, Red. What about your sister? What would Kenna do without you?"

254

I'd still be me. Ugh, I couldn't have this conversation in wolf form. So much for a relaxing run... I squeezed my eyes shut and pictured my human form. A moment later, I sat on the bottom step of the stairwell, fully naked.

Ransom's appreciative gaze raked over me, sending a chill over my bare flesh.

"You know, if we'd completed the bond, we could've just spoken to each other through the mate link instead of me having to shift back every five seconds," I grumbled.

The corner of his lip tipped up into a smile. "You're right. That would make things much easier." His dark eyes sparkled with mischief. "You are naked... we could just do it now—"

I shot him a narrowed glare. "I shifted back to tell you that I wouldn't be abandoning my sister if I became a vampire. I'd still be me... wouldn't I?"

He nodded slowly. "Eventually. But it's a long, hard road for the first few years, as we've both experienced first-hand."

"I'd like to believe I have stronger willpower than *you*."

He chuckled. "Maybe. But no one knows for sure until the change comes on. I like to think I'm the same man I was before, but I'm not entirely sure I will ever be." He tugged his shirt off and handed it to me with a grin.

"Based on the stories I've heard from Hunter and Sierra, you weren't that awesome before you died."

His shoulders shook, a deep belly laugh vibrating his chest. "You've obviously been lied to. And, I think you need to stop spending so much time with them." He nudged his shoulder against mine. "I like to think you've changed me for the better."

"Damn, right, fanger." I smirked.

"Do you remember when Seline died, and I asked if you

would've wanted me to turn you if it had been you instead of her?"

My head dipped slowly.

"You said no. You didn't want to be a vampire. So what's changed?"

I stared down at my hands, threading my fingers together. "What's changed is that if becoming a vampire means I can save the people of Nocturnis and even Azar, then it's something I need to at least consider. Plus, when we had that talk, it was before I admitted to you, hell, to myself, that I loved you. It's stupid, I know, but it makes a difference. Getting to spend forever with you makes the idea of immortality more bearable."

Ransom cupped my cheek, diverting my eyes to his. "I'd love you in any form—vampire, wolf, sea nymph... it wouldn't matter to me. But it might matter to you in the long run." His eyes dipped from mine and ran down my chest and landed on my belly. "You'd never be able to have children."

My brows slammed together. At nineteen, it wasn't something I thought much about. Plus, with my career choice I wasn't sure I'd live to see twenty let alone motherhood. And Ransom, I'd never be able to have children with him anyway.

He lifted his gaze back to meet mine, and it was like staring into the farthest depths of the galaxy. Like getting sucked into a beautiful black hole.

"But you can't have children either," I whispered.

His lips puckered. "That doesn't mean I wouldn't want it for you."

A surge of regret pummeled through the bond, the longing, the ache unmistakable.

"You *want* kids? I thought you just loved to practice?"

He lowered his head, a hint of crimson tingeing his

cheeks. "I'd never thought twice about kids before I met you. It's this damned mate bond. It comes built in with this burning desire to reproduce. I've heard about it from friends, but I never believed it until now." He shook his head, a rueful grin flashing across his lips. "Seeing Sierra pregnant, I don't know, it just did something to me."

Mind. Blown.

"And now with my s—" He chomped down on his lower lip, his fang drawing blood.

"What?" I reached for the crimson droplet and swept it from his chin.

"Nothing. I just want you to consider all the possibilities."

Never in a million years would I have thought Ransom wanted little vamp-pups of his own. We'd have to adopt or get a surrogate or something. My mind raced with the prospect. I needed to put a break on these crazy thoughts. Babies with Ransom was the last thing I needed to be thinking about right now.

But it was too late...

I hopped into his lap, straddling him. "I love you," I whispered against his lips. "You're reckless and cocky as hell, and I'm pretty sure you're slightly insane but gods' help me I love you."

His mouth captured mine, and I weaved my arms around the back of his neck, drawing him closer. It was never close enough. The burgeoning mate bond was relentless. As his hands moved over my body and his mouth worshipped mine, the bond hummed between us. My heart swelled as our heady emotions tangled. An odd sense of clarity came over me as we kissed, our bodies entwined. Somehow it would work, I was certain of it. I wasn't sure how we'd accomplish it logistically, but somehow, we'd complete the mate bond and be tied together for life. He was mine, and I was his. Forever.

I'd never been more certain about anything than I was in that moment.

"What?" Ransom released my swollen lips, his hooded lids peering up at me.

"Nothing." I shook my head and claimed his mouth once again.

Tomorrow, we'd find Thanatos. Tonight, we'd spend entangled in each other's arms until there was no more him or me but only us.

P *hoenix*

"I HATE the idea of using Nix as bait." Vera pouted as she leaned her head on her hand at the kitchen table. Cal sat beside her, rubbing her shoulders. They were so cute sometimes.

"I couldn't agree with you more, little witch." Ransom folded his arms over his chest and leaned against the wall.

"Well, we're running out of options." I marched the length of the couch, my thoughts spinning. Talon had come back this morning after another unsuccessful search of the Darklands. Azara had been missing for three days now, and the dragon was going nuts.

"So what are we going to do exactly?" Spark asked. "Just wander the streets until he finds you?"

"We could go to one of Ronin's old clubs," I answered. "They're probably still infested with Children of the Night. We could go undercover like the old days." I slanted a look at Ransom. "Bring out the bloodwhore outfit for one more night?"

"Oh, Red, you always know exactly what to say." His lips curled into a grin.

"We could all go." I scanned my team, plus the surly dragon. "With Ronin's death, there must be some instability amongst the Children. It would be a good recon mission."

"Or Thanatos has already swooped in with his shiny scythe and easily taken the rebel king's place," said Cal.

"Either way, I bet we'll find out if we go to that gentleman's club." My skin puckered as memories of the first time I came face to face with Ronin flitted across my mind.

"I'm in," said Talon.

Archer shrugged. "I'll take any excuse to get out of the penthouse for a while."

Vera and Cal both nodded as well, and my gaze turned to Spark. "Come on, Sparky, are you in?"

A rueful smile spread his lips. "You're the boss, Nix. I go where you do."

"Hey, that's my line." Ransom draped his arm across my shoulders. I hadn't even noticed him move. He dipped his lips to my ear and whispered, "I hope you still have those boots from the safehouse because Red, dreaming about you in those things was the only thing that got me through my time in captivity."

I jabbed my elbow into his gut, and he folded over with a satisfying grunt. "Control yourself, fanger."

"That's not what you said last night—"

I slapped my hand over his mouth as he chuckled darkly. "Okay, everyone get ready. We go out tonight."

IF I HADN'T BEEN SO desperate to get Ransom on board with this mission, I never would've agreed to resurrect this outfit. My boobs were spilling over the top of the corset and the daggers strapped to my thighs were practically peeking out from under my obscenely short leather skirt. One wrong move and I'd impale myself, removing the question of children in the future all together. I still couldn't quite wrap my head around the fact that Ransom wanted a family, kids, the whole nine yards with me.

As I moved, the gleam of bardy's blade flickered beneath the moonlight, catching my eye and drawing my thoughts to the present. Now was not the time to consider a future I wasn't a hundred percent certain we'd have.

"Stop." Ransom halted and I nearly barreled into him, my thoughts still scattered. The rest of the team froze, pressing their backs against the wall. He paused at the edge of the crumbling building and peered around the corner. "There it is." Ransom ticked his head at the inconspicuous door at the end of the dim alleyway. Unlike most of Ronin's establishments spread around Nocturnis, this one was super VIP, an invite-only type place. Luckily, Ransom's Royal bloodline allowed him to compel most vampires.

"Ransom and I will go first and once he's taken care of the guard, I'll give you the sign."

Vera, Archer and Talon nodded. Despite major grumblings, Spark and Cal were to remain outside as backup. The seven of us going in together was too conspicuous, and it would've taken too much of Vera's power to cloak the entire team. A dragon, an angel, a Fae and a witch would not have gone unnoticed despite our best efforts. So Archer was playing the part of the vampire and Vera his willing blood-whore. Talon had refused to remain outside, but with his towering form and the heat that radiated from his dragon, he'd also never pass as a vamp. So he was going to wing it and if things got nasty, he'd use his SIA credentials to get himself out of a jam. Or at least that was the plan anyway.

"Ready?" Ransom's approving gaze raked over me.

"I'm ready to get this night over with so I can get home and take off this ridiculous outfit."

"You and me both, Red." His dark eyes sparkled with mischief. He offered me his arm, and I weaved mine through his.

As we marched toward the door, my thoughts flitted to the past. I never in a million years would've thought I'd be returning to this place willingly. Or with my vampire-wolfy mate at my side. Funny how things had changed.

The vamp guard at the door eyed us as we approached, his eyes narrowing. I could almost feel it, the moment Ransom's power swirled to life. I felt a tug at my core as if our connection was drawing from my power to fuel his.

The guard's jaw softened, and his eyes glazed over by the time we reached him. Ransom gave the guy a smile. "Good evening. We'd like to enjoy your fine establishment."

"Are you on the list?" the male asked as his eyes dipped to the tablet pressed against his black suit.

"Keep your eyes on me, my friend." Ransom tipped the guy's chin up and locked his eyes on the target. Power pulsated, and deep crimson eclipsed the endless black. "I'm not on the list yet, but I'd like you to add me to it now. Ransom De La Sangue and guests."

The guard's head dropped, and his fingers flew over the screen.

I looked over my shoulder and motioned for Talon, Vera

and Archer to approach. As my Fae teammate sauntered closer, I shot my witchy friend a smile. She'd done an incredible job cloaking him. From the pale, dewy complexion and the fangs peeking out from under his lip, he had fanger written all over. Vera wore a tight black dress with sky-high chunky stripper heels, and she'd conjured up bite marks across her neck and collarbone. She looked every bit the sexy bloodwhore.

Talon on the other hand just looked pissed. The compelled vamp guard staggered back as the dragon marched past. I couldn't blame the guy. With fury carved into his features and silver flames flickering across his irises, the shifter looked about a second away from burning the place down.

"Thank you, my friend." Ransom patted the guard on the shoulder as we strode past. "You never saw us tonight. Especially not the big dragon."

The male nodded slowly, eyes still glazed over.

Once we were inside, we dipped into a small niche in the corridor. "We'll split up from here," I instructed. "Everyone's got their com on?" I flicked the device behind my ear, and a chorus of yeses rang out loud and clear. "Keep an eye out for any of Ronin's men and obviously any word of Thanatos or Azara."

Everyone nodded.

Talon moved first. His eagerness to search the club radiated from the tense set of his shoulders.

"Poor guy," I mumbled as he stalked into the sprawling warehouse.

"We'll find her," said Vera. She weaved her arm through Archer's and shot him an adoring smile, then nuzzled into his chest. "Ready, oh great one?"

Archer raised a bemused smile. "Cal is one lucky guy."

263

As the pair walked ahead of us, Ransom threw me a smirk. "She sure knows how to play the part of a blood-whore. Perhaps you should take a lesson or two from the little witch."

"Oh, shut up." Shaking my head, I strutted down the hallway, my boots slapping the floor.

The moment the corridor opened up into the sprawling space, my mind flitted to the past. The couch we'd sat at the night I'd first seen Ronin face to face was open. Ransom's hand moved to the small of my back, and he directed me to our spot. A few vampires stood at the adjacent bar, while two or three other couples filled the circle of loveseats.

From the corner of my eye, two familiar males caught my attention. *Mother fangers.* Their heavy gazes bored into the side of my face, but I forced myself to keep moving. Had they recognized me? We'd spent quite some time speaking to the two old vamps that night.

"Did you see—"

"Yes," Ransom hissed. "Just keep walking. Let them make the first move." He settled onto the couch and drew me into his lap. I squirmed as he dipped his head to my neck, and his hands rested on my thighs. His fingers skimmed beneath the hem of my skirt. "Remember, you're a good little blood-whore." He ran his fangs over my flesh and my breath hitched, goosebumps exploding down my arms. "That's right, baby."

I tipped my head back and exposed my neck to him. A sharp hiss echoed around the circle of sofas. I hazarded a peek beneath slitted lids, and all eyes were on me.

"It's just your scent, Red," he whispered.

"Right..." I mumbled. You would've thought after all the bloodsharing, Ransom's scent would've fully masked mine by now.

"Don't look now, our friends are coming this way."

A shot of nervous energy zipped through my veins. Or maybe it was the thrill of Ransom's touch.

The older male stopped in front of us, a hint of saliva pooling at the corner of his lips. "I'm surprised to see you here, Ransom De La Sangue. I'd heard all kinds of rumors from our fallen king."

Ransom shifted me to one leg, his arm tightening around my waist. "Desante, right?"

The old vampire nodded then motioned to the other male. "And my partner Giorgiu."

"Of course. I remember."

Desante reached for me, and Ransom's body stiffened, his arm like a steel band around my torso. The twinkle in his eye vanished, and something much darker surfaced.

The fanger pulled his arm back, and a rueful chuckle broke the tense moment. "I see you're as possessive as ever over your little bloodwhore." He clucked his teeth. "What a shame."

He gave him a smile, flashing pointy fangs. "She's *mine,* and I don't share."

"Yes, you've made that quite clear." He huffed out a breath. "It saddens me as she still smells exquisite. I'd hoped with the arrival of Thanatos, you would've had a change of heart to our ways."

My ears perked up at the name.

"So, you're with him then?" Ransom asked.

"How could one not be?" Giorgiu responded. "He is a god after all, and our creator. Ronin failed, but Thanatos will not. We will finally be restored to our former power."

I chomped down on my lower lip to suppress a grunt. These ancient fangers were delusional.

From the corner of my eye, I caught movement. A hulking

form stalked toward us, much faster than anyone that size should be able to. I glared at Talon, shaking my head but it was too late. His big hand clamped on Desante's shoulder, and he spun the vamp around.

"Where can I find Thanatos?" he growled, the sound more beast than man. He dug his fingers into the vampire's shirt collar and lifted him off his feet. *Dammit, guess the dragon was out of the bag.* Silver scales rippled across Talon's arms, and his pupils narrowed to angry slits.

"Who let the dragon loose in here?" Desante's eyes widened, and crimson flooded the darkness. "Let go of me now, you brute." Power laced his tone, his words pulsating between the minute space.

Ransom scooted me off his lap and rose to stand beside Talon.

He clenched his jaw as he fought the vampire's influence, but the dragon's raw strength was no match against the ancient immortal. His fingers loosened, jaw slackening, before he released him.

Straightening his collar and flattening out his ruffled shirt, Desante turned to Ransom, lips twisted. "I'm not sure I enjoy the company you keep."

Ransom shrugged. "I would say the same if we weren't surrounded by them."

I scanned the circle of vampires who'd suddenly appeared around us. My fingers ached for bardy. Why had I let Ransom convince me to leave him home? Just outside the ring of immortals, my gaze landed on a pair of familiar faces. Vera nodded at me. She and Archer were just beyond the inner ring. By the hard set of her jaw, she was ready.

"What are you doing here, Mr. De La Sangue?" the old vamp tipped up a silver brow.

"Like my shifter friend said, we're looking for Thanatos."

Giorgiu chuckled. "For what?"

"He has my mate," Talon snarled.

"A dragon?" In Desante's defense, he really looked like he had no idea what was going on.

"No. Azara is the dark lord of the Underworld."

The male's head snapped back. Guess we were the only ones in on the ingredients needed to break the shadow curse. "Do you even know that Thanatos doesn't have what he needs to break the curse?" I blurted.

Ransom shot me a sidelong glance.

"We do not question the god of death," Desante answered.

"Perhaps you should." Ransom gave him a smug grin. "Even he may not be able to deliver all that was promised."

"Ronin didn't even come close," I muttered through clenched teeth.

"How dare you speak of the rebel king in such a manner, you bloodwhore." Giorgiu cried out as he lifted his hand.

Ransom's fingers curled around his wrist before his palm made contact. "Don't *you* dare speak to her like that," he snarled. "That bloodwhore tore Ronin's head off." A wicked smile spread his lips as dread pooled in my gut.

Probably not the best place to brag about killing the rebel king.

"You?" Desante's eyes widened, his mouth curving into a capital O. "*You're* the wolf with the mortal bite?"

Well, I guess my cover was blown. This whole mission had been a bust. I leapt up and stood beside Ransom and Talon. Auburn fur rippled over my arms, the crimson glow lighting up my skin. If we had to fight our way out, I was ready.

"It's incredible." Desante's dark eyes razed over me. There was something about the ancient vampire's look that sent the hair on the back of my neck on end. "She's the perfect weapon. With a scent like that... you must have to fight them off. And then she turns the table. One bite and it's over." A sneer curled his lips. "I wonder..." His eyes narrowed as he regarded me, his true age betrayed in those haunting irises. The old vamp turned to the Children who'd tightened the noose around our threesome. "Let them leave, unharmed. The she-wolf's purpose has yet to be fulfilled, and there's no reason for carnage tonight."

My brows knitted. My purpose? Say what, fanger? I thought he didn't know about the spell.

"Let's not miss out on the opportunity the kind Desante has gifted us." Ransom curled his fingers around my arm and tugged me toward the exit. I nodded at Vera and Archer who'd remained just beyond the circle of vampires. They turned toward the door, trailing a few feet behind us. Talon was the last to move.

"If any of you see Thanatos, you tell him I'm coming for him," Talon shouted. "And if he's harmed even a single hair on my mate's head, I'll rip him apart from head to toe. I don't care if he is immortal. It'll only make the torture sweeter."

His heavy footfalls reverberated behind us, and Ransom hurried me along beside him.

"That wasn't exactly how this was supposed to play out," he growled at Talon.

"It was too late once those vamps recognized you. At least now Thanatos knows we're coming for him."

That was exactly what I was afraid of.

Ransom whipped the door open, and the cool night air drifted over my heated skin. My wolf settled back into my core, and I released a breath. Spark and Cal raced over as soon as they saw us, and the Nephilim's arms weaved around Vera.

"Well, that was a disaster," said Archer.

"You did not enjoy your evening, Fae?" A voice boomed in the distance, and every hair on my body stood at attention.

CHAPTER
THIRTY-FOUR

R*ansom*

THANATOS BLEW in atop a chariot of gleaming skulls and bones with that luminous scythe clenched in his fist. *The Reaper.* The skeletons writhed and hissed beneath the god's boots, propelling him forward. The dark cowl fell back, revealing Thanatos in all his glory. Wild, raven hair tumbled over his shoulders, blowing with an invisible wind. Likely the same mystical gusts that were animating his skeletal soldiers.

"That is so creepy," Spark muttered.

I tugged Red into my side and judging by the jealous gleam in her eye as she regarded Thanatos's weapon, she was likely cursing me for forcing her to leave bardy home. The ultimate showdown between the two medieval weapons was not what we needed tonight.

The god's fathomless eyes met mine, and my thoughts

began to swim. Strong fingers pushed into my mind. I focused on the internal walls I'd built as a wolf when I sought to keep nosy alphas out of my head, but Thanatos was nothing like my father or even Hunter.

I felt my control slip as his eyes bored into mine.

"Ransom, Ransom, don't you dare leave me!" A sharp jerk of my arm pushed the haze aside. I blinked quickly, and my eyes focused on Red. "Snap out of it," she snarled.

"I'm okay," I mumbled, fighting my way through the haze.

Thanatos's dark gaze darted from me to Red and back. His eyes narrowed, and fear lanced through my spine. Did he know about me? Could he feel my soul?

"How is it that you're able to block my influence, vampire?" Thanatos glared down at me from his throne of bones, the weight of his gaze like a two-ton unipeg sitting on my chest.

"Just special, I guess." I shot him a smirk.

"I understand you were looking for me." The mass of skeletons that made up his unearthly chariot disassembled. He leapt to the ground, onyx wings folding behind his back and eyes intent on my mate. A deep growl vibrated my insides, and my fangs lengthened. He couldn't control me. I'd never let him get his hands on her.

Talon moved between Thanatos and us, silver scales shimmering across his thick arms. "I'm the one looking for you."

"And who are you?" he hissed.

His pupils narrowed to reptilian slits. "I'm the man who's going to send you back to hades or wherever the hell you came from if you don't return my mate immediately."

Thanatos's thick brows furrowed for a moment before

his head dipped in understanding. "The female warlock is yours?"

"She's *my mate*."

"Hmm, interesting." He crossed his arms over the dark cloak that covered his body. The black fabric moved like shadows over his form. "I'm not quite finished with her yet."

"Oh yes, you are." Silver flames exploded from Talon's half-shifted maw. They licked up the god's cloak, the fire dancing over the dark material. But it didn't burn. He may have just doused the god with bath water for all it affected him.

Talon let out a sharp growl, and dragon wings burst from his back.

"Talon, no!" Red shouted, but her cry fell on deaf ears. I couldn't blame the male. If it were my mate, I would've done the same.

He lunged at Thanatos, but the Reaper darted to the side, his moves faster than any vampire. Talon hit the floor with a thud, skidding across the crumbling asphalt. He jumped back up and attacked again. This time, the god swung his weapon.

"No!" Red screeched. She lunged forward, but I clamped my arm across her torso, holding her back. There was no way I'd let her get between the battling males.

Somehow, Talon shifted at the last second, and the blade slammed into his shoulder instead of his neck. He let out a grunt, and the big dragon dropped to the asphalt with a ground-shaking thud.

"Enough!" Red cried out. Then she spun at Cal and ticked her head at Talon. "Go, help him."

Cal and Vera raced over to the fallen dragon, but I kept my eyes trained on my mate, who I knew was about to do something incredibly stupid. And brave.

Thanatos fixed his bottomless irises on Red, and a shudder wracked my core. He regarded her with a hunger I knew well. "You're the little wolf that bested Ronin."

She nodded. "And I'm about to *best* you." She ticked her head at Vera and opened her palm. Bardy appeared in a flash of smoke. The glistening blade shimmered beneath the moonlight as she held it high above her head.

"You are a fearsome warrior, and it pains me to end your life when its only just beginning."

Fear's claws wrapped around my ribcage, and I inched closer to Red. Only the fact that he needed her alive to complete the spell kept me in control.

"So you do need to kill us for the spell to work?"

He shrugged. "The warlock Drakin isn't certain. Until we have all the pieces we need, there is no way to say."

"Let Azara go!" Talon's weak growl echoed from behind me. "Take some of her blood and release her."

"I'm afraid that's impossible."

Red stepped forward, just out of my reach. "I'll go with you if you release Azara."

"No," I hissed.

"You don't seem to understand, little wolf. I need you both."

Red released the stake from the sheath at her thigh and pressed it against her neck. The steady rise and fall of Thanatos's chest halted. His jaw clenched, and lips drew into a thin line.

"What are you doing?" I cried.

"And if I kill myself, you'll never get what you want. There is no other wolf like me. There *is* another female warlock." She pressed the pointy tip into her throat, and my nostrils flared. Blood pooled at the tip. "Take us to her. Let Talon confirm she's okay, and you can have me."

273

My fingers curled into fists at my side, and another growl rumbled deep in my core. I'd never let that happen. I wouldn't let Thanatos take our mate.

"What's to stop me from taking you now?" Death smiled.

"I am." Spark stood in the shadows with a crossbow trained at the back of Red's head.

No...

"If you make a move, I'll fire. She'll be dead on the spot, and you'll never get what you want."

They'd planned this. Red had gone behind my back and made a pact with the dragon. He wouldn't. That overgrown lizard didn't have the balls... Fury tumbled through my insides, a mix of fear and panic writhing through every inch.

"Please, take me to her." Talon's voice was weak, but from the looks of it, Cal's angel healing had stopped the blood loss. "I'll do whatever you want."

Thanatos dismissed him with a wave and turned to Red once again. "If I take you to Azara, you will stay?"

Red nodded, and I resisted the urge to strangle her. "You will not!" I growled.

"If you release her, I will. Take some of her blood, and you'll always know where you can find more." She glanced at Talon. "Right?"

He nodded slowly. "If it means saving her life, I'd give you whatever you asked for."

"Azara wouldn't approve of any of this," I snarled. "I met the girl for a few days, and I already know that. Don't do this."

Thanatos eyed me, and his nostrils flared. I pressed my arms across my chest as if I could somehow hide my tiny soul. He couldn't know or he would've acted by now. "Only the she-wolf and the dragon may come."

"Absolutely not," I barked. "I go where she goes."

Red's team muttered protests, but she whirled on them, steel carved into the hard line of her jaw. "I need you to keep the others safe. If we don't return, tell the queen everything."

Vera raced over and pulled her into a hug. "Don't do this, Nix."

"I have to." She whispered something to her friend, but I couldn't make it out over the roar of my thundering heart.

Archer and Cal moved in next, each giving their leader a solemn nod.

"I can't believe you guys are okay with this," I howled. "You can't let her do this." Grabbing Red's hands, I squeezed her fingers. "He'll never let you go."

"I know," she whispered.

"Then what are you doing?"

She leaned in and brushed her lips against the shell of my ear. "Just trust me, like I trust you."

Trust her? Was she out of her mind? She was jumping headfirst right into a trap.

Sparky appeared behind her and pulled her into a hug. "Be careful."

"How can you let her do this?" I shouted at the stupid dragon.

"Because I trust her." He shot me a smug grin, and it took all my restraint not to bite him.

"So that's it? You're just going to blindly follow the *god of death* wherever he may take you?"

"Us. I'm going to follow him wherever he'll take *us*. Because I know you'll do the right thing when the time comes."

What the hell did that mean? Did she want me to turn her?

She pivoted to Thanatos. "Ransom comes too or no deal."

Death rolled his eyes and let out a grunt. Like life was so

rough for the immortal being. "Fine, fine." The chariot of bones reassembled, and he walked up the skeletal steps onto his throne. Once seated, he spread his hands out, and a dark mist crawled up from the ground. It snaked up my legs, then Red's, a fine layer of frost working its way up my appendages. I reached for Red and held her tight against my chest as the dark shadows consumed us.

CHAPTER
THIRTY-FIVE

P *hoenix*

THE COLD CREPT through every inch of my body until not even Ransom's warm arms curled around me made a difference. But as quickly as it had come, the icy tingles vanished, and a room materialized around us. Or maybe it was the other way around, and we'd actually materialized in the dark chamber.

Obsidian made up the walls, the lanterns hung along the stone casting the dim room in shadows. Thanatos sat atop a throne made of the same creepy bones that had served as his mystical chariot, and to his right, stood Drakin. The warlock watched us, his fingers twitching in excitement.

Talon coalesced beside me a moment later, and a swell of relief filled my chest at the sight of him. The wound across the front of his shoulder had begun to heal, only the tattered shirt and blood splatter remained. Thank the gods for Cal and his half-angel healing power.

"Where is Azara?" Talon barked.

Thanatos wiggled his fingers at Drakin, and the warlock stomped out of the room with a dramatic eyeroll. Damn, that warlock was pretty ballsy. Or Thanatos was less scary than he seemed. Or the god really needed Drakin to break the curse.

"So, what's your grand plan?" Ransom whispered.

That was an excellent question. The truth was I didn't have one. I was just winging it. Getting Azara away from Thanatos was as far as I'd gotten, and I had been completely serious about giving myself up for her. But I couldn't tell my vampire mate that or he would go ballistic.

"It's a surprise," I finally muttered.

"Red, I'm not sure I'm going to like this surprise."

I weaved my fingers through his and gave his hand a squeeze. "Just remember I love you."

A shot of his panic surged through our bond. "Don't say that, Red. Nothing ever good happens when the hero says that in the movies."

"Well, then, it's a good thing I'm the *heroine*."

Drakin reappeared, tugging Azara along behind him. Or what used to be Azara. Dark circles lined her eyes, and a thick layer of dirt and mud covered her arms and legs. Thick iron manacles were fastened around her ankles and wrists and judging by the potent odor of magic in the air, they were no ordinary handcuffs.

Talon sucked in a sharp breath as she staggered in. He raced toward her, but Drakin's hand shot up and the dragon bounced off an invisible wall and flew back. "No further, shifter."

"Talon," Azara murmured when her mate hit the floor.

"What have you done to her?" he growled as he pushed off his hands and knees to stand.

"What I had to in order to keep her subdued," Drakin answered. His dark navy irises pulsed. "She's quite powerful. I daresay she might come close to my abilities, but her demon side makes her volatile."

"Take these cuffs off, and I'll show you how volatile I can be," Azara hissed.

I squared my shoulders at the dark deity. "Let her go, Thanatos. That was the deal, me for her."

Azara's hazy eyes lifted to mine, and she slowly shook her head. "No..."

Drakin spun at Thanatos, arms flailing. "You can't be serious. We are so close."

The god waved a nonchalant hand. "Just take a healthy serving of the female warlock's blood. The she-wolf is far more valuable to us."

"But Thanatos, we still don't know how much we need."

"We'll know where to find her, and there's always her mother. There is only one wolf with the kiss of death, and I won't lose the opportunity to capture her."

"This is foolish," Drakin grumbled under his breath.

Thanatos's eyes darkened to twin pools of obsidian, and he leapt off the throne. "You dare question me, you insignificant warlock? You don't think I could replace you with ten others? You have no idea what the future holds for the girl. Only I do."

Drakin's eyes narrowed, but he lowered his gaze.

Me?

Ransom's panic streaked through the bond. "Don't do it, Red," he murmured. "Please, I can't lose you. I won't."

"Take the female warlock's blood and get out of my sight," Thanatos shouted.

Drakin revealed a dagger from the folds of his robe and dragged it across Azara's wrist. She winced but didn't make a sound as her blood began to spill.

"No, I won't let this happen." Ransom pressed his lips to mine and before I could blink, he was gone. A dark blur darted across the room.

All the air siphoned out of my lungs as Ransom leapt at Azara and knocked her to the ground. His fangs lengthened, and he chomped down on her throat.

Talon let out a strangled cry, and an odd choking sound burst from my mouth. "Ransom, no!" I finally shouted once I dragged in enough air to speak.

Chaos exploded across the room. Drakin and Talon lunged for Ransom, and Thanatos darted toward me. His speed was uncanny. I searched my core for my wolf and before Death could reach me, I was down on all fours. Flames danced over my fur, the crimson fire illuminating across my periphery.

All around I could just make out the bones and skulls reassembling into animate forms. The scary skeletal soldiers closed in around us, their creepy unseeing orbs trained on me. When Thanatos reached me, he froze, his dark gaze raking over me.

"Good goddess," he muttered. "What has she done?"

He reached for me, but I darted out of the way and tiny flames jumped off my fur and landed on his black cloak. He let out a curse as the mystical flames singed the fabric.

Yes! Point for my wolf.

I raced across the room searching for Ransom and Azara. Oh gods, please don't let her be dead. Anger and fear for my mate spiraled inside, a wicked tornado battering my insides. How could he have done this? He swore...

Azara lay on the floor, blood dripping from her neck and

wrist. Talon crouched beside her, anguish contorting his handsome face. I slid down beside him and cocked my wolfy head.

"She's alive," he whispered, "but barely."

Drakin held Ransom in a glowing crimson orb, and if I hadn't been so furious with my mate, I would've found the sight comical. He smacked at the invisible edges, like a mime with a seriously bad attitude. His panicked eyes met mine, Azara's blood still dripping from his chin, and he mouthed something I couldn't quite make out. Warring sensations surged through the bond, and my heart stuttered out an erratic rhythm. My human form sprang out of my wolf, the shift instantaneous. The fact that I was naked barely registered amidst the chaos.

"How could you?" I mouthed at Ransom. He shook his head still shouting through the invisible barrier. "What is he saying?" I yelled at Drakin.

"Who cares?"

"I need to know!"

Thanatos appeared beside me with his army of skeletal soldiers. "Let's hear what the traitor has to say before I take his life."

Drakin snapped his fingers, and Ransom's shouts blasted through the bubble. "I'm the vampire with the soul!"

My eyes widened, and icy fear crawled up my spine. I started shaking my head, but it was too late.

Thanatos moved closer. "Release him now," he called out.

"But..."

"Do it now, Drakin. I thought I sensed something earlier..."

The bubble burst, and Ransom slumped forward. "I'm

the vampire you need, and now I have the blood of the last three pieces you were missing running through *my* veins."

My jaw nearly came unhinged. "No..."

"The wolf and I have been bloodsharing for months. My blood is as much hers as it is mine. And I nearly drained the female warlock. You should have plenty. Now, let them go."

My hand wrapped around Ransom's arm, and I spun him toward me. "What are you doing?"

"I'm saving you. I'm finally going to be the mate you deserve. Better late than never, right?" A rueful smirk curled up the corners of his lips as he tugged his shirt over his head and pulled it over mine. The gesture was so familiar, so sweet, tears burned my eyes.

"Don't do this, Ransom." Emotion tightened my throat.

His strong hands framed my face, and a tear trailed down his cheek. "I love you, Red. It was all worth it to spend these last few months with you."

"But you promised. You promised me forever."

He smiled, a heartbreaking smile that would forever be emblazoned in my mind. "Never trust a vampire." He released me and shouted at Thanatos. "Do we have a deal?"

Thanatos grinned, flashing a row of perfect white teeth. "Let the others go, Drakin. We finally have what we need."

"No, no, no!" I reached for Ransom, but he spun out of my grasp.

"I love you," he mouthed, then he turned to Talon. "Get her out of here, now!"

Talon's arms snaked around my waist, and I let out a shriek, struggling against his hold. "Let go of me!" Azara was slung over his shoulder and still somehow, I couldn't escape his steel grip. "Talon, let go!"

"I'm sorry, I can't." His wings snapped out, and my stomach bottomed out. As he flew across the room, my gaze chased to Ransom's. A serene smile stretched across his face despite the fear crushing my lungs.

"Ransom, please!" I cried out. "Don't leave me. I love you!"

The chamber disintegrated around us, and cool night air blanketed my feverish skin. Ransom's smile was the last thing I remembered before the icy chill returned and everything went black.

To Be Continued...

READ on for a special sneak peek of the final book, Vampish: Blood Mate, which will release on August 23rd!

SNEAK PEEK OF VAMPISH: BLOOD MATE

Chapter 1

Ransom

I saved her.

For once in my life, I did the right thing, and I didn't care what it cost me. Death could bleed me dry for all I cared. As long as Red was safe. My heart fluttered out a triumphant beat despite the agony tearing through our bond. I kept my gaze fixed to Red's as Talon flew higher. She struggled against his hold, and I did my best to shoot reassuring vibes through our connection. "I love you," I mouthed. Her screams echoed across my eardrums as she grew further and further away until Thanatos's dark magic wrapped around their forms and presumably transported them home.

I gritted my teeth refusing to succumb to the hot tears burning my eyes. I'd see Red again someday, whether in this life or the next. The only comfort was that we hadn't completed the mate bond. Losing me would be painful, but it wouldn't be a death sentence. In time, our tie would fade, and she'd be able to move on.

I forced my feet to move from the spot. Red was gone. It was time to get this over with. I whirled around to face Thanatos and Drakin. The warlock eyed me suspiciously as the god leaned against his skeletal throne. It was clear Drakin wasn't onboard with this blood thing. He would've preferred to have all three of us in person and live. But I had enough of Red's blood coursing through my veins and after taking a bite of the dark lord, Azara's neck, I should have plenty of hers as well.

It had been a gamble for sure. I wasn't certain Thanatos would agree to let the girls go, I still didn't trust him not to go back on his word. But he was a god, and his honor had to count for something.

I squared my shoulders at the dark deity and smiled. "So are we going to do this thing, or what?"

Thanatos' dark gaze lanced over me, his brilliant blue eyes unearthly in their radiant glow. His obsidian wings fluttered behind him as he spoke, "You really love the girl, don't you?"

I nodded, not feeling the urge to get into my love life with Death.

"It's incredible the lengths a male will go for the sake of a woman. It's twisted, really." His lips quirked in amusement. "It must be your soul..." His brows drew together as he continued to scrutinize me. "Of all my children, I've never met one like you. I sincerely hope that you will survive what's to come."

"Thanks," I muttered. "But I suppose that's ultimately up to you, isn't it?"

The corners of his mouth dipped. "No, it's not. It's up to the requirements of the spell."

"So you really don't know how much blood you'll need?" I slanted a look at the warlock.

The male's dark brows slammed together, and I was fairly certain had his skin not been a deep ebony, crimson would've tinged his cheeks. "No," he snarled. "Breaking a curse such as this is unheard of. I will be the first to attempt a spell of this magnitude."

Arrogant little a-hole.

"So let's do it." I clapped my hands. "If all goes well, I could get home in time for dinner with my girl, right?"

Thanatos clucked his tongue. "Not so fast, my child. Now that we have all the ingredients, we must wait for the blood moon."

Ugh, why is it always about blood?

I glanced at my wrist, searching for a non-existent watch. "So when will that be?"

"In five days," Drakin responded.

I folded my arms across my chest and grunted. "Well, what the hades are we going to do until then?"

Thanatos ticked his head at the warlock. "Bring him to the dungeon with the others."

Dungeon? "Seriously?" I planted my feet as Drakin moved for me, sparks of neon energy sparking between his palms. "I gave myself to you willingly. I won't run because that would only put Phoenix at risk. There's no need to imprison me. Can't we talk upgrades?"

The hint of a smile curled the Reaper's lips. "I believe you, Ransom, but I can't have you walking freely through my home."

"Why not?" I glanced around the massive chamber. By the looks of it, his home was some sort of medieval castle. The question was where? "I swear I'll be the perfect guest."

He grunted. "If I could compel you, things would be

different." His eyes narrowed once again as they regarded me. He hated that his powers didn't work on me.

"Hmm, I wonder why that is?" I rubbed at my chin with a cheeky grin. It was Red. I was certain of it. Our bond was stronger than whatever hold he had over me. "Regardless, I swear I won't run."

Drakin whirled at Thanatos. "Don't listen to him. He'll run as soon as he has the chance. His love for the girl cannot possibly run that deep. He's a vampire after all. I'd bet he'll save his own hide and abandon the wolf."

"Never," I snarled. My wolf surged to the surface, his ghostly presence nudging at my insides. Gods, he was close. I was almost certain if Red and I had completed the bond, he would've found his way back to the world of the living. I massaged the sore spot in the middle of my chest. This time it was mine. Red had gone silent, passed out most likely from the blast of Death's magic.

"It's clear you've never truly loved, Drakin." Thanatos narrowed his eyes at the warlock, and I recognized something in his gaze. Loss. Heart shattering loss. The god of death had actually loved?

I saved that little tidbit of knowledge to explore later. Love was life-altering, all-consuming, infinite, and it also made one vulnerable. And a vulnerability in a god was something worth investigating.

"So what will you have me do with him?" Drakin growled.

Thanatos leapt at him, his powerful body blurring to nothing more than darkness and shadows. His hand curled around the warlock's throat and the male's navy eyes bulged. "I'll have you change your tone. I've warned you before, and I won't do it again. You warlocks are replaceable. I doubt you're the only one of your kind. Not like my vampire." He turned his dark gaze on me, and the hair on the back of my neck prickled. Slowly, he loosened his hold around Drakin's neck until his feet touched the floor once more. "Take him to my wing after you've drawn his blood. He can remain in the room adjacent to my own, spelled shut, of course. I trust him not to leave, but I don't trust he wouldn't attack me if given the opportunity."

My lips curled into a smile. "You give me too much credit, Thanatos. You think *I* could hurt *you*?"

"I do not. But I wouldn't blame you for trying." His thumb moved in slow circles across the staff of his mighty scythe. The tender gesture reminded me of Red and bardy and a pang shot through my heart. I swallowed it down, forcing it into the dark depths. *I saved her. I saved her.*

He spun the weapon in his palm, his onyx wings curling around his back. "Go with Drakin and do not give him any trouble. If you do as told, I will be sure to see that your stay here is comfortable."

I nodded, dipping into a bow. "As you say, my liege."

This Thanatos was an interesting guy. I looked forward to getting to know him better in the coming days. Maybe, just maybe, I could convince him not to break the curse. Maybe his arrival in Azar could serve a better purpose.

The Reaper spun on his heel, and his army of skeletons reassembled and followed behind him. Freaky fangers.

As soon as he was gone, Drakin whirled on me, fury coursing through those deep navy irises. "Don't let him fool you," he growled. "He'll use you just like he does everyone. You saw what he allowed happen to Ronin."

"I did. I had a front row view as my girl ripped his head off." I couldn't help the smile from splitting my lips. I was so proud of Red.

Drakin scowled, his arms pressing across his chest, and it

occurred to me the warlock actually cared about Ronin. Hence, the piss poor attitude with Thanatos. Hmm... another thing to exploit. "Watch your tongue, vampire, or I'll see to it that your girl meets the same fate."

Fury surged through my veins, and a growl tore from my clenched lips. I lunged for the warlock, but his hands shot up and a shimmering shield coalesced between us. I bounced off the invisible and flew backward.

As I pushed myself off the ground, Drakin wagged a finger at me. "Tsk, tsk, Ransom. Thanatos might trust you, but I do not. Don't challenge me or I might accidentally drip you dry."

I dusted myself off and sauntered closer, my pulse roaring through my eardrums. "*Never* threaten her again or I can assure you that you won't make it to see the blood moon. Because you're right not to trust me, warlock. I may play nice with Death but you? Just give me a chance, and I'll rip your throat out."

He swallowed hard, his Adam's apple bobbing. Lowering his gaze, he motioned toward the doorway. "This way to my laboratory."

I shot him a smirk and moved in front of him. As I walked down the corridor, the glowing orb of his shield accompanied us. *Coward.* The warlock was right. I'd play along as best I could, but if the chance came to take down Thanatos I wouldn't hesitate. I may have wanted to protect Red at all costs, but I sure as hell didn't have a death wish.

Now I just had to figure out how one goes about killing a god.

To be continued...

The final book, Vampish: Blood Mate will be released on August 23rd and you can preorder it now! Don't forget to join GK DeRosa's Supe Squad on Facebook for a chance to win an ARC and chat about all the bookish things!

ALSO BY G.K. DEROSA

Wolfish (World of Azar)

Wolfish: Moonborne

Wolfish: Curseborne

Wolfish: Mateborne

Wolfish: Fateborne

Darkblood Prison (World of Azar)

Darkblood Prison: Demon On A Dime

Darkblood Prison: Demon Double-Agent

Darkblood Prison: Demon At Large

Darkblood Prison: Demon Dark Lord

Royally Hitched Series (World of Azar)

Royally Hitched: The Fae Prince

Royally Hitched: The Fae Twins

Royally Hitched: The Fae Princess

Darkblood Academy (World of Azar)

Darkblood Academy: Half-Blood

Darkblood Academy: Supernatural Slayer Squad

Darkblood Academy: Demons

Darkblood Academy: Prophecies

The Hitched Series (World of Azar)

Hitched: The Bachelorette

Hitched: The Top Ten

Hitched: The Final Five

Hitched: The One

The Vampire and Angel Wars (Stand Alone Series)

Wings & Destruction

Blood & Rebellion

Souls & Salvation

The Vampire Prophecy (Stand Alone Series)

Dark Fates

Dark Divide

Dark Oblivion

The Hybrid Trilogy (Spin Off of the Guardian Series)

Magic Bound

Immortal Magic

Beyond Magic

Magic Bound: The Hybrid Trilogy The Complete Collection

The Guardian Series

Wilder: The Guardian Series

Wilder Destiny

Wilder Revelation

Wilder Legacy

Wilder: The Guardian Series The Complete Collection

ACKNOWLEDGMENTS

A huge and wholehearted thank you to my dedicated readers! I could not do this without you. I love hearing from you and your enthusiasm for the characters and story. You are the best!

A special thank you to my loving and supportive husband who always understood my need for escaping into a good book (or TV show!). He inspires me to try harder and push further every day. And of course my mother who is the guiding force behind everything I do and made me everything I am today. Without her, I literally could not write—because she's also my part-time babysitter! To my father who will always live on in my dreams. And finally, my babies, Alexander and Stella, who bring an unimaginable amount of joy, adventure and craziness to my life everyday.

A big thank you to my talented graphic designer, Sanja Gombar, for creating a beautiful book cover and to Samaiya Beaumont for the lovely header designs and all the swag. A special thank you to my dedicated beta readers/fellow authors Jena, Mary Ellen, and Lydia who have been my sounding board on everything from cover ideas, blurbs, and story details. And to all of my beta readers, Stacie, Cheryl, Sarah and Tess, who gave me great ideas, caught spelling errors, and were all around amazing.

Thank you to all my family and friends, author and

blogger friends who let me bounce ideas off of them and listened to my struggles as an author and self-publisher. I appreciate it more than you all will ever know.

~ G.K.

ABOUT THE AUTHOR

USA Today Bestselling Author, G.K. De Rosa has always had a passion for all things fantasy and romance. Growing up, she loved to read, devouring books in a single sitting. She attended Catholic school where reading and writing were an intense part of the curriculum, and she credits her amazing teachers for instilling in her a love of storytelling. As an adult, her favorite books were always young adult novels, and she remains a self-proclaimed fifteen year-old at heart. When she's not reading, writing or watching way too many TV shows, she's traveling and eating around the world with her family. G.K. DeRosa currently lives in South Florida with her real life Prince Charming and their little royals.

www.gkderosa.com

Printed in Great Britain
by Amazon

16193125R00178